The Perfume River

The Perfume River

An Anthology of Writing from Vietnam

EDITED BY

CATHERINE COLE

UWA PUBLISHING

First published in 2010 by
UWA Publishing
Crawley, Western Australia 6009
www.uwap.uwa.edu.au

UWAP is an imprint of UWA Publishing
a division of The University of Western Australia

THE UNIVERSITY OF
WESTERN AUSTRALIA
Achieving International Excellence

A full CIP record for this book is available from
the National Library of Australia.

ISBN: 978 1 921401 48 0

Cover design by Becky Chilcott, Chil3, Perth
Typeset in 12pt Bembo by Lasertype
Printed by McPherson's Printing Group

The Perfume River turns into liquor, I come to drink
I am sober, the royal palaces stumbingly drunk...

Nguyen Trong Tao
Memory of Black Eyes

Contents

Contents

Contents

Introduction

This anthology, named *The Perfume River* after one of Vietnam's most poetic waterways, draws together writing 'from Vietnam' in every sense. The writers live in Vietnam and a number of other countries. Some are of Vietnamese background, others are not. For all Vietnam has defined itself as a voice of inspiration, of homeland, memory and discovery.

Vietnam first wove its magic for me in 1994. I went there because a friend had told me that Hanoi was very like Paris. Its colonial buildings and wide tree-lined streets, the shutters and decorative grilles on the windows, the zinc bars in the cafés – all spoke of the city's colonial history just as the poverty and war damage spoke of war. I had grown up calling the conflict the 'Vietnam' war and the Vietnamese friends I would make on subsequent visits called it the 'American' war. Regardless of the semantics, for everyone involved in the conflict it was a watershed era. Young men and women fought, protested, fled. Suddenly, a country few of us had been much aware of was on our television screens every night and throughout the years after the war's end we saw the plight of 'boat people' fleeing the new regime.

A great deal has happened in Vietnam since I first explored the streets of Hanoi's Old Quarter. There is a new prosperity, a place for Vietnam on the world's economic stage, a great surge in tourism and infrastructure change. Time also has offered a return for many of the people who fled, for their children and grandchildren born in new homelands and a wider engagement for the country's internet-savvy youth who are drawn to the freedoms of global communications and for whom a war which shaped the political lives of previous generations in Vietnam and abroad, is just a historical epoch with little to offer their own bright new lives.

Yet despite all this change, Vietnam remains a complex and contradictory place. It's a national homeland for which millions of Vietnamese died and a lost home to which fleeing Vietnamese return cautiously, a place to which young men from Australia, New Zealand and America were sent to fight in a war against which their compatriots protested. Hordes of these former soldiers have gone back to Vietnam to discover something of their younger selves, as have the anti-war protesters who once marched in Vietnam's support.

A tourist Mecca. A centre of business and culture. A communist country with its own brand of *laissez faire* capitalism – Vietnam, it could be argued, is in a constant state of flux and Australia's cultural relationship with it shifts with each of these new developments.

One key thing, though, which strikes a writer who visits Vietnam, is the country's passionate interest in writers and writing. Conversations about Vietnamese, French and Russian writers await anyone keen to talk to Vietnam's writers and literary scholars – the older generation of which grew up with the close study of French literature. If there is a sadness in these conversations it is that readers in the West know so little of Vietnamese writing – the country's long cultural and literary traditions exemplified most potently for tourists in Hanoi's *Van Mieu* – The Temple of Literature. The Vietnamese writers included in this anthology represent just a small sampling of Vietnam's most engaging 'younger' generation or writers whose work has been translated into English or European languages such as French.

How best then to compile an anthology of writing which reflects the complex layers of this experience? Writing about a place like Vietnam offers new ways of examining and understanding the relationships shared between countries. Questions are inevitably posed. What do our stories tell us about the manner in which a country's writers approach their writing? How are collective memories of a war rendered in fiction? What role do place and nation play in a country's narratives?

The theorist Shaden Tageldin has claimed that fiction offers an important site of memory from which to renegotiate the meanings of the past in order to imagine a future. Cultural practice, particularly the methods by which writers research, imagine and write, also holds a mirror up to an understanding of nation, often with surprising consequences. In Australia the Vietnam War and all we associate with it formed a kind of rent in the national psyche. Why were we there? What did we achieve? What have we left behind and what will our new relationships with the country offer?

The war and its legacy continue to play out in the fiction of a new generation of Vietnamese writers in Vietnam, Australia and overseas, offering a means of exploring how authors use creativity to speak of their times, as a locus for examining the ways in which loss of a homeland surfaces in fictional texts and how these are mediated by a new country's culture. In many such stories, loss, exile and nostalgia seem to be an attempt to come to terms with the past in different historical and geographical contexts, giving play to this in highly stylised and attenuated images of lost landscapes or writing nostalgically of dispossession. And of course, as the idiosyncratic style of some of Vietnam's contemporary writers shows, many writers don't want to write about war at all.

Unlike America, where the Vietnam War has been a potent source of writing across all genres, it could be argued that a dearth of fictional texts about the war in Australia reflected more a desire to forget the past than to commemorate it. In the decade immediately after the cessation of war, Vietnam seemed to find its way into surprisingly few Australian novels and for those in which the country did feature, the war was often explored thematically, with hermeneutical intent, primarily seeking answers to questions about Australia's involvement in the war and its impact on those who fought.

Yet as this volume attests, Vietnam has been quietly making its presence felt in fiction, through poetry and short fiction and essays. Whether the anthology's writers are of Vietnamese background or from another cultural heritage, all have 'claimed' Vietnam in surprising ways, often self-consciously or perplexed by the country. From Pam Brown's 'Hanoi Cycle', written in the year in which I first discovered Hanoi and offering the bemused and untarnished eye of a first encounter, to Chi Vu's, 'Vietnam: a psychic guide', in which a young woman sees her old city through new eyes.

And what of writers from other countries? The collection offers a fluidity of movement in that regard, which seems a metaphor for the ways in which writers move away from and towards Vietnam tidally. Canada's

Vincent Lam has a strong familial connection with Australia as well as Vietnam. Nam Le lives in Australia and the USA and his collection of short stories, *The Boat,* has been translated into sixteen languages internationally. Fiction writer and journalist, America's Andrew Lam, moves between Australia, Vietnam and his adopted homeland, the USA, his writing and internet presence mapping his re-engagement with a lost past with an often exquisitely painful honesty.

In Vietnam, fiction writing can be viewed generationally from that of the older generation aligned to the State to the work of younger writers who refuse to mark the war temporally as the social and cultural watershed it was for their parents. Bao Ninh's 1991 novel, *The Sorrow of War,* offered many Western readers their first glimpse of the impact of the Vietnam War on the writers who fought in it and lived to enjoy a victory of sorts. The book, the first grim section of which opens this anthology, has been compared to Stephen Crane's *The Red Badge of Courage,* the Moravian writer, Bohumil Hrabal's, *Closely Observed Trains* and the German, Eric Remarque's *All Quiet on the Western Front,* in the manner in which, taking its place in a multinational pantheon of novels that examine the cruelty of war, it refuses to glorify wars' pollutant affect on the lives of all who fight in them. Yet *The Sorrow of War* is of little interest to many young Vietnamese for whom new media, mobile phones and internet writing offer a contemporary voice.

Nostalgia, it has been argued, is an inevitable by-product of conflicts such as the wars Vietnam has fought against France and the United States and her allies. The French novelist and psychoanalyst, François Lelord, has written extensively about France's post-colonial nostalgia for Vietnam, its manifestations in French writing and film and its interplay with and impact on nostalgic tourism. The French–Vietnamese filmmaker, Tran Anh Hung, also gives full play to such nostalgia in the aestheticised settings of his films, *The Scent of Green Papaya,* which was shot in Paris, and *Vertical Rays of the Sun,* shot in Hanoi. In Adam Aitken's piece, 'Beyond Khe Sanh', the author weaves a nostalgic memoir with a keen analysis of Greene's *The Quiet American.* As Alison Murray has asserted, for writers such as many of those in this anthology, nostalgia can be an attempt to 'come to terms with the facts and fantasies of colonial domination in different historical and geographical contexts'. Pham Duy Khiem meets a Vietnamese *Tiên* in Paris. Andrew Lam's palm reader reads palms as one reads lost terrains. The lost is thus relocated in the highly stylised and attenuated images of the idealised landscape or, if the physical landscape refuses to offer itself to the myth of belonging, the inner landscapes of refugees imprisoned in a state of irretrievable dispossession of which, 'the migrant's impossible nostalgia is but a symptom'.

In many of these stories we also see how migrant Vietnamese negotiate their new country's customs while holding onto the old. Viet Lê's 'Strawberries for Sale', Hoa Pham's 'The Daughters of Au Co' and Isabelle Thuy Pelaud's 'Eurasian' speak of the painful negotiations between two cultures. Similar engagements with the past, it can be argued, continue to influence a writer's cultural relationship with Vietnam. Stories, films, plays and poetry featuring Vietnam become sites 'where problems of historical consciousness are worked out, and, as such, are both reflective and constitutive of collective memory'[1]. The past is a symbolic place. It is found in the narratives of exile, reflecting perhaps, a migrant's need 'to reach deeper into the past and further into the future to retrieve the longed for object'[2].

Nostalgia has much to do with a visitor's cultural response to Vietnam, particularly in the tourism undertaken by the ex–servicemen and women who return to the sites of their war experience. Vietnamese–Australians who return to Vietnam on holidays or to visit their relatives, have also reshaped the manner in which the two countries view one another. But the relationship is a contradictory one. The Saigon from which many of Australia's Vietnamese fled may have been reshaped by Vietnam's economic revolution – the *doi moi* renovation – but every year on the 30th of April, Liberation Day, the city also continues to display the triumphalism associated with the city's fall.

Identity is negotiated through public spaces and public culture. In Sydney's Vietnamese communities, in Hanoi's Old Quarter or HCM City's mélange of past and contemporary structures, tourists and returning Vietnamese often find something that defies their notion of Vietnam and Vietnamese culture. A decade after Pam Brown's visit, poets such as Steve Kelen and Jane Gibian capture a symbolic meaning in the landscape. John Urry has argued that identity almost everywhere has to be produced partly out of images constructed for tourists, asserting that '…it is not just that places are transformed by the arrival or potential arrival of visitors. It is also that…people are themselves transformed'[3].

The youthful tourists who backpack through South East Asia or international students who participate in exchange programs with Australian universities have influenced younger generations uninterested in a conflict that happened decades before they were born. Without eliding the locals from the setting, tourism throws up a hybrid nostalgia manifesting itself in the renovated buildings of the colonisers, the pith helmets and colonial uniforms of France's colonial powers worn unselfconsciously by Vietnamese staff in hotels such as Hanoi's Metropole today.

Whatever we take to or bring away from Vietnam, the country offers metaphors of loss and love, of past glories and new beginnings. In many ways the pragmatic is interwoven with this. Diplomatic, unwilling to offend the tourists who arrive open to new experiences, Vietnam offers its travellers a mirror of their own expectations. Or perhaps it's more like a set of binoculars through which the distance moves closer in tantalising and disruptive ways. The ancient cultural images of temples and faeries and mandarins, or a damp green landscape with rice paddies, ducks and water buffaloes, colonial cities with cyclos and French-inspired cafés, or rap-loving, internet-using, hip, young Vietnamese. All of these images are underpinned with the keening of those who suffered and fled. Idealised, perplexing, open, closed Vietnam – as we read about it we might understand what we've lost, what we're looking for and what we've found.

CATHERINE COLE

1. A. Murray, 'Women, Nostalgia, Memory: *Chocolat, Outremer,* and *Indochine',* *Research in African Literatures,* no. 2, vol. 33, 2002, p. 238.

2. S. Boym cited in S. M. Tageldin, 'Reversing the Sentence of Impossible Nostalgia: The Poetics of Postcolonial Migration in Sakinna Boukhedenna and Agha Shahid Ali', in *Comparative Literature Studies,* no. 2, vol. 40, 2002, pp. 233.

3. J. Urry, *Consuming Places,* Routledge, New York, 1995, p. 65.

Bao Ninh

The Sorrow of War

On the banks of the Ya Crong Poco River, on the northern flank of the B3 battlefield in the Central Highlands, the Missing in Action Remains-Gathering Team awaits the dry season of 1975.

The mountains and jungles are water-soaked and dull. Wet trees. Quiet jungles. All day and all night the water streams. A sea of greenish vapour over the jungle's carpet of rotting leaves.

September and October drag by, then November passes, but still the weather is unpredictable and the night rains are relentless. Sunny days but rainy nights.

Even in early December, weeks after the end of the normal rainy season, the jungles this year are still as muddy as all hell. They are forgotten by peace, damaged or impassable, all the tracks disappearing bit by bit, day by day, into the embrace of the coarse undergrowth and wild grasses.

Travelling in such conditions is brutally tough. To get from Crocodile Lake east of the Sa Thay river, across District

67 to the crossroads of Cross Hill on the west bank of the Yar
Crong Poco – a mere fifty kilometres – the powerful Russian
truck has to lumber along all day. And still they fall short of
their destination.

Not until after dusk does the MIA Zil truck reach the
Jungle of Screaming Souls, where they park beside a wide
creek clogged with rotting branches.

The driver stays in the cab and goes straight to sleep. Kien
climbs wearily into the rear of the truck to sleep alone in a
hammock strung high from cab to tailgate. At midnight the
rains start again, this time a smooth drizzle, falling silently.

The old tarpaulin covering the truck is torn, full of holes,
letting the water drip, drip, drip through onto the plastic
sheets covering the remains of soldiers laid out in rows below
Kien's hammock.

The humid atmosphere condenses, its long moist, chilly
fingers sliding in and around the hammock where Kien lies
shivering, half-awake, half-asleep, as though drifting along
on a stream. He is floating, sadly, endlessly, sometimes as if on
a truck driving silently, robot-like, somnambulantly through
the lonely jungle tracks. The stream moans, a desperate
complaint mixing with distant, faint jungle sounds, like
an echo from another world. The eerie sounds come from
somewhere in a remote past, arriving softly like featherweight
leaves falling on the grass of times long, long ago.

Kien knows the area well. It was here, at the end of the
dry season of 1969, that his 27th Battalion was surrounded
and almost totally wiped out. Ten men survived from the
Lost Battalion after fierce, horrible, barbarous fighting.

That was the dry season when the sun burned harshly,
the wind blew fiercely, and the enemy sent napalm spraying
through the jungle and a sea of fire enveloped them, spreading
like the fires of Hell. Troops in the fragmented companies
tried to regroup, only to be blown out of their shelters

again as they went mad, became disorientated, and threw themselves into nets of bullets, dying in the flaming inferno. Above them the helicopters flew at treetop height and shot them almost one by one, the blood spreading out, spraying from their backs, flowing like red mud.

The diamond-shaped grass clearing was piled high with bodies killed by the helicopter gunships. Broken bodies, bodies blown apart, bodies vaporised.

No jungle grew again in this clearing. No grass. No plants.

'Better to die than surrender, my brothers! Better to die!' the battalion commander yelled insanely; waving his pistol in front of Kien he blew his own brains out through his ear. Kien screamed soundlessly in his throat at the sight, as the Americans attacked with submachine guns, sending bullets buzzing like deadly bees around him. Then Kien lowered his machine gun, grasped his side, and fell, rolling slowly down the bank of a shallow stream, hot blood trailing down the slope after him.

In the days that followed, crows and eagles darkened the sky. After the Americans withdrew, the rainy season came, flooding the jungle floor, turning the battlefield into a marsh whose surface water turned rust-coloured from the blood. Bloated human corpses, floating alongside of incinerated jungle animals, mixed with branches and trunks cut down by artillery, all drifting in a stinking marsh.

When the flood receded everything dried in the heat of the sun into thick mud and stinking rotting meat. And down the bank and along the stream Kien dragged himself, bleeding from the mouth and from his body wound. The blood was cold and sticky, like blood from a corpse. Snakes and centipedes crawled over him, and he felt death's hand on him. After that battle no one mentioned the 27th battalion any more, though numerous souls of ghosts and devils were born in that deadly defeat. They were still loose, wandering in every corner and bush in the jungle, drifting along the stream, refusing to depart for the Other World.

From then on it was called the Jungle of Screaming Souls. Just hearing the name whispered was enough to send chills down the spine. Perhaps the screaming souls gathered together on special festival days as members of the Lost Battalion, lining up in the little diamond-shaped clearing, checking their ranks and numbers. The sobbing whispers were heard deep in the jungle at night, the howls carried on the wind. Perhaps they really were the voices of the wandering souls of dead soldiers.

Kien was told that passing this area at night one could hear birds crying like human beings. They never flew, they only cried among the branches. And nowhere else in these Central Highlands could one find bamboo shoots of such a horrible colour, with infected weals like bleeding pieces of meat. As for the fireflies, they were huge. Some said they'd seen firefly lights rise before them as big as a steel helmet – some said bigger than helmets.

Here, when it is dark, trees and plants moan in awful harmony. When the ghostly music begins it unhinges the soul and the entire wood looks the same no matter where you are standing. Not a place for the timid. Living here one could go mad or be frightened to death. Which was why in the rainy season of 1974, when the regiment was sent back to this area, Kien and his scout squad established an altar and prayed before it in secret, honouring and recalling the wandering souls from the 27th Battalion still in the Jungle of Screaming Souls.

Sparkling incense sticks glowed night and day at the altar from that day forward.

This is an extract from the novel The Sorrow of War. *Translated by Phan Thanh Hao.*

Nam Le

Love and Honour and Pity and Pride and Compassion and Sacrifice

My father arrived on a rainy morning. I was dreaming about a poem, the dull *thluck thluck* of a typewriter's keys punching out the letters. It was a good poem — perhaps the best I'd ever written. When I woke up, he was standing outside my bedroom door, smiling ambiguously. He wore black trousers and a wet, wrinkled parachute jacket that looked like it had just been pulled out of a washing machine. Framed by the bedroom doorway, he appeared even smaller, gaunter, than I remembered. Still groggy with dream, I lifted my face toward the alarm clock.

'What time is it?'

'Hello, Son,' he said in Vietnamese. 'I knocked for a long time. Then the door just opened.'

The fields are glass, I thought. Then tum-ti-ti, a dactyl, end line, then the words *excuse* and *alloy* in the line after. *Come on*, I thought.

'It's raining heavily,' he said.

I frowned. The clock read 11:44. 'I thought you weren't coming until this afternoon.' It felt strange, after all this time, to be speaking Vietnamese again.

'They changed my flight in Los Angeles.'

'Why didn't you ring?'

'I tried,' he said equably. 'No answer.'

I twisted over the side of the bed and cracked open the window. The sound of rain filled the room – rain fell on the streets, on the roofs, on the tin shed across the parking lot like the distant detonations of firecrackers. Everything smelled of wet leaves.

'I turn the ringer off when I sleep,' I said. 'Sorry.'

He continued smiling at me, significantly, as if waiting for an announcement.

'I was dreaming.'

He used to wake me, when I was young, by standing over me and smacking my cheeks lightly. I hated it – the wetness, the sourness of his hands.

'Come on,' he said, picking up a large Adidas duffel and a rolled bundle that looked like a sleeping bag. 'A day lived, a sea of knowledge earned.' He had a habit of speaking in Vietnamese proverbs. I had long since learned to ignore it.

I threw on a t-shirt and stretched my neck in front of the lone window. Through the rain, the sky was as grey and striated as graphite. *The fields are glass*...Like a shape in smoke, the poem blurred, then dissolved into this new, cold, strange reality: a windblown, rain-strafed parking lot; a dark room almost entirely taken up by my bed; the small body of my father dripping water onto hardwood floors.

I went to him, my legs goose-pimpled underneath my panamas. He watched with pleasant indifference as my hand reached for his, shook it, then relieved his other hand of the bags. 'You must be exhausted,' I said.

He had flown from Sydney, Australia. Thirty-three hours all up – transiting in Auckland, Los Angeles, and Denver – before touching down in Iowa. I hadn't seen him in three years.

'You'll sleep in my room.'

'Very fancy,' he said as he led me through my own apartment. 'You even have a piano.' He gave me an almost rueful smile. 'I knew you'd never really quit.' Something moved behind his face and I found myself back on a heightened stool with my fingers chasing the metronome, ahead and behind, trying to shut out the tutor's repeated sighing, his heavy brass ruler. I realised I was massaging my knuckles. My father patted the futon in my living room. 'I'll sleep here.'

'You'll sleep in my room, Ba.' I watched him warily as he surveyed our surroundings, messy with books, papers, dirty plates, teacups, clothes – I'd intended to tidy up before going to the airport. 'I work in this room anyway, and I work at night.' As he moved into the kitchen, I grabbed the three-quarters-full bottle of Johnnie Walker from the second shelf of my bookcase and stashed it under the desk. I looked around. The desktop was gritty with cigarette ash. I threw some magazines over the roughest spots, then flipped one of them over because its cover bore a picture of Chairman Mao. I quickly gathered up the cigarette packs and sleeping pills and incense burners and dumped them all on a high shelf, behind my Kafka Vintage Classics.

At the kitchen swing door I remembered the photo of Linda beside the printer. Her glamour shot, I called it: hair windswept and eyes squinty, smiling at something out of frame. One of her ex-boyfriends had taken it at Lake MacBride. She looked happy. I snatched it and turned it facedown, covering it with scrap paper.

As I walked into the kitchen I thought, for a moment, that I'd left the fire escape open. I could hear rainwater gushing along gutters, down through the pipes. Then I saw my father at the sink, sleeves rolled up, sponge in hand, washing the month-old crusted mound of dishes. The smell was awful. 'Ba,' I frowned, 'you don't need to do that.'

His hands, hard and leathery, moved deftly in the sink.

'Ba,' I said, half-heartedly.

'I'm almost finished.' He looked up and smiled. 'Have you eaten? Do you want me to make some lunch?'

'*Hoi*,' I said, suddenly irritated. 'You're exhausted. I'll go out and get us something.'

I went back through the living room into my bedroom, picking up clothes and rubbish along the way.

'You don't have to worry about me,' he called out. 'You just do what you always do.'

★ ★ ★

The truth was, he'd come at the worst possible time. I was in my last year at the Iowa Writers' Workshop; it was late November, and my final story for the semester was due in three days. I had a backlog of papers to grade and a heap of fellowship and job applications to draft and submit. It was no wonder I was drinking so much.

I'd told Linda only the previous night that he was coming. We were at her place. Her body was slippery with sweat and hard to hold. Her body smelled of her clothes. She turned me over, my face kissing the bedsheets, and then she was chopping my back with the edges of her hands. *Higher. Out a bit more.* She had trouble keeping a steady rhythm. 'Softer,' I told her. Moments later, I started laughing.

'What?'

The sheets were damp beneath my pressed face.

'What?'

'*Softer*,' I said, 'not *slower*.'

She slapped my back with the meat of her palms, hard – once, twice. I couldn't stop laughing. I squirmed over and caught her by the wrists. Hunched forward, she was blushing and beautiful. Her hair fell over her face; beneath its ash-blond hem all I could see were her open lips. She pressed down, into me, her shoulders kinking the long, lean curve from the back of her neck to the small of her back. 'Stop it!' her lips said. She wrested her hands free. Her fingers beneath my waistband, violent, the scratch of her nails down my thighs, knees, ankles. I pointed my foot like a ballet dancer.

Afterward, I told her my father didn't know about her. She said nothing. 'We just don't talk about that kind of stuff,' I explained. She looked like an actress who looked like my girlfriend. Staring at her face made me tired. I'd begun to feel this way more often around her. 'He's only here for three days.' Somewhere out of sight, a group of college boys hooted and yelled.

'I thought you didn't talk to him at all.'

'He's my father.'

'What's he want?'

I rolled toward her, onto my elbow. I tried to remember how much I'd told her about him. We'd been lying on the bed, the wind loud in the room – I remember that – and we were both tipsy. Ours could have been any two voices in the darkness. 'It's only three days,' I said.

The look on her face was strange, shut down. She considered me a long time. Then she got up and pulled on her clothes. 'Just make sure you get your story done,' she said.

* * *

I drank before I came here too. I drank when I was a student at university, and then when I was a lawyer – in my previous life, as they say. There was a subterranean bar in a hotel next to my work, and every night I would wander down and slump on a barstool and pretend I didn't want the bartender to make small talk with me. He was only a bit older than me, and I came to envy his ease, his confidence that any given situation was merely temporary. I left exorbitant tips. After a while I was treated to battered shrimps and shepherd's pies on the house. My parents had already split by then, my father moving to Sydney, my mother into a government flat.

That's all I've ever done, traffic in words. Sometimes I still think about word counts the way a general must think about casualties. I'd been in Iowa more than a year – days passed in weeks, then months, more than a year of days – and I'd written only three and a half stories. About seventeen thousand words. When I was working at the law firm, I would have written that many words in a couple of weeks. And they would have been useful to someone.

Deadlines came, exhausting, and I forced myself up to meet them. Then, in the great spans of time between, I fell back to my vacant screen and my slowly sludging mind. I tried everything – writing in longhand, writing in my bed, in my bathtub. As this last deadline approached, I remembered a friend claiming he'd broken his writer's block by switching to a typewriter. You're free to write, he told me, once you know you can't delete what you've written. I bought an electric Smith Corona at an antique shop. It buzzed like a tropical aquarium when I plugged it in. It looked good on my desk. For inspiration, I read absurdly formal Victorian poetry and drank Scotch neat. How hard could it be? Things happened in this world all the time. All I had to do was record them. In the sky, two swarms of swallows converged, pulled apart, interwove again like veils drifting at crosscurrents. In line at the supermarket, a black woman leaned forward and kissed the handle of her shopping cart, her skin dark and glossy like the polished wood of a piano.

The week prior to my father's arrival, a friend chastised me for my persistent defeatism.

'Writer's block?' Under the streetlights, vapours of bourbon puffed out of his mouth. 'How can you have writer's block? Just write a story about Vietnam.'

We had come from a party following a reading by the workshop's most recent success, a Chinese woman trying to immigrate to America who had written a book of short stories about Chinese characters in stages of immigration to America. The stories were subtle and good. The gossip was that she'd been offered a substantial six-figure contract for a two-book deal. It was meant to be an unspoken rule that such things were left unspoken. Of course, it was all anyone talked about.

'It's hot,' a writing instructor told me at a bar. 'Ethnic literature's hot. And important too.'

A couple of visiting literary agents took a similar view: 'There's a lot of polished writing around,' one of them said. 'You have to ask yourself, what makes me stand out?' She tag-teamed to her colleague, who answered slowly as though intoning a mantra, 'Your *background* and *life experience*.'

Other friends were more forthright: 'I'm sick of ethnic lit,' one said. 'It's full of descriptions of exotic food.' Or: 'You can't tell if the language is spare because the author intended it that way, or because he didn't have the vocab.'

I was told about a friend of a friend, a Harvard graduate from Washington, D.C., who had posed in traditional Nigerian garb for his book-jacket photo. I pictured myself standing in a rice paddy, wearing a straw conical hat. Then I pictured my father in the same field, wearing his threadbare fatigues, young and hard-eyed.

'It's a license to bore,' my friend said. We were drunk and walking our bikes because both of us, separately, had punctured our tires on the way to the party.

'The characters are always flat, generic. As long as a Chinese writer writes about *Chinese* people, or a Peruvian writer about *Peruvians*, or a Russian writer about *Russians*...'

he said, as though reciting children's doggerel, then stopped, losing his train of thought. His mouth turned up into a doubtful grin. I could tell he was angry about something.

'Look,' I said, pointing at a floodlit porch ahead of us. 'Those guys have guns.'

'As long as there's an interesting image or metaphor once in every *this* much text' – he held out his thumb and forefinger to indicate half a page, his bike wobbling all over the sidewalk. I nodded to him, and then I nodded to one of the guys on the porch, who nodded back. The other guy waved us through with his faux-wood air rifle. A car with its headlights on was idling in the driveway, and girls' voices emerged from inside, squealing, 'Don't shoot! Don't shoot!'

'Faulkner, you know,' my friend said over the squeals, 'he said we should write about the old verities. Love and honour and pity and pride and compassion and sacrifice.' A sudden sharp crack behind us, like the striking of a giant typewriter hammer, followed by some muffled shrieks. 'I know I'm a bad person for saying this,' my friend said, 'but that's why I don't mind your work, Nam. Because you could just write about Vietnamese boat people all the time. Like in your third story.'

He must have thought my head was bowed in modesty, but in fact I was figuring out whether I'd just been shot in the back of the thigh. I'd felt a distinct sting. The pellet might have ricocheted off something.

'You could *totally* exploit the Vietnamese thing. But *instead*, you choose to write about lesbian vampires and Colombian assassins, and Hiroshima orphans – and New York painters with haemorrhoids.'

For a dreamlike moment I was taken aback. Catalogued like that, under the bourbon stink of his breath, my stories sank into unflattering relief. My leg was still stinging. I imagined sticking my hand down the back of my jeans, bringing it to my face under a streetlight, and finding it gory, blood-spattered. I imagined turning around, advancing wordlessly up the porch steps, and drop-kicking the two kids. I would tell my story into a microphone from a hospital bed. I would compose my story in a county cell. I would kill one of them, maybe accidentally, and never talk about it, ever, to anyone. There was no hole in my jeans.

'I'm probably a bad person,' my friend said, stumbling beside his bike a few steps in front of me.

★   ★   ★

If you ask me why I came to Iowa, I would say that Iowa is beautiful in the way that any place is beautiful: if you treat it as the answer to a question you're asking yourself every day, just by being there.

That afternoon, as I was leaving the apartment for Linda's, my father called out my name from the bedroom.

I stopped outside the closed door. He was meant to be napping.

'Where are you going?' his voice said.

'For a walk,' I replied.

'I'll walk with you.'

It always struck me how everything seemed larger in scale on Summit Street: the double-storied houses, their smooth lawns sloping down to the sidewalks like golf greens; elm trees with high, thick branches – the sort of branches from which I imagined fathers suspending long-roped swings for daughters in white dresses. The leaves, once golden and red, were turning brown, dark orange. The rain had stopped. I don't know why, but we walked in the middle of the road, dark asphalt gleaming beneath the slick, pasted leaves like the back of a whale.

I asked him, 'What do you want to do while you're here?'

His face was pale and fixed in a smile. 'Don't worry about me,' he said. 'I can just meditate. Or read.'

'There's a coffee shop downtown,' I said. 'And a Japanese restaurant.' It sounded pathetic. It occurred to me that I knew nothing about what my father did all day.

He kept smiling, looking at the ground moving in front of his feet.

'I have to write,' I said.

'You write.'

And I could no longer read his smile. He had perfected it during our separation. It was a setting of the lips, sly, almost imperceptible, which I would probably have taken for a sign of senility but for the keenness of his eyes.

'There's an art museum across the river,' I said.

'Ah, take me there.'

'The museum?'

'No,' he said, looking sideways at me. 'The river.'

We turned back to Burlington Street and walked down the hill to the river. He stopped halfway across the bridge. The water below looked cold and black, slowing in sections as it succumbed to the temperature. Behind us six lanes of cars skidded back and forth across the wet grit of the road, the sound like the shredding of wind.

'Have you heard from your mother?' He stood upright before the railing, his head strangely small above the puffy down jacket I had lent him.

'Every now and then.'

He lapsed into formal Vietnamese: 'How is the mother of Nam?'

'She is good,' I said – too loudly – trying to make myself heard over the groans and clanks of a passing truck.

He was nodding. Behind him, the east bank of the river glowed wanly in the afternoon light. 'Come on,' I said. We crossed the bridge and walked to a nearby Dairy Queen. When I came out, two coffees in my hands, my father had gone down to the river's edge. Next to him, a bundled-up, bearded figure stooped over a burning gasoline drum. Never had I seen anything like it in Iowa City.

'This is my son,' my father said, once I had scrambled down the wet bank. 'The writer.' I glanced quickly at him but his face gave nothing away. He lifted a hot paper cup out of my hand. 'Would you like some coffee?'

'Thank you, no.' The man stood still, watching his knotted hands, palms glowing orange above the rim of the drum. His voice was soft, his clothes heavy with his life. I smelled animals in him, and fuel, and rain.

'I read his story,' my father went on in his lilting English, 'about Vietnamese boat people.' He gazed at the man, straight into his blank, rheumy eyes, then said, as though delivering a punch line, '*We* are Vietnamese boat people.'

We stood there for a long time, the three of us, watching the flames. When I lifted my eyes it was dark.

'Do you have any money on you?' my father asked me in Vietnamese.

'Welcome to America,' the man said through his beard. He didn't look up as I closed his fist around the damp bills.

★   ★   ★

My father was drawn to weakness, even as he tolerated none in me. He was a soldier, he said once, as if that explained everything. With me, he was all proverbs and regulations. No personal phone calls. No female friends. No extracurricular reading. When I was in primary school, he made me draw up a daily ten-hour study timetable for the summer holidays, and punished me when I deviated from it. He knew how to cane me twenty times and leave only one black-red welt, like a brand mark across my buttocks. Afterward, as he rubbed Tiger Balm on the wound, I would cry in anger at myself for crying. Once, when my mother let slip that durian fruit made me vomit, he forced me to eat it in front of guests. *Doi an muoi cung ngon*. Hunger finds no fault with food. I learned to hate him with a straight face.

When I was fourteen, I discovered that he had been involved in a massacre. Later, I would come across photos and transcripts and books; but that night, at a family friend's party in suburban Melbourne, it was just another story in a circle of drunken men. They sat cross-legged on newspapers around a large blue tarpaulin, getting smashed on cheap beer. It was that time of night when things started to break up against other things. Red faces, raised voices, spilled drinks. We arrived late and the men shuffled around, making room for my father.

'Thanh! Fuck your mother! What took you so long – scared, no? Sit down, sit down.'

'Give him five bottles.' The speaker swung around ferociously. 'We're letting you off easy, everyone here's had eight, nine already.'

For the first time, my father let me stay. I sat on the perimeter of the circle, watching in fascination. A thicket of Vietnamese voices, cursing, toasting, braying about their children, making fun of one man who kept stuttering, 'It has the power of f-f-five hundred horses!' Through it all my father laughed good-naturedly, his face so red with drink he looked sunburned. Bowl and chopsticks in his hands, he appeared somewhat childish squashed between two men trading war stories. I watched him as he picked sparingly at the enormous spread of dishes in the middle of the circle. The food was known as *do an nho*: alcohol food. Massive fatty oysters dipped in salt-pepper-lemon paste. Boiled sea snails the size of pool balls. Southern-style shredded chicken salad, soaked in vinegar and eaten with spotty brown rice crackers. Someone called out my father's name; he had set his chopsticks down and was speaking in a low voice:

'Heavens, the gunships came first, rockets and M60s. You remember that sound, no? Like you were deaf. We were hiding in the bunker underneath the temple, my mother and four sisters and Mrs Tran, the baker, and some other people. You couldn't hear anything. Then the gunfire stopped and Mrs Tran told my mother we had to go up to the street. If we stayed there, the Americans would think we were Viet Cong. "I'm not going anywhere," my mother said. "They have grenades," Mrs Tran said. I was scared and excited. I had never seen an American before.'

It took me a while to reconcile my father with the story he was telling. He caught my eye and held it a moment, as though he were sharing a secret with me. He was drunk.

'So we went up. Everywhere there was dust and smoke, and all you could hear was the sound of helicopters and M16s. Houses on fire. Then through the smoke I saw an American. I almost laughed. He wore his uniform so untidily – it was too big for him – and he had a beaded necklace and a baseball cap. He held an M16 over his shoulder like a spade. Heavens, he looked nothing like the Viet Cong, with their shirts buttoned up to their chins – and tucked in – even after crawling through mud tunnels all day.'

He picked up his chopsticks and reached for the *tiet canh* – a specialty – mincemeat soaked in fresh congealed duck blood. Some of the other men were listening now, smiling knowingly. I saw his teeth, stained red, as he chewed through the rest of his words:

'They made us walk to the east side of the village. There were about ten of them, about fifty of us. Mrs Tran was saying, "No VC no VC." They didn't hear her, not over the sound of machine guns and the M79 grenade launchers. Remember those? Only I heard her. I saw pieces of animals all over the paddy fields, a water buffalo with its side missing – like it was scooped out by a spoon. Then, through the smoke, I saw Grandpa Long bowing to a GI in the traditional greeting. I wanted to call out to him. His wife and daughter and granddaughters, My and Kim, stood shyly behind him. The GI stepped forward, tapped the top of his head with the rifle butt and then twirled the gun around and slid the bayonet into his throat. No one said anything. My mother tried to cover my eyes, but I saw him switch the fire selector on his gun from automatic to single-shot before he shot Grandma Long. Then he and a friend pulled the daughter into a shack, the two little girls dragged along, clinging to her legs.

'They stopped us at the drainage ditch, near the bridge. There were bodies on the road, a baby with only the bottom half of its head, a monk, his robe turning pink. I saw two bodies with the ace of spades carved into the chests. I didn't understand it. My sisters didn't even cry. People were now shouting, "No VC no VC," but the Americans just frowned and spat and laughed. One of them said something, then some of them started pushing us into the ditch. It was half full of muddy water. My mother jumped in and lifted my sisters down, one by one. I remember looking up and seeing helicopters everywhere, some bigger than others, some higher up. They made us kneel in the water. They set up their guns on tripods. They made us stand up again. One of the Americans, a boy with a fat face, was crying and moaning softly as he reloaded his magazine. "No VC no VC." They didn't look at us. They made us turn back around. They made us kneel back down in the water. When they started shooting I felt my mother's body jumping on top of mine; it kept jumping for a long time, and then everywhere was the sound of helicopters, louder and louder like they were all coming down to land, and everything was dark and wet and warm and sweet.'

The circle had gone quiet. My mother came out from the kitchen, squatted behind my father, and looped her arms around his neck. This was a minor breach of the rules. 'Heavens,' she said, 'don't you men have anything better to talk about?'

After a short silence, someone snorted, saying loudly, 'You win, Thanh. You really *did* have it bad!' and then everyone, including my father, burst out laughing. I joined in unsurely. They clinked glasses and made toasts using words I didn't understand.

Maybe he didn't tell it exactly that way. Maybe I'm filling in the gaps. But you're not under oath when writing a eulogy, and this is close enough. My father grew up in the province of Quang Ngai, in the village of Son My, in the hamlet of Tu Cung, later known to the Americans as My Lai. He was fourteen years old.

$$\star \quad \star \quad \star$$

Late that night, I plugged in the Smith Corona. It hummed with promise. I grabbed the bottle of Scotch from under the desk and poured myself a double. *Fuck it*, I thought. I had two and a half days left. I would write the ethnic story of my Vietnamese father. It was a good story. It was a fucking *great* story.

I fed in a sheet of blank paper. At the top of the page, I typed 'ETHNIC STORY' in capital letters. I pushed the carriage return and scrolled down to the next line. The sound of helicopters in a dark sky. The keys hammered the page.

$$\star \quad \star \quad \star$$

I woke up late the next day. At the coffee shop, I sat with my typed pages and watched people come and go. They laughed and sat and sipped and talked and, listening to them, I was reminded again that I was in a small town in a foreign country.

I thought of my father in my dusky bedroom. He had kept the door closed as I left. I thought of how he had looked when I checked on him before going to bed: his body engulfed by blankets and his head so small among my pillows. He'd aged in those last three years. His skin glassy in the blue glow of dawn. He was here, now, with me, and already making the rest of my life seem unreal.

I read over what I had typed: thinking of him at that age, still a boy, and who he would become. At a nearby table, a guy held out one of his iPod earbuds and beckoned his date to come sit beside him. The door opened and a cold wind blew in. I tried to concentrate.

'Hey.' It was Linda, wearing a large orange hiking jacket and bringing with her the crisp, bracing scent of all the places she had been. Her face was unmaking a smile. 'What are you doing here?'

'Working on my story.'

'Is your dad here?'

'No.'

Her friends were waiting by the counter. She nodded to them, holding up one finger, then came behind me, resting her hands on my shoulders. 'Is this it?' She leaned over me, her hair grazing my face, cold and silken against my cheek. She picked up a couple of pages and read them soundlessly. 'I don't get it,' she said, returning them to the table. 'What are you doing?'

'What do you mean?'

'You never told me any of this.'

I shrugged.

'Did he tell you this? Now he's talking to you?'

'Not really,' I said.

'Not really?'

I turned around to face her. Her eyes reflected no light.

'You know what I think?' She looked back down at the pages. 'I think you're making excuses for him.'

'Excuses?'

'You're romanticising his past,' she went on quietly, 'to make sense of the things you said he did to you.'

'It's a story,' I said. 'What things did I say?'

'You said he abused you.'

It was too much, these words, and what connected to them. I looked at her serious, beautifully lined face, her light-trapping eyes, and already I felt them taxing me. 'I never said that.'

She took a half step back. 'Just tell me this,' she said, her voice flattening. 'You've never introduced him to any of your exes, right?' The question was tight on her face.

I didn't say anything and after a while she nodded, biting one corner of her upper lip. I knew that gesture. I knew, even then, that I was supposed to stand up, pull her orange-jacketed body toward mine, speak words into her ear; but all I could do was think about my father and his excuses. Those tattered bodies on top of him. The ten hours he'd waited, mud filling his lungs, until nightfall. I felt myself falling back into old habits.

She stepped forward and kissed the top of my head. It was one of her rules: not to walk away from an argument without some sign of affection. I didn't look at her. My mother liked to tell the story of how, when our family first arrived in Australia, we lived in a hostel on an outer-suburb street where the locals – whenever they met or parted – hugged and kissed each other warmly. How my father – baffled, charmed – had named it 'the street of lovers'.

I turned to the window: it was dark now, the evening settling thick and deep. A man and woman sat across from each other at a high table. The woman leaned in, smiling, her breasts squat on the wood, elbows forward, her hands mere inches away from the man's shirtfront. Throughout their conversation her teeth glinted. Behind them, a mother sat with her son. 'I'm not playing,' she murmured, flipping through her magazine.

'L,' said the boy.

'I said I'm not playing.'

★　★　★

Here is what I believe: We forgive any sacrifice by our parents, so long as it is not made in our name. To my father there was no other name – only mine, and he had named me after the homeland he had given up. His sacrifice was complete and compelled him to everything that happened. To all that, I was inadequate.

At sixteen I left home. There was a girl, and crystal meth, and the possibility of greater loss than I had imagined possible. She embodied everything prohibited by my father and plainly worthwhile. Of course he was right about her: she taught me hurt – but promise too. We were two animals in the dark, hacking at one another, and never since have I felt that way – that sense of consecration. When my father found out my mother was supporting me, he gave her an ultimatum. She moved into a family friend's textile factory and learned to use an overlock machine and continued sending me money.

'Of course I want to live with him,' she told me when I visited her, months later. 'But I want you to come home too.'

'Ba doesn't want that.'

'You're his son,' she said simply. 'He wants you with him.'

I laundered my school uniform and asked a friend to cut my hair and waited for school hours to finish before catching the train home. My father excused himself upon seeing me. When he returned to the living room he had changed his shirt and there was water in his hair. I felt sick and fully awake – as if all the previous months had been a single sleep and now my face was wet again, burning cold. The room smelled of peppermint. He asked me if I was well, and I told him I was, and then he asked me if my female friend was well, and at that moment I realised he was speaking to me not as a father – not as he would to his only son – but as he would speak to a friend, to anyone, and it undid me. I had learned what it was to attenuate my blood but that was nothing compared to this. I forced myself to look at him and I asked him to bring Ma back home.

'And Child?'

'Child will not take any more money from Ma.'

'Come home,' he said, finally. His voice was strangled, half swallowed.

Even then, my emotions operated like a system of levers and pulleys; just seeing him had set them irreversibly into motion. 'No,' I said. The word shot out of me.

'Come home, and Ma will come home, and Ba promises Child to never speak of any of this again.' He looked away, smiling heavily, and took out a handkerchief. His forehead was moist with sweat. He had been buried alive in the warm, wet clinch of his family, crushed by their lives. I wanted to know how he climbed out of that pit. I wanted to know how there could ever be any correspondence between us. I wanted to know all this but an internal momentum moved me, further and further from him as time went on.

'The world is hard,' he said. For a moment I was uncertain whether he was speaking in proverbs. He looked at me, his face a gleaming mask. 'Just say yes, and we can forget everything. That's all. Just say it: Yes.'

But I didn't say it. Not that day, nor the next, nor any day for almost a year. When I did, though, rehabilitated and fixed in new privacies, he was true to his word and never spoke of the matter. In fact, after I came back home he never spoke of anything much at all, and it was under this learned silence that the three of us – my father, my mother, and I – living again under a single roof, were conducted irreparably into our separate lives.

★ ★ ★

The apartment smelled of fried garlic and sesame oil when I returned. My father was sitting on the living room floor, on the special mattress he had brought over with him. It was made of white foam. He told me it was for his back. 'There's some stir-fry in the kitchen.'

'Thanks.'

'I read your story this morning,' he said, 'while you were still sleeping.' Something in my stomach folded over. I hadn't thought to hide the pages. 'There are mistakes in it.'

'You read it?'

'There were mistakes in your last story too.'

My last story. I remembered my mother's phone call at the time: my father, unemployed and living alone in Sydney, had started sending long emails to friends from his past – friends from thirty, forty years ago. I should talk to him more often, she'd said. I'd sent him my refugee story. He hadn't responded. Now, as I came out of the kitchen with a heaped plate of stir-fry, I tried to recall those sections where I'd been sloppy with research. Maybe the scene in Rach Gia – before they reached the boat. I scooped up a forkful of marinated tofu, cashews, and chickpeas. He'd gone shopping. 'They're *stories*,' I said, chewing casually. 'Fiction.'

He paused for a moment, then said, 'Okay, Son.'

For so long my diet had consisted of chips and noodles and pizzas I'd forgotten how much I missed home cooking. As I ate, he stretched on his white mat.

'How's your back?'

'I had a CAT scan,' he said. 'There's nerve fluid leaking between my vertebrae.' He smiled his long-suffering smile, right leg twisted across his left hip. 'I brought the scans to show you.'

'Does it hurt, Ba?'

'It hurts.' He chuckled briefly, as though the whole matter were a joke. 'But what can I do? I can only accept it.'

'Can't they operate?'

I felt myself losing interest. I was a bad son. He'd separated from my mother when I started law school and ever since then he'd brought up his back pains so often – always couched in Buddhist tenets of suffering and acceptance – that the cold, hard part of me suspected he was exaggerating, to solicit and then gently rebuke my concern. He did this. He'd forced me to take karate lessons until I was sixteen; then, during one of our final arguments, he came at me and I found myself in fighting stance. He had smiled at my horror. 'That's right,' he'd said. We were locked in all the intricate ways of guilt. It took all the time we had to realise that everything we faced, we faced for the other as well.

'I want to talk with you,' I said.

'You grow old, your body breaks down,' he said.

'No, I mean for the story.'

'Talk?'

'Yes.'

'About what?' He seemed amused.

'About my mistakes,' I said.

★ ★ ★

If you ask me why I came to Iowa, I would say that I was a lawyer and I was no lawyer. Every twenty-four hours I woke up at the smoggiest time of morning and commuted – bus, tram, elevator, usually without saying a single word, wearing clothes that chafed against me and holding a flat white in a white cup – to my windowless office in the tallest, most glass-covered building in Melbourne. Time was broken down into six-minute units, friends allotted eight-unit lunch breaks. I hated what I was doing and I hated that I was good at it. Mostly, I hated knowing it was my job that made my father proud of me. When I told him I was quitting and going to Iowa to be a writer, he said, *Trau buoc ghet trau an.* The captive buffalo hates the free buffalo. But by that time, he had no more control over my life. I was twenty-five years old.

The thing is not to write what no one else could have written, but to write what only you could have written. I recently found this fragment in one of my old notebooks. The person who wrote that couldn't have known what would happen: how time can hold itself against you, how a voice hollows, how words you once loved can wither on the page.

'Why do you want to write this story?' my father asked me.

'It's a good story.'

'But there are so many things you could write about.'

'This is important, Ba. It's important that people know.'

'You want their pity.'

I didn't know whether it was a question. I was offended. 'I want them to remember,' I said.

He was silent for a long time. Then he said, 'Only you'll remember. I'll remember. They will read and clap their hands and forget.' For once, he was not smiling. 'Sometimes it's better to forget, no?'

'I'll write it anyway,' I said. It came back to me – how I'd felt at the typewriter the previous night. A thought leapt into my mind: 'If I write a true story,' I told my father, 'I'll have a better chance of selling it.'

He looked at me a while, searchingly, seeing something in my face as though for the first time. Finally he said, in a measured voice, 'I'll tell you.' For a moment he receded into thought. 'But believe me, it's not something you'll be able to write.'

'I'll write it anyway,' I repeated.

Then he did something unexpected. His face opened up and he began to laugh, without self-pity or slyness, laughing in full-bodied breaths. I was shocked. I hadn't heard him laugh like this for as long as I could remember. Without fully knowing why, I started laughing too. His throat was humming in Vietnamese, 'Yes…yes…yes,' his eyes shining, smiling. 'All right. All right. But tomorrow.'

'But' –

'I need to think,' he said. He shook his head, then said under his breath, 'My son a writer. *Co thuc moi vuc duoc dao.*' Fine words will butter no parsnips.

'*Mot nguoi lam quan, ca ho duoc nho,*' I retorted. A scholar is a blessing for all his relatives. He looked at me in surprise before laughing again and nodding vigorously. I'd been saving that one up for years.

* * *

Afternoon. We sat across from one another at the dining room table: I asked questions and took notes on a yellow legal pad; he talked. He talked about his childhood, his family. He talked about My Lai. At this point, he stopped.

'You won't offer your father some of that?'

'What?'

'Heavens, you think you can hide liquor of that quality?'

The afternoon light came through the window and held his body in a silver square, slowly sinking toward his feet, dimming, as he talked. I refilled our glasses. He talked above the peak-hour traffic on the streets, its rinse of noise; he talked deep into evening. When the phone rang the second time I unplugged it from the jack. He told me how he'd been conscripted into the South Vietnamese army.

'After what the Americans did? How could you fight on their side?'

'I had nothing but hate in me,' he said, 'but I had enough for everyone.' He paused on the word *hate* like a father saying it before his infant child for the first time, trying the child's knowledge, testing what was inherent in the word and what learned.

He told me about the war. He told me about meeting my mother. The wedding. Then the fall of Saigon. 1975. He told me about his imprisonment in re-education camp, the forced confessions, the indoctrinations, the starvations. The daily labour that ruined his back. The casual killings. He told me about the tiger-cage cells and connex boxes, the different names for different forms of torture: the honda, the airplane, the auto. 'They tie you by your thumbs, one arm over the shoulder, the other pulled around the front of the body. Or they stretch out your legs and tie your middle fingers to your big toes.'

He showed me. A skinny old man in Tantric poses, he looked faintly preposterous. During the auto he flinched, then, a smile springing to his face, asked me to help him to his foam mattress. I waited impatiently for him to stretch it out. He asked me again to help. *Here, push here. A little harder.* Then he went on talking, sometimes in a low voice, sometimes grinning. Other times he would blink – furiously, perplexedly. In spite of his Buddhist protestations, I imagined him locked in rage, turned around and forced every day to rewitness these atrocities of his past, helpless to act. But that was only my imagination. I had nothing to prove that he was not empty of all that now.

He told me how, upon his release after three years' incarceration, he organised our family's escape from Vietnam. This was 1979. He was twenty-five years old then, and my father.

When finally he fell asleep, his face warm from the Scotch, I watched him from the bedroom doorway. I was drunk. For a moment, watching him, I felt like I had drifted into dream too. For a moment I became my father, watching his sleeping son, reminded of what – for his son's sake – he had tried, unceasingly, to forget. A past larger than complaint, more perilous than memory. I shook myself conscious and went to my desk. I read my notes through once, carefully, all forty-five pages. I reread the draft of my story from two nights earlier. Then I put them both aside and started typing, never looking at them again.

Dawn came so gradually I didn't notice — until the beeping of a garbage truck—that outside the air was metallic blue and the ground was white. The top of the tin shed was white. The first snow had fallen.

★ ★ ★

He wasn't in the apartment when I woke up. There was a note on the coffee table: *I am going for a walk. I have taken your story to read.* I sat outside, on the fire escape, with a tumbler of Scotch, waiting for him. Against the cold, I drank my whiskey, letting it flow like a filament of warmth through my body. I had slept for only three hours and was too tired to feel anything but peace. The red geraniums on the landing of the opposite building were frosted over. I spied through my neighbours' windows and saw exactly nothing.

He would read it, with his book-learned English, and he would recognise himself in a new way. He would recognise me. He would see how powerful was his experience, how valuable his suffering — how I had made it speak for more than itself. He would be pleased with me.

I finished the Scotch. It was eleven-thirty and the sky was dark and grey-smeared. My story was due at midday. I put my gloves on, treaded carefully down the fire escape, and untangled my bike from the rack. He would be pleased with me. I rode around the block, up and down Summit Street, looking for a sign of my puffy jacket. The streets were empty. Most of the snow had melted, but an icy film covered the roads and I rode slowly. Eyes stinging and breath fogging in front of my mouth, I coasted toward downtown, across the College Green, the grass frozen so stiff it snapped beneath my bicycle wheels. Lights glowed dimly from behind the curtained windows of houses. On Washington

Street, a sudden gust of wind ravaged the elm branches and unfastened their leaves, floating them down thick and slow and soundless.

I was halfway across the bridge when I saw him. I stopped. He was on the riverbank. I couldn't make out the face but it was he, short and small-headed in my bloated jacket. He stood with the tramp, both of them staring into the blazing gasoline drum. The smoke was thick, particulate. For a second I stopped breathing. I knew with sick certainty what he had done. The ashes, given body by the wind, floated away from me down the river. He patted the man on the shoulder, reached into his back pocket and slipped some money into those large, newly mittened hands. He started up the bank then, and saw me. I was so full of wanting I thought it would flood my heart. His hands were empty.

If I had known then what I knew later, I wouldn't have said the things I did. I wouldn't have told him he didn't understand – for clearly, he did. I wouldn't have told him that what he had done was unforgivable. That I wished he had never come, or that he was no father to me. But I hadn't known, and, as I waited, feeling the wind change, all I saw was a man coming toward me in a ridiculously oversized jacket, rubbing his black-sooted hands, stepping through the smoke with its flecks and flame-tinged eddies, who had destroyed himself, yet again, in my name. The river was behind him. The wind was full of acid. In the slow float of light I looked away, down at the river. On the brink of freezing, it gleamed in large, bulging blisters. The water, where it still moved, was black and braided. And it occurred to me then how it took hours, sometimes days, for the surface of a river to freeze over – to hold in its skin the perfect and crystalline world – and how that world could be shattered by a small stone dropped like a single syllable.

Lam Thi My Da

A Sky in a Bomb Crater

Your friends said that you, a road builder,
had such a love for our country, you rushed
down the trail that night, waving your torch
to save the convoy, calling the bombs down on yourself.

We passed the spot where you died,
tried to picture the young girl you once had been.
We pitched stones up on the barren grave,
adding our love to a rising pile of stone.

I gazed into the centre of the crater
where you'd died and saw the sky in the pool
of rain water. Our country is so kind:
water from the sky washes the pain away.

Now you rest deep in the ground,
quiet as the sky that rests in the crater.
At night your soul pours down,
bright as the stars.

I wonder, could it be your soft skin
changed into columns of white clouds?
Could it be that when we passed that day,
it was not the sun but your heart breaking through?

This jungle trail now bears your name;
the skies reach down to your death and touches it;
and we, who never saw your face,
each wear a trace of you, bright on our cheek.

Translated by Ngo Vinh Hai and Kevin Bowen

Chi Vu

Vietnam: A psychic guide

Art is a lie that makes you realise the truth.
Picasso

airport

The City is located within a large airport. Metal and leather armchairs occupy the kilometres-long lobby. Waiting, always waiting, people will pass away the time by asking you where you had arrived from and which ticket you had purchased to get there.

A small friendship is struck, cheering up both parties momentarily. Complete strangers will ask to see each other's tickets. With the little glossy paper in our hands we build centuries of history from each other's seat number.

———————————————————————

Dear all,

You can never get a parking ticket; you can u-turn anywhere; the weather is warm; the beer is cold; the food is fabulous. If sexy is defined as that strange combination of awkwardness, an old and emerging new paradigm, then Hanoi is 'sexy'. You can get exquisite French tailoring and Vietnamese embroidery next to a vendor selling sticky brown tamarind procured with a long chopstick. I am staying in a hotel room with large white tiles and carved wooden furniture. If feels strange to have to submit the key to my room every time I leave the hotel. But I guess I am used to privacy a lot more. The room has a balcony that overlooks a little laneway, a sparrow's hop from the main lake – *Ho Hoan Kiem*. It is inner Hanoi and there the old cathedral, the lake itself and some of the most cosmopolitan new shops in Hanoi. Vietnam seems to have really discovered boutique shopping, for good or for bad.

The pavement is cracked, everywhere, as though Hanoi is a large grey and brown snake undergoing the shedding of its skin. And so for the time being the new pink skin is side by side with the old flakes of white skin.

I am also close to the Old Quarter, which has streets named after the old guilds of Hanoi. I am on *Hang Hanh* – the guild which sold onions. There is also *Hang Bac* (silver street), *Hang Gai* (hemp street), and *Hang Ngang* – a play on words for those of you who know Vietnamese. Of course not all the street names correspond to what is now being sold. Otherwise there would be a lot more streets called *Hang Internet*. The nouveau-riche ride about on spunky new motorbikes – the Spacey, the Majestic which has the elevated rear seat so that your *Vinababe*, wearing pink platform shoes, can look like she's straddling your neck as you both ride around the city.

The rural poor commute to the city during the day, walk around with baskets balanced on their bamboo sticks. Baskets heavy and bobbing with mandarins, lettuce, or tamarind candy. The rural people walk around all day, their bare feet black and cracked and swollen. Dry thick skin cracked just like the streets of the city.

Hanoi is a snake shedding its skin, regrowing the old patterns, changing its shape and slither. Its descendents came from the mating of an angel and a dragon you know...

Love, Michelle.

———————————————

Hi Hai,

When I rang her, she said that she would come and meet me for coffee.

'Do you want to see the aeroplane that came down during the time of the American air raids?'

'Yes?' I said.

So we got there, a short motorbike ride away, down an alleyway, and suddenly back out in the open air. A blue-black pile of metal flesh lay in a stagnant water pond of eerie green. Plastic bags and thick black insects floated at the edge of the pond. Around us were concrete houses. The older ones had just the one level with black flecks of mould growing in the walls. Several newer buildings three or four stories high, with a red-wood trimming on the doors and windows. These had been done-up for foreigners to rent. She said that when she was a little girl this pond was used to grow flowers, the most beautiful flowers. I asked whether they were then transported to *Hang Bong* (flower) street and sold, like in the movie *Three Seasons*.

'No, they were sold all throughout Hanoi.' Then she paused.

'What did you think of *Three Seasons*,' I asked.

'I did not like it very much.'

'Oh. Do many people here not like it as well?'

'No.' And she paused. I stood there too, and tried to think about it from her point of view – the way Vietnamese people were portrayed – a prostitute, a cyclo driver, beggar children. But I couldn't be sure what her silence meant.

'Yes, I think some characters were speaking very strangely,' I said, thinking like a scriptwriter; all the characters spoke formal Vietnamese as though reading a textbook. She still wasn't saying anything. 'Westerners like it because of the beautiful scenery,' I concluded, giving up on the topic.

'Perhaps because I live here I take that scenery for granted,' she said, as though we were standing in one of the delicious locations from the film.

'They showed a lot of rural scenes, farmers,' she said. 'But we are modern now.' She gestured to those tall buildings for foreigners to rent, 'We have tall buildings.'

The height of those buildings seemed to be trying to pull that wreck of metal out of the stagnant green pond.

Michelle.

Dear Kim,

After a week of being asked to buy postcards every time I see him, a particular postcard seller named Khiem, I have started to avoid the Old Quarter all together. Yesterday when I saw him he had a smile on his face. Khiem handed over the small booklet wrapped in brown paper. It was a hand-bound book of some sort, a traveller's guide written in English. I sat more forward on the steel fold-up chair. I opened the guidebook.

'These are hand-drawn,' I said.

'Yes, a one-off,' he sat with legs wider, confident.

There were scribblings in fine and thick black lines. The words all appeared backwards, as though a small, frail man with a beard and glasses had sat by *Ho Hoan Kiem* and written them all by the reflection of the lake, carefully choosing the different light at different times in the day to assist his purpose.

'They're backwards,' I said.

'Yes,' he said, 'To better lie. To better tell the truth.'

I held the page up to the light and read the backwards writing. I read:

> The journey of importance is not the physical one. The real journey is in the heart and in the mind. This is a guidebook of a different kind. It is the psychic guide to Vietnam.

Each section had a small heading, and contained strange hand-drawn pictures. As I read, Khiem looked around the café. He watched fellow postcard sellers and drew his box closer to his body. Suddenly Khiem pulled the book from my hands, placed his elbows on it, and leant forwards on the table, talking.

'You are here for a few weeks? Do you want to see pagoda?'

'Yeah I was, umm...' I was confused.

The *cong an*, a uniformed policeman, watched the two of us, his face etched in stone. Then he went.

'How much?' I asked.

'They're not even from here. You don't want to buy them.' Khiem said.

I took a sip from the *coc* of draught beer, it too sweating beads of perspiration in this heat.

'I may not.'

'You may not,' he said coolly. His eyelids were blue. Perhaps they were dusted with shimmery powder, perhaps they were broken veins of soft bruising.

Be good,
Mich.

---

intersections scream

With hands hanging onto possessions – a large blue backpack, an old plastic suitcase a relative had lent with the specific instruction of disposing of it once the destination had been reached – the traveller is carried along in a giant aluminium shell gliding through a series of pulses, heartbeats, screams. At the meeting of twin rivers of sound, the screaming is a song of hesitation, or polite resignation; created by hands on horns and bells; by exotic finches with Egyptian eyes held captive in shapely bamboo cages; by geckos in the middle of the night posing as walls laughing; by the street vendors crying out their monotonic calls. In the city of Hanoi no one bothers to scream with their throats.

---

grandma vanishings

There were whispers around town. Nothing fast and flaming like the ones used for lovers who met under trees in the evenings. No these were whispers of matter-of-factness: *It happened again. Did you hear? Just around Hang Bac street yesterday evening.*

Another grandmother had been standing there among the dust, the cracked streets and water-drains. Stooped back and wool-vested, she took her wrinkled hand and lifted her geometric hat, and held it out, entreating the traveller. The traveller looked away. In that instance, at that very spot another grandmother had vanished into the very night itself – there, but not there. A section of her tattered conical hat was turned into a tasteful 'collage' postcard of old Hanoi.

---

string conversations

Many visitors, who come from colder climates, communicate by tying long threads of silky black string to the object of which they speak. Two friends sat at a café and discussed the flora and caged birds around them. The speaker would hook the thread from the tip of his finger, his eye or his tongue, and run the line to connect with the leafy tree that he is speaking of. The listener would garner from the direction and tautness of the string the topic that was being spoken of and the feelings of the speaker towards it. Any conversation could have threads running from mouth to walls, to the balustrades of old colonial buildings, to the many lakes that dot the beautiful and serene city. In contrast, the inhabitants of Hanoi are renowned lovers. Their way is to tie strings to each other when they speak. In a casual lunchtime conversation, the black threads are knotted with nimble fingers to each other's eyelids, mouths and ears. This way the conversationalists always move together, in a jumbled, intimate, jungle of thread, at once restrictive and comfortingly secure.

One time a Hanoi inhabitant sat at the dinner table of the visitors. He had tied his strings onto his fellow diners, who were chirpy, friendly and inquisitive enough. But at the moment of completing his second knot onto his neighbour's sleeve, he looked up to find that they had already turned away – their hands busily tying black threads to trees, abstract street signs, to the brick and sand-work of the city around them. The Hanoian sat there in smiling, polite horror. It was the first time that no one had tied their strings back to him.

Dear all,

Hanoi is a city of lakes. Almost every district seems to have its own lake. Mist hangs around on days such as today – making Hanoi seem like London with conical hats. The Hanoians are loathe to get any bit of the warm drizzle on their heads, and so will wear all sorts of head-gear to protect themselves – straw hats; green-cloth army helmets; baseball caps worn by women; little hoods of plastic ponchos; or even clear plastic shopping bags with the handles tied into little knots to create a fitted head-cover. But what I really like best, and what I think exemplifies Hanoi style, is riding on the back of a motorbike holding an open umbrella for you and your fella, as you ride through the streets at 8 kilometres an hour. There is a little old man dressed in a worn-out suit. Around his shoulders and chest is a wooden box with Vietnamese words written in black texta on it – it seems to say something about peanuts, and he rings a little brass bell with a certain rhythm that is distinctly his, 'Tinga-tinga-tinga ting!' Crossing *Hang Bac* (silverware street), another old man was peddling a rusted tricycle with four battered vacuum flasks, selling tea, or *'che'* as the Hanoians call it. He calls out his song, low and drawn out, *'Che nong hoi. Che,'* swallowing the words into one another. It is not like the frantic heckling from fruiterers at Victoria market, 'Watermelons, watermelons, juicy red watermelons! On fire,' using large hand gestures, the metaphors becoming more suggestive when a female shopper passes by. No, this tea-seller's slow call is more like the song of the brown and yellow birds they keep in the small bamboo cages here; intermittent and consisting of one melody, over and over. One of the phrases of the birds is like the start of a love song my father wrote, over forty years ago. 'Ahh dad, you've been pinching melodies from the birds,' I think to myself.

Love, Michelle.

Dear Kim,

I'm losing my English so have been transcribing bits from a book I bought off a postcard seller (*A psychic guide*). It's getting harder to read – he seems to be shrinking – his words I mean.

Will send you that lacquer stuff. Was it the red-red or the brown-red?

Ciao, Michhh

---

the friendship of birds

Within the city of Hanoi there are those who seek a pleasure, which would make listeners blush if they could even imagine it. Its practitioners had searched and searched furtively between the lines of poetry, and in the scriptures of great meditations from sages across the ages. They could not find the word for it. As the word did not exist, it could not be spoken about. So the pleasure-seekers found a useful solution. Around the city are many types of birds confined in shapely bamboo cages. These fine plumed creatures could produce the sounds which most resonated, resembled the missing, non-invented word. These pleasure-seekers began to have long, sensuous, serious conversations with the red and gold parrots; the bright orange canaries; and the large sour-looking peckers, all of whom had had much training conversation from the poachers and pirates who had captured them from the wilds and brought them in cages to the city of Hanoi. Amongst themselves the pleasure-seekers rarely acknowledge each other beyond a nod or a glance. Unable to find the missing word they rarely speak with one another, instead preferring to approximate the language of birds.

Strangers who watch and do not know, see only shy men or women seated at the many parks and lakes around the city, speaking with great melody to their plumaged companions caught in delicate cages.

Dear all,

I am in the splendour of Halong Bay, the rocky outcrops the spine of a dragon floating in a sea of jade. A small boat speeds up alongside our ferry. The boy, with his mother and younger brother, holds up fresh fish and prawns in bamboo baskets; he holds up green shapely coral. He looks about eleven to me. I ask him how old he is. He is sixteen. I ask him if he and his mother catch these fish and prawns, and dive to the bottom of the China Sea for the coral. He says that they do not, and tells me where they get them.

'They buy it from the market and resell it here,' I translate for my fellow traveller.

'Oh,' she says disappointed, 'Thanks for spoiling the illusion for me.'

Some travellers go to exotic places to pretend that people do not suffer deeply from their poverty and that they do not at times cheat and lie to try to escape it. Some people travel to let go of understanding what's happening around them, to be as nude and deluded as children. It is easy to watch them walk with an air of stupidity about them, smiling at everything.

There are those who travel to exotic places to feel sorry for the natives. 'They do not have any colouring pencils or crayons for the children to be creative,' they cry. They don't see the inventiveness of games created out of tin cans, rubber thongs, and bits of metal from the machines of war.

Love, Michelle.

Dear Kim,

I spotted a *xe-om* driver and negotiated a price with him. 'How much?'

'One US Dollar.'

'Too much. Local price is 40 cents.'

'You are not local.'

'My family came from here,' I smile.

'Alright.' He smiles.

I hopped on and he started his motorbike. He said, 'Vietnam is very poor. There is much suffering here. Is there suffering in your country?'

We were speeding through the city, jumping the open gutters and the cracks of the city streets. I thought of old

people dying alone in nursing homes in my foreign country.
I thought of people chasing status down endless aisles in a
giant shopping mall.

'Suffering. To be human is to suffer.' I looked at him
carefully to see if he was satisfied with this answer. I wondered
if he would get angry at me. He lowered his head for a
moment and thought. Then he nodded to himself, and wove
through the traffic with renewed energy and speed. As I sat on
the back seat, I knew what I said was both true and untrue.

hugs, Michelle.

---

city of face

In the deep east beyond the river of honey, and the jungle of
variegated jade, there is the city of Face.

Once you arrive there, large sculptures of white clay
with rounded mouths and Buddha cheeks are placed around
the circumference of the city, and at regular points along the
radii of the 'spokes' that reach in towards the centre. Each
had been beautifully hand chiselled by an artist and two
assistants, one of whom is solely there to sweep away the
beautiful alabaster chips of hardened clay and burn them on
small fires near to the sculpture.

It's face, after face, after face, as you walk towards the
centre of the city. One who speaks and forgets to mention
the white sculptures will have the polite inhabitants of Hanoi
turn away, blush and look downwards, fall into silence or
even vacate the premises without a further word.

If the traveller follows the radius of the white clay faces to
its very heart, there is a small circle of these sculptures. One

hears the voice of a beautiful, long-haired woman weeping in the middle of the night next to a small fire.

Dear K,

It is night and I am on a train heading to the mountains. I have mastered the art of disappearing. They looked but they didn't know where to find me. In being very still and small, I have managed to vanish. I am in a cabin with the local people. Next door, the foreigners have paid three times the price for the same journey. They are rowdy and sing. I am in a soft sleeper, and we sit in silence. There are seven of us, in this six-person cabin.

Suddenly the train conductor races in, followed by a young official. The official pulls down an empty, new Korean-made suitcase from the top bunk. The conductor puts his leathery hand on the suitcase. They struggle wordlessly for a few moments over the new suitcase. Then the conductor says politely, containing the great strain in his body, 'Please, leave this suitcase here.'

The official is angrier and younger. He says, 'I am taking it.' They continue to struggle silently. Everyone else in the cabin is watching, and not watching. No one bothers to say anything with their throats.

'So this is what it feels like to disappear,' I thought. I lie there and pretend that my invisibility has made me mute and blind as well. And heartless. But I do have a heart, and so do the other people in this cabin.

Love, M.

---

city of words

I am building a city of words to replicate the city of things around me – of dust, of polyester shirts and trousers, of teeming humanity. Every day I pace the space of the city in my long walks in order to measure out the dimensions for my replica city of scribble.

Except my city of words is built with the square, angular exact bricks of your language, while the inhabitants of the city itself build theirs with the slippery, rounded, sing-song stone marbles of the Hanoian language. These round stones create their architecture not by their shape, but by their placement. I had failed before I had begun.

Dear Kim,

There are four words to a war. *Cach Mang* is the word northern soldiers used for themselves; *Bo Doi* is the word used in the south. The southern word for one of their own is *Linh Cong Hoa*. The northern word for the same soldier is *Nguy*. 'Did your parents not teach you the words of a war?' The taxi driver in *Da Nang* said to me.

'No,' I said, 'We talked of school, getting high grades, and buying a house so that no one can look down on us.'

His red eyes looked ahead, expressionless. 'It is not anyone's fault which side of a war they fight on. Where you live is who you fight for,' he said, erasing the eight years of hiding in the mountains for fighting for the losing side.

I entered the museum of sadness today.

Yours, Mich.

Dear Hai,

All my photos came out shit. I could hardly take photos of strangers as though their features, dress, or ways of living are completely foreign to me. That would be like me going to Sydney and taking photos of strangers there. Vietnamese photos are only for taking photos of relatives or friends, and certainly not lumps of rock by themselves. No, you have to get a relative or friend to stand in front of a piece of important rock or monument, in a stiff but friendly pose. For a Westerner you want a piece of untouched landscape, objective, silent, uninterrupted, lonely. Have you seen the traffic in Vietnam?

I could not take photos because I didn't know who the person pressing the button was.

Michelle

Dear all,

I am sitting in the café of Babel. There is a pretty girl sitting on my right reading swirls and squiggles. I ask her which language it is. She tells me, smiling, that it is Hebrew. An older couple argue with each other by talking too loudly at their Vietnamese tour guide. They take turns being extra nice to him – entreating him to drink some beer with them, asking him whether he likes Western coffee or not. They are scared out of their wits in this strange environment, and are to boot, unhappily married.

The layers of language in this café are wonderful and scary. Perhaps the snake that is Hanoi is swimming along a river flowing out to sea. My uncle told me that in such a river there is a region of several kilometres where the sweet water of the river mixes with the saltwater of the sea. In this zone, a special type of fish thrives. This is the meeting of east and west. It is the mixing of two mediums. It is where the other fish die.

The tour guide is bored, but attempting to be surprised by the old couple's questions about 'Vietnamese culture'. His eyes dart around the café. He looks at the girl reading the Jewish text for a while. He looks at an older Caucasian man with his hair combed over his bald patch learning Vietnamese poetry from a young tutor.

The tutor is pleased with the progress of this mature-aged student, and leans closer into the table. Just where the Caucasian man thinks he's going to use *gap em o Chua Huong*,* I don't know. They are both drinking Tigers. It is a hot day. It is only 10 am and the sunlight is already golden pink, filtering through the doorway of the café in *Pho Co*.

Yours, Mich.

* From an epic poem about two young lovers gazing at each other for the first time. Translation: *I met her at the temple gate.*

---

the prism heart

If you take a sharp knife to dissect my heart for the grit and sludge of hatred and prejudice, you will find it there. If you carve my heart in search of the red blood and scented flesh of compassion, forgiveness and courage, you will see that too. I am a prism of possibilities. And as you move, and as my breath moves me, the colours of the refraction is shifting, shimmering, shifting.

I have written these words by the many lakes of the city. During days of fear and paranoia, my handwriting shrivelled up into little black dots and swirls, barely readable by my own eyes or by any unwelcomed readers. My spine too, curled up like that of a circular insect. Sometimes I thought twice before writing down a thought or not. Maybe one can conceal conscious thoughts, even to oneself. But one cannot suppress feelings. And so my hand would betray me, and draw the thought anyway. Perhaps this is why there are so many artists in the city.

I have captured, in scribble, the various reflections in the water. To tell you a lie, to tell you a truth.

Phan Huyen Thu

Hue

Night slithers slowly into the Perfume River
an elongated note breaks under the Trang Tien Bridge

A Nam Ai dirge of widowed concubines
fishing for their own corpse from a boat on the river

To be king for a night in the imperial capital
go now, make a poem for purple Hue

Shattering symmetry voluntarily
with a tilted conical hat
      an askew carrying pole
           eyes looking askance
Hue is like a mute fairy
crying silently without speaking.

I want to murmur to Hue and to caress it
but I'm afraid to touch the most sensitive spot on Vietnam's
body.

Translated from the Vietnamese by Linh Dinh

Ho Anh Thai

Installation

A photograph.
A bottle of medicine capsules.
A tourist bag, Samsonite brand.
A shirt and a trousers hanging in the sideboard.

The guest who had been in room number 37 left only these things. At ten o'clock in the morning, the room-service maid entered after the guest had gone. A man. The clothes in the sideboard confirmed it. The trousers about 1.1 metres long. The shirt size 42. The man must be rather tall and well built. A lingering male odour.

The black and white photograph must have been taken over twenty years ago. The West Lake. The other shore seemed as far away as the other side of a bay, not as it does today, as narrow as a village pond. The young man and the girl look like two students. One of his hands is on her shoulder, lying tentatively. His fingers are half hidden behind her shoulder, as if to demonstrate their close friendship while at the same time they seem about to fly off her from embarrassment. The girl also looks shy, as if she wants to stand some distance from him. Obviously they are just friends or maybe even lovers. But they are definitely not husband and wife.

The photo had been left on the nightstand, next to a bedside lamp. The maid turned on the lamp and the faces of the two youths brightened. She seemed lively and natural, her cheeks elegantly dimpled. His eyes were damp with a vague melancholy.

Next to the photo was a small bottle of medicine – the capsules inside crackled when the bottle was shaken. The label was in a strange language and the maid could not tell what kind of medicine the bottle contained.

On the sofa was a tourist's overnight bag. An airlines sticker had been wrapped around the handle, marked with a barcode and the plane's route: Ho Chi Minh – Ha Noi. The maid picked it up in order to clean the sofa. The bag was zipped up. Fully.

★ ★ ★

The above said things.

Plus a pair of underwear briefs hanging to dry in the bathroom.

A set of syringes.

Two unused Insulin tubes.

The maid was startled to see the set of syringes. Then she regained her calm. It wasn't heroin. The man had diabetes. And the syringe looked pretty good, not the kind scattered under bushes by the West Lake, just outside the hotel.

The photo had fallen on its side by the lamp pole, causing the couple to lie side by side in an awkward position. She was on top. He was at bottom. The maid turned the photo right side up. As she looked into the young man's damp and soulful eyes, the maid flipped through her memories of her own boyfriends' faces. There had to be one with eyes like that.

Suddenly she was startled again. Remembered. Yesterday at dusk, when she was about to leave after her shift, she passed a woman coming into the hotel. Her face was a bit familiar.

The maid thought the woman was just one of the guests in the hotel and forgot about her. Now, looking again at the photo, she remembered that the woman she saw yesterday had two dimples on her cheeks. She was the very girl in this photo. Yesterday she came to meet this man.

In the rubbish basket there were two broken Insulin tubes. Three used condoms. The maid poured them into a big rubbish bin and took it away.

After dark, she found some extra work so she could stay on and see the man's face. If she was lucky enough, she would see the woman again as well; the woman might come again to meet the man. Finally, though, she had to give it up and go home without seeing anybody.

★ ★ ★

The photo fell face down on the nightstand, exposing the numbers written in ball-pen on the other side: May 2, 1982.

Two broken Insulin tubes.
Two used condoms.
All were in the rubbish basket.
In the corner of the bathroom, there were black ashes in which twisted, burned papers could be seen.

The maid washed the ashes away. Some pieces of paper had not been burned totally. They were from an old letter covered with girlish handwriting, done with a student's purple ink. She could make out the words 'understanding' and 'missing you'. Parts of an invoice with several numbers that didn't seem to signify anything. The maid put the unburned papers into the rubbish basket.

The bottle of capsules, the set of syringes, the underwear drying in the bathroom, the clothes hung in the mirrored sideboard — all had disappeared. They must have been all packed up in that fully zipped bag. The guest must be checking out of the hotel. He must be returning to Ho Chi Minh City.

After cleaning the room, the maid looked again at the photo. She had to confess to herself that she was attracted to this handsome man. She adjusted the photo vertically at the base of the lamp before locking the room and leaving.

Noon. The Hour of the Horse. The time the Water King takes the lives of the people who are still in the water. From the West Lake there was a clamour. People running helter skelter. A shout that someone had drowned. It happened sometimes. The working maids didn't dare to go out to see; they just poked their heads out of the windows. Canopies of leaves blocked their view. They yelled to each other, asking who had died, and when, and whether the corpse was face up or face down. Each one had a different version of the story. After all the noisy questions and speculative answers, still no one was sure if the victim was really dead or still alive. They only knew that the victim was a man.

The maid's heart thudded. So strange! A premonition of an accident nearby. As if forced by something, she ran back to room 37, unlocked the door. The bag was in the same place – probably everything had been put inside. The photo flew down from the nightstand. She hurriedly picked it up and only now she could see a paper next to the base of the lamp. Handwritten with a fountain pen. Two lines.

No one would be blamed.

I have decided my fate.

The third line was a signature.

The fourth line was the man's full name.

★ ★ ★

The woman.

The maid.

A heap of used pillow cases and bed sheets just taken out from rooms.

The next day the maid was carrying the used pillowcases and bed sheets down to the front courtyard. As she was about to take them into the laundry room, the woman came in. She had two dimples on her cheeks. The maid had seen her so many times in the photo. She had walked out of the border of the photo and become this woman. Who apparently had not known what happened yesterday with the guest in room 37.

The maid felt sorry for the boy and the girl in the photo. She did not want the woman to find out what had happened from the receptionist. She would invite the woman to step outside. She would tell her everything. The story is over. Finished. Please leave the hotel, auntie. If you want, you can look for him somewhere else. Otherwise, you if go into the hotel and ask for him, the police will come to question you and nose around for the details.

I know you. The maid said in short.

Really? Thank you. The woman said, as if she didn't know what she was saying. Her eyes were dry.

I know you, the maid repeated when the woman had gone out of sight. In her wallet, the maid had the photo of the erstwhile boy and girl. When she had hurried to inform the hotel owner about the note in the room 37, she hid the photo for herself. She didn't know why.

★ ★ ★

Room 37's door was sealed.
A woman with a Southern accent.
Three handkerchiefs in the handbag.
The hotel owner.
The maid.

That afternoon, the hotel owner told the maid to unlock room 37. With him was a woman just flown in from Ho Chi Minh city. They broke the seal, opened the door, and returned the bag to the woman. Poor him, poor him, she repeated continuously. Tears streamed from her eyes. As she was about to pat them with her handkerchief, she saw that it was already soaked. She opened her handbag and rummaged inside for another handkerchief. The maid stared, surprised that the woman had another handkerchief.

The seal was removed. The stains were scraped up. Cleaned out. And then room 37 was ready for a new guest.

★ ★ ★

A photo.
A bottle of medicine capsules.
A tourist bag, Samsonite brand.
Two shirts and two trousers hanging in the sideboard.

Half a year later. The maid opened room 36 and entered. Shock. The same tourist bag, though the airlines sticker had been removed. One of the sets of clothing in the sideboard was the same – the maid remembered the size of the shirt and the length of the trousers. The capsules inside the bottle crackled when it was shaken. On the bottle was the same strange language so she could not tell what kind of medicine.

The maid couldn't believe what she was seeing. But the photo lying at the base of the lamp confirmed it. In the photo, there was still the erstwhile girl and boy, but now they were with three other boys. The three friends were mischievously pressing the shoulders of the girl and the boy, forcing them to stand side by side to take the picture, while the two struggled to move away. It was the same damp-eyed boy. And the same girl with dimples in her cheeks.

I know you, uncle, the maid whispered to the man. As if he was standing in the room in front of her.

How can you know a man when you haven't seen his face?

I know you. I haven't seen you for a long time.

The man only smiled. Vietnamese can use a smile to cover any dilemma.

Today the maid would fabricate the excuse that her family had all gone to the country on vacation and she didn't want to go home alone. She would ask for extra work to stay in the hotel. And she would wait until she could see the man who last time was in room 37 and this time was in room 36. She would not be shy about talking to the man. I know you, she would tell him.

★　★　★

The installation artist would remind the author of this story that the author has forgotten the set of syringe and the diabetes medication. And that he has forgotten the photo which is still in the maid's wallet.

Certainly I have forgotten those things and others and some characters also. In installation art, materials and elements sometimes disappear without a trace. And the artist also disappears.

Translated by Ho Anh Thai and Wayne Karlin

Steve Kelen

The No-Food Restaurant

I'm Popeye the Sailor
I pay my respects at the no-food cafe
there's no meat or vegetable
the noodles have been spirited away
and the rice is second-hand,
cold from the previous customers' bowls.
A boiled carp appears, it tastes like poison
its miserable lips frozen in a slight smile
I place a cigarette butt between them.

Red Dzao Village

No guide book describes the ecstasy
brought on by a breeze blowing down terraced fields
of rice green, green full of water—Asia green.
The Dzao people's rough houses snuggle in the valley.
Dawn to dusk, most of the village
women are in the fields, working for the rice
some are at home making things to sell at the market,
drying, dyeing and weaving hemp, fine embroidering
the young girls' hands and feet are blue
from crushing indigo, young boys turn yellow
with spice, they all take turns pumping water
from the well, feeding pigs and chickens
guiding buffalo from field to river
the men search the forest for medicine
tend a few poppies away from official eyes
and come home, melt down old coins
beat the silver into jewellery to sell at the market
they hunt game in the forest, few animals
and birds remain so they must work hard
these days to keep the mountains friendly.
At night, a curtain of black sky falls.
Spirits play and hear rice sing
the way the Red Dzao do.

Books are rare, maybe one or two in the headman's
house, useful only to the young who have to go to school.
Real writing is left to the shaman who paints Chinese
characters
on thin strips of paper the Dzao pin to the walls and doors
of their houses
charm against the curses many worlds throw at a house:
this calligraphy must sometimes shout
to keep evil spirits, burglars away
ward off tigers and bears straying from the cloud world.
In the old days a powerful charm
could take a living tiger by the scruff of the neck
and whisper *move on quietly* –
the leopards read it once, and never returned.
To disobey the words meant the worst oblivion.

A bottle cannot read or listen
and is untroubled by good magic
no matter how powerful the
characters written on the charm
which, in any case,
cannot recognise a bottle
and save a house from what a bottle can bring.
Once every ten years or so
bottles appear in odd corners
and are rarely noticed and bring a being
whose name is never mentioned
with a voice like spider silk
and all the guile a piper needs
to tempt children away.
Children love to play
with the shiny glass changing colours
listen to silky voice in the bottle say,
'let me out and see something great'.

Unstopped, the being dazzles
bright baubles the child picks up
attach and tendrils enter
take the blood, all the moisture
a body has, and the powder remaining
of the child passes to its own bottle
that appears in odd corners
of houses, the child's dreaming
becomes a silky voice, the love of life's
an appetite to make another into powder.
Thus the Dzao keep few bottles.

At the Ho Chi Minh Mausoleum

Uncle Ho was a cool guy, now he's an ancestor...
Ancestors say free energy
   clear spirit pure charisma glow
     at peace, relaxed
     doing and saying it all
       for the country.
            All Vietnam
              fought for freedom
           Ho had
        the charisma come
       by way of
          gentleness
           & ferocity –
           the two
             sides – in
             villages,
                  seaports
                    cities maze
                     on land's
                        resilience
                       people
                       who've spent
                       millennia
                       working for
                       the rice
                       tough as nails
                     the people
                      are everyone
                      on the planet
                    a map of Peace
                   a shot-down bomber,
                  soldier, sailor, farmer,
             tinker, office, factory
         pamphleteer, dreamer
          worker, poet, leader –
         the aftermath a god
     protecting young children
    – men and women, boys and
     girls will build – they love him, still
     queue for miles feel his glow
     fighter – waiting, he is the land
     he is everyone

Le Minh Khue

The Professor of Philosophy

Thanh Ha! Blue River – it seemed such a good name to give the child, quite uncommon. In that remote village by the sea, the village teacher had dreamed that his daughter would flow through the surrounding hedge of bamboo and reach as far as she could into the world of humanity. His dreams floated in the name he gave her, Thanh Ha.

But when she went to the university, wherever she looked she found other rivers. Even two of the boys in her class were called Ha. And her professor of philosophy in her last year at the college of technology was Duong Ha (Sea and River).

★   ★   ★

Every morning at ten, Ha caught a bus that took her from the south side of the city to her college, on the north side. The bus stop was always draped with so many sleeping bodies it looked like a dormitory. This morning, Ha looked across the street, where a group of muscular young men was waiting for someone to hire them. She recognised several recent college graduates.

63

There were unemployed graduates everywhere these days. A friend of hers, a girl named The, had told her it was because there were too many teachers and they needed as many students as they could get, in order to keep themselves employed. Too often, their students left the college almost as ignorant as when they entered. Her other girl friend, Thu, recounted getting a letter full of basic diction mistakes from a college boy.

Thu and The had come from the same village and had graduated at the top of their class, but both were working now as bar girls. They let Ha live with them, rent-free. Every evening, The would always cake her face thickly with make-up – she was working a bar near the train station. She would look over at Ha and tell her, 'Keep studying. No matter whatever happens, its good to have a college diploma.'

Every night after midnight, the two bar girls came back by motorcycle and slept together in a single bed. Ha placed a bench near the door and slept there. The whole room was only twelve square metres. Mosquitoes hummed in the girls' ears. In front of their building was a pond, which had been sold to a man from down town. Soon the pond would be filled in, and in the blink of an eye a four-story house, thin as a nail, would tower over the small buildings of the neighborhood, making the roofline resemble a row of rotten teeth. It was like that everywhere Ha looked.

The bus that she caught every morning ran from the south side of the city to the north side. The fact that the driver and conductor wore uniforms didn't make the passengers any neater or more orderly. The upholstery had been stripped off the seats, the floor was thick with mud and littered with grapefruit peel and cigarette butts. Ha quietly rose from her seat and went to stand behind the driver. She admired the way he controlled the bus. How could he manoeuvre so smoothly when everyone on the road seemed intent on committing suicide? Motorcyclists wove around the bus, determined to overtake it. Pedestrians completely ignored the horn. Yet the driver's face remained icy and calm. Probably only the cold-blooded could do this kind of work, on these dusty streets packed with sweating people. A gregarious passenger, standing next to Ha, was trying to speak to the driver. Too many motorbikes, he said. Yeah. The country's Gee Dee Pee was seeing unprecedented growth this year. Yeah. Man, we're living in paradise and don't even know it! Yeah.

Yeah and yeah, said the icy-faced driver, until Mr. Gregarious was gradually beaten into silence.

The bus ground to a dead halt in front of the College of Transportation. The world is always full of cheap ironies. There was always a traffic jam in front of the College of Transportation. Morning, noon and night. A half-hour wait. Ha took out her notebook and began to read her notes, but wasn't able to understand a word. Everything was jumbled up and confused.

★   ★   ★

Every day she saw the man walking calmly from the teachers' residential quarters to the front gate of the college. The professor of philosophy. Compared to the other faculty, the teachers of practical subjects who were tremendously busy, always invited to lecture here and there, he appeared nonchalant and preoccupied in his badly wrinkled shirt and dust-coloured vest. His hair was greying. She knew he was still a bachelor and shouldn't lack for money, and his sloppiness seemed reprehensible to her. Often, as Ha was on her way to school for an afternoon class, she would spot him going to eat in a 'dust inn' (a popular café). She'd see his rumpled hair and unwashed face as he slipped quietly into the café. He seemed to have a seat reserved for him. He'd always sit in it and eat the same meal, which was always ready for him. God knew why Ha bothered to watch.

65

LIVERPOOL JOHN MOORES UNIVERSITY
LEARNING SERVICES

Perhaps it was because of her mental state: she was a lonely country girl in the big city; she didn't want to go back to the roots (the country), nor did she know how to cling to the top (the city). Besides, there was something different about this professor. When he came to class, he always dressed more neatly, though he still looked distracted. At the beginning, he would lecture in a desultory manner, but bit-by-bit he'd become impassioned, even though his lectures were about matters no longer of any concern to today's youth. What did he care if the students were listening or not? If they didn't pass his subject, they'd be eating gruel the rest of their lives. The professor lectured on. He knew people were indifferent to what he said. And so was Ha.

★　★　★

Hearing Ha describe the professor, Thu was surprised. 'That's not possible. How could we let a teacher like that live alone?'

'Some girls tried to be with him, but they left after a while,' Ha said. 'They said he lived like a soldier.'

She was sitting, self-absorbed, on the bed of the two older girls, watching the rain falling on the pond outside – the future foundation of the future nail. Her mind was in turmoil. She was about to take her final exam. About to graduate. About to look for a job.

The two ex-students present-bar girls stared at her. 'How many square metres to his flat?' The asked pointedly.

'I just passed by it, didn't get a clear look. But it seems big enough. The living room is probably ten square metres. I'm not sure about the inner room.'

The raised her eyebrows, which were trimmed as neatly as a model's. 'Listen, this is an order from your elder sisters. You have to move into the philosophy professor's flat.'

'I couldn't do that. He's too old.'

'Maximum, only forty years older than you. I'd be ready to marry an eighty year old if he'd get me a job.'

'Don't be silly. I'm just a country girl. He'd never accept me.'

'Don't put yourself down. Look into that mirror again. If that teacher is the way you described him, believe me you'll suit him. You're honest, a bit shy and a little foolish. Try.'

Thu broke into peals of laughter. 'You have nothing to lose. You need to find a way to stay in this city.'

They talked on and on. They disagreed and agreed and so on. Finally, the two older girls issued a resolution: Ha had to go to the college earlier than usual. And she had to go to lunch in the dust inn.

★   ★   ★

The café was set below the surface level of the road. Its tables were covered with red-checked plastic tablecloths. Ha glanced at her wristwatch and took a place on the wobbly bench where the professor usually sat. She ordered some fried tofu and soup with two slices of meat: 3,000 *dong*. A fairly reasonable student price.

From then on, she came every day. At first, the professor couldn't place her. The college had thousands of students, and his subject was in such little demand that he only taught one class a week. But seeing that quiet, shy, considerate girl sitting near him every day when he came for lunch made him pay attention. Finally, one day he asked her name.

'My name is Ha.'

'Then you're my namesake.'

'Interesting.'

'Where are you from? Ah – now I remember you. I'll be teaching your class again next month.' And then one day he said: 'Please come closer. It's sad to eat alone.'

He ordered more courses, and chopsticked food into Ha's bowl. He only ate a little himself. The dish he liked best was tofu in tomato sauce and marinated mustard leaf. As he ate, he sipped a glass of vodka. He began talking about this and that. About B52 bombardments. About someone who had saved his life when he was fighting on Highway 9 in 1969. Then about his village, which this season had been inundated by floods. He was living alone, but soon his flat would be teeming with guests. He had to help out by taking care of the children of his brothers and sisters, but he didn't know how he would make ends meet. They assumed he was a rich bachelor and expected his help as a matter of course.

Ha in turn would talk about her village. About the bus she took to the college. About the pond and her rented room. Then one day it was so hot that the two of them couldn't finish their lunch. 'Come have tea in my flat,' he invited her.

He had a living room filled with books. Professors of philosophy read many books, he explained, and then they write much nonsense. One steals ideas from the other. They scavenge scraps here and there and put mortar to pestle and mash them all together and claim them as their own thinking. That was how the field of philosophy went in these times. As much a jumble as the cheap goods sold in the market. But Professor Duong Ha didn't bother to write anything. After he'd taken off his army uniform, he'd gone abroad to study philosophy, and though he studied a great deal, he still had felt like a frog sitting at the bottom of a well. To drive away his sadness, he read, and in his spare time played chess with a high school history teacher who lived on the street next to the college. The two would become absorbed in the game. In this way, his youth had passed. Now he was 'prefix four, suffix maximum' – forty-nine.

He smiled sadly. Ha noticed that the only thing he seemed diligent about was shaving. Maybe he was afraid if he didn't shave for five days, no one would recognise him anymore. When she made tea, she saw that his refrigerator was empty and dirty, caked thickly with ice. If she wanted to fix something else for him, she wouldn't find it here. Not that it mattered.

No sooner had the professor had his tea than he lay down on the sofa and dozed off. It was too hot. The ceiling fan only pushed the burning, wet air around the room. In the heat, Ha could faintly smell the heavy odour of an unwashed, older man. A typical smell. The smell of age. But she had started her adventure and now she had to jump into it, even if it was a pit of boiling lime.

While the professor slept, Ha estimated the size of his flat. She could put a double bed in the middle of the room, with his desk on one side, and a shaded stand-up lamp on the other. Lamp-shaded light would make the room look different. She could paint the walls blue. Hang some posters. The kitchen shouldn't be set up like that…in a word, everything had to be rearranged.

★   ★   ★

Thu and The choked with laughter when Ha told them about the professor's feet. Long nails, black as coals. Sandals also coal-black. His collar looked terrible. He didn't care…

Everything else was going well. 'Next month, when it's cooler, I'm going to ask him if we can cook in the flat. Just so we start taking our meals together; it's not like I'm scheming to make anything happen, right?'

'Okay. But remember you're graduating this year. Graduates in your field are as crowded together as piglets in a pen. Or do you want to become a bar girl, like us?' Thu asked.

The winced. 'These days, there's not much money in being a bar girl either. The time's passed when those countryside bosses would come in and throw around government money, get anything they wanted. Now, if they have to spend their own money to buy a coffee, they howl like they've been castrated. How can they be big spenders in a karaoke bar if they have to shell out dough from their own pockets? Look at us – we can't even rent a decent room. Just trying to save up a lousy 200,000 *dong* a month to send our parents leaves us broke. You've got to get money. You've got to get that professor.'

Ha listlessly boarded the bus. She planned her future distractedly. Day after day. Hot and dusty. Patiently she waited for the professor at the café. He gave her money in advance to pay for his meals. When the weekend came, she gave him back the correct change. And while they ate their meals, he slowly opened up to her and told her the secrets of his life. During the war he had fallen in love with a girl in signals. It seemed suitable, an artillery soldier and a signals girl. But after she was demobilised, she left him without saying why.

From then on, he couldn't keep a girlfriend. It was as if he was predestined for that kind of bad luck. Girls would come to his flat, and chatter for a while, and then disappear. Maybe he had a malevolent guardian star. He reached thirty, and he kept trying to find a woman, as any man would. Tried but achieved nothing. So now he played chess to help the time go by.

Ha smiled sadly. At their meals, which they always ate at the same time every day, he seemed little by little to be turning into a new man. Day by day, gradually. He wore shoes. He got a haircut. He seemed to bathe more often.

Thu commented that the fish was slowly but surely approaching the hook. Ha didn't understand why she didn't like it when Thu and The talked that way about him. She turned her back on them as she did her homework.

★ ★ ★

She was back at the bus stop when the professor pulled up, riding a borrowed motor scooter. When he saw Ha, he called out pleasantly, mimicking dialect: 'You'll have to eat alone today. I won't bee eateeng.'

'Where are you off to, teacher?'

'The railway station,' he said, and laughed ironically. 'I'm receiving my sweet fruits, my relatives, from my village. I have to take them shopping, then get them back to the village. They get married there even in the hot season.'

He laughed as he spoke. Ha saw a sparkle in his eyes: They were innocent and twinkling. He was wearing quite a smart shirt today also. She wondered if he'd found a girl friend.

She said goodbye and had turned to leave when he called out her name. 'Ha!' Turning, she saw him still standing there. His face looked thoughtful, truly thoughtful, not simply absent from life as it had before. Her feet suddenly felt reluctant to walk away from him.

'Tomorrow I have to go back to my village for several days. I know it's hard for you to live so far from school. Please come and tidy up my flat. And you could feed the cat for me. Stay there. Make yourself at home,' he said.

He gave her the key. As Ha took it, she wondered about the cat; she'd never seen it though she'd been going there for some time.

The cat turned out to be just like its owner, quiet and inactive. It hung around outside and came back only to lie inside a box lined with a blanket, as if submitting to its fate. Whenever Ha opened the box, it would look out, but wouldn't raise its head or feel the need to utter a meow.

During the days the professor was absent, she cleaned the patterned tile floor. First she washed away the coat of dirt covering it, and then scrubbed it again and polished it with a jute sack until it sparkled. The tiles were from the seventies and had never been mopped. Looking at their colours emerging, Ha felt touched. They had been as dusty and shrouded from life as the professor.

He kept a soldier's belt hanging from a hook in the wall. Maybe it reminded him of what had once been most meaningful to him. It didn't look new, nor did it ever seem to get older. But nothing else in the room really seemed to mean much to him. Ha washed and polished a beautiful ceramic vase and filled it with lotus flowers. She hung a brand-new curtain that rustled in the breeze of the standing fan. It took her three afternoons to tidy up the flat. When the sheets were finally dry, Ha made his bed. Looking at the single pillow lying there, Ha reproached herself. What was she worried about? By a lucky chance, this flat could belong to her. All she had to do was stick with the teacher.

The cat glided silently past her feet. Its disdain made her feel guilty.

★   ★   ★

The once again broke into peals of laughter. 'If I were you, after I'd washed the sheets and made the bed, I would have put myself in it. And then just waited.'

It wasn't really that the two older girls were experienced. They just wanted to mock everything. To slight everything. It was all simple to them. If the professor nodded, Ha would stay. If he shook his head, she would go.

But Ha was beginning to feel obstinate. Slowly, her heart had started to awaken. She supposed it had begun on the day he had asked her home to have tea. She'd had to go look for the tea since it hadn't been prepared. After the tea she saw the professor lean his dappled silver hair on the back of the sofa and start to doze off. There was something of a disappointed boy in the way he was sitting and napping. Another day, she had noticed how coal-black the collar of his shirt was. On yet another, she came up and caught him cleaning his muddy toe nails. He seemed as pathetic as a single boiled egg in one of the meals he had at the café. Ha had planned to trap him, move into his flat. But gradually, everything had changed. By now, she had been impatiently waiting for five days, but there was still no sign of him. Did he really have a girl somewhere?

Thu and The winked at each other and then looked at Ha.

'Go and sleep in his flat tonight. He asked you to look after it. How strange you are! You just cleaned it and locked it up?'

'There's nothing to guard there. Who'd want to steal books?'

'But your affair is coming along.'

'I'm not going back. I gave the key to a neighbour.'

'You're crazy!' the two girls exclaimed in unison.

Ha walked over to the door. The pond had almost been completely filled in with dirt. If only her life could be arranged as fast as that. Forget it. The day before she had received a letter from her father telling her that after graduation she could come back and help him grow straw mushrooms, which were selling like hotcakes. All right then! There'd be no more chances to meet the professor.

'Girl, you raise a pig just to give it to a tiger to devour. You straighten up and clean his flat, and wash his clothes, and make him into someone brand new – just so some other girl will pounce on him. Don't be so foolish,' The said, sing-songing her words as she powdered her face.

★　★　★

Love comes as suddenly as pain. At first it's vague, secret and soft, and then it suddenly squeezes one's heart. Ha stood, leaning against the inner wall of the bus, watching motionless as the uniformed conductor spat on the floor with blatant indifference, as if he were standing in the middle of a garbage dump. She got off and walked some of the way to school. Probably the professor had come back and had unlocked his flat. The cat's bowl had been filled with milk, which the cat probably hadn't even finished yet. She had done just as he had asked.

A group of her classmates on the path ahead called to her boisterously.

'Ha, the philosophy professor has been looking for you like a fireman searching for his hose. He said to tell you to come see him soon.'

'Did you buy that shirt for him?'

'What a smart hanging rope you bought him. What a tie. We've been classmates for years – I never knew you had such good taste.'

They jostled each other, trying to talk and laugh with her. Like a flock of laughing thrushes. She felt as if she were intoxicated, half-asleep. She got permission from the class monitor to be absent; it was the last day of the week anyway, and went to the college entrance to wait for the bus. For once, she didn't take it back to the south side of the city, but instead, holding onto her briefcase, she got off on a less frequented street downtown. Here the finest row of trees in the city seemed to hold onto its own sky, far above. The clean pure colour of the leaves stained the air green. Orchids, growing deep beyond iron fences, surrounded the villas along the street. I will never know this world, Ha thought, and she suddenly wanted to sob. How ironic that he should be the first man with whom she fell in love. Anyway, she should not have tried to find her luck in this way.

She wandered through the city until dusk. Then she boarded the nearly empty bus. The pond had been filled in completely. Nearby, a cluster of people stood talking about something. The room was fully lit. Maybe Thu had guests.

How strange – by this time, the two girls should have locked up the room and gone to the bar.

Thu was sitting with her back to the door. On the bench where Ha slept, a strange man was sitting and talking to her room mate. A mature man, his hair cut short, the long sleeves of his shirt rolled up. The shirt that she had chosen and bought and left on the bed sheets which she had washed with love.

Thu turned around and grinned. 'Here she is.'

★ ★ ★

As it was, the bowl she'd left for the cat was dry. If the professor had returned a few days later, the cat would have had to look for mice.

It was cool today. Sometimes, in the summer, there were days like this. The sky was a pale blue. The faint scent of magnolia blossoms hung in the air. The two people could guess from where that fragrance came. They were surprised at how they both felt like whispering.

Ha sat leaning against the back of the cane chair that the professor had just bought. Something round and warm brushed her feet. Ah, the cat. Jump up to my lap. Okay, now lie still. My teacher, the cat is like you – suddenly it has become active, Ha joked.

Her laugh was as clear as ringing crystal. The professor was standing quietly at the gate, looking back at his brightly illuminated flat and feeling strange, as if he were looking into someone else's home. His life, which he'd thought incomplete, had finally been arranged.

Well. Now he would try to live like everyone else.

Translated by Ho Anh Thai and Wayne Karlin

Pham Thi Hoai

Sunday Menu

On Sundays I visited grandma in her attic, a room windowless except for a ventilation hole in the wall where a brick had been removed just above grandpa's altar, as if to give grandpa some fresh air. Through the opening you could see white clouds floating outside, just like TV. Grandma lay on two timber planks placed next to each other and laid across a stack of Buddhist prayer books and tiny trunks among a collection of jars, bottles, sandals, thongs, a lime pot, mouldy oranges, a fine china potty and a cheap plastic one. She spread herself grandly over her possessions, watching the clouds floating past. A stick of incense, which I lit for grandpa every week, was enough to fill this tiny matchbox of a room up with smoke. I said to her 'Last week on Monday we had Chicken with Golden Flowers, on Tuesday it was Phoenix Embryo, Dragon's Beard for Wednesday, Golden Sand Abalone for Thursday, Hibiscus Fried Crab on Friday, White Bird Returning to Nest on Saturday and today, Sunday, we had Duck with Holothurian.' On each visit I told her a different menu so that, until her two timber planks were used for another purpose, she could rest assured that her aristocratic culinary heritage hadn't been wasted.

My mother used to work in a state-owned restaurant, but she now ran a food stall serving cyclo drivers. Every Sunday she gave me two 5,000-*dong* notes and said 'You can take the day off. Go and travel with grandma.' Grandma and I would travel back a whole lifetime, further and further back in time until we came face to face with a red lacquered tray of food covered with a muslin cloth. For my part, I tried to prove a worthy companion by talking about culinary dishes, the substance of which I was not sure, but the names of which sounded like they had been conjured up by someone in the Sino-Vietnamese Academy. I would quietly place the two 5,000-*dong* notes on grandpa's altar – somehow it seemed more polite to make a donation to the dead than to the living. Then I'd withdraw, leaving grandma in her own world with the stuffed bean sprouts of her glorious turn-of-the-century haute cuisine.

Our cyclo-driver food was soupy in summer and fatty in winter, but throughout the year the essential staple was pickled vegetables and fried tofu. For variety, sometimes we would have fish or meat, shrimps, an omelette or stir-fried vegetables. Everything that mother had learnt from her stint with the state-owned restaurant proved very useful: her soup was diluted by a ratio of three to one, fish sauce five to one, her omelettes were as fluffy as the pillows on a wedding night, and the modest slices of meat were always displayed conspicuously as if they were offerings to the gods. When Mother decided to open this eatery I thought, *Oh no, what a shame*, Mother's culinary art, which our family had suffered for twenty years, was about to be inflicted upon the public! Mother told me 'If Grandma asks, tell her that we have opened a specialty cuisine restaurant.' On the second day of the previous New Year, Mother had made a special effort to cook a mushroom-in-aspic dish and told me to take it to Grandma. When Grandma upturned the dish onto a plate the sloppy jelly wobbled but luckily it stayed in one piece. Normally, Mother's aspic jelly is so runny that I would faint just looking at it. I was pleased and waited for grandma to eat it, but she didn't. Instead she said 'Take it back to your mother and tell her to use a fine cloth as a sieve to drain the pork skin first; the peppers should be roasted lightly – swirl them around twice only in a hot pan; the mushrooms should be pared right to the base; and tell her to stop trying to poison me with indiscriminate use of gourmet powder.'

I threw the lot into Hoan Kiem Lake on the way home but told Mother that Grandma had enjoyed it. I wanted to bring mother and grandma a little closer – cyclo-driver food served on a red-lacquered tray would mark the beginning of a new trend in culinary fashion. But I worried unnecessarily. Mother knew herself that she wasn't the best daughter-in-law that ever lived, and never pretended to be so. Her motto was 'sacrifice for the people' – 200 *dong* would buy something; the most expensive dish a thousand five hundred – and customers came flocking to us in such numbers that there weren't enough tables and chairs for them all and they overflowed onto the footpath. From outside looking in, all you saw was a crowd of people noisily chomping their food and a blur of chopsticks flying from their dipping sauce to their mouth and back again; dipping, licking, dipping, quite an amusing sight. All the work was done by just the three of us: Mother, me and Thai, a cousin from my father's side living in the Buoi area. Thai did all the heavy work such as drawing water, carrying the pots, disposing of the rubbish, lighting the fires, washing up, and maintaining order because our clientele were not the gentle folk who would chew their food gently for fear of hurting the grains of rice. A couple of drinks, a few peanuts, or a piece of tofu, any minor thing out of place and anything could start and nobody could tell what might happen. Thai didn't like his work, except the keeping order. As soon as any trouble began to brew, he'd be right in there, machete in hand, and if Mother tried to calm him down he'd sulk and go into the kitchen to piss into the pot of soup. Mother was frightened that sacking him may be worse, so she tried to put up with him and occasionally even gave him money, telling him to go to those karaoke inns to have a good time because if he was to pour out his heart at our eatery it'd be like spitting into the face of our clientele – not a polite thing to do. He sang only one song, 'Sad Autumn Afternoons'. I told Grandma that our specialty restaurant employed a special security guard who had been to Japan to study, who in one breath could say a whole Japanese phrase: *Karaoke-toshiba-ajinomoto-toyota-honda-yamaha-mitsubishi-ohayo-tokyo.* Grandma said that it sounded better than *merci beaucoup.* She blamed the French for the corruption of Vietnamese culinary taste.

I took great care not to mention food such as *roti* and *phaxi* together with butter, milk, sausages and bacon so as not to shake her onion-garlic-fish-sauce-flavoured patriotism. Mother's crime was worse than that of the French. Her crime was that of destruction. I guessed when the time came, Grandma would take with her the Chinese porcelain potty with beautiful figures of goddesses to protect her Eastern cultural heritage, and bequeath the cheap plastic one to us, children of an era that the Sino-Vietnamese Academy would describe as a period of mongrelisation, from food intake to waste output.

'If things had continued in this way there would have been nothing for me to complain about. I had no dreams of working in a tight skirt, wriggling my pretty bottom, approaching white-napkined tables to offer a menu in three languages as an aperitif. The girls of my age working in those places always looked so proud, their lips so wet, as if they were kissed all day long. I wondered what it would feel like to be kissed. At our food stall, Mother and I were the only women. The rest were men, and rough men at that. I got my fair share of pinches on the bottom, but kisses were rare. Thai was a crude, rough and sulky man. Sometimes he went overboard and chased me into the kitchen and dropped eggs down my blouse just to watch me panic and take off my blouse to save the eggs from breaking. That's about as far as he got. It was not a happy place but it wasn't a depressing place either. Sometimes I felt quite close to the customers as if I had shared my meals with them all my life. Our meals weren't always the best but they certainly were filling. In any case, our customers were busy people constantly on the move.

Many of them were quite unpleasant to look at, squatting down on their haunches as if on a toilet, picking their teeth with the scratching movements of a market-sweeper, cursing freely and with almost unbearable crudeness, but Mother said 'The customer is always right. Even if they shit right there, we'd still have to put up with it and smile, my child.' I had to acknowledge that the world view of the harsh and sharp-tongued former state-run trader had gained a certain humorous and humanistic edge.

The days floated past in a crazier fashion than the clouds drifting in the *tivi* at Grandma's. From ten thirty onwards there wasn't enough time to think about anything. Only in the mornings, squatting down at work in the kitchen, did I have time to mindlessly recite to myself the Sunday menus so that I could look at the pots without cold shivers shooting up my spine. I knew for a fact that today's soup was yesterday's soup disguised by freshly chopped shallots, and yesterday's was really the day before's; that inside that pot over there, happily simmering away and gently browning to a mahogany colour, were the 2.1 kilos of rotten, fly-blown meat bought at the market at the end of the day – the flies and their egg-sacks dotted that piece of meat like black beans and sesame seeds. But our customers led such busy lives that food never stayed in their mouth for long, and nobody had the time to discern yesterday's soup in today's soup. I simply sat and recited to myself my Sunday menu Moonlit Flowers, Magnolia Palace Fishballs, Snow White Soup, Chicken with Holothurian... which helped to overcome the shivers threatening to travel up my spine. I didn't know what a holothurian was but I'd heard that it was quite nutritious. And if it's nutritious it's good, on this both Mother and Grandma agreed.

That's all. I am not difficult like Grandma, not insouciant like Mother. Grandma's turn-of-the-century and Mother's end-of-the-century culinary art agreed in another aspect as well: they both tried to deceive the eaters. Grandma's fish bladder was exaggerated to become dragons' beard. Mother's fish balls were overfilled with flour. Grandma satisfied them by ear and eye, Mother by filling up their stomachs. They both respected protein highly. When my turn comes in the twenty-first century, I might combine their methods of deception to immortalise both Mother and Grandma in my own food fashion which could be called 'Vietnamese Blend of Old and New Culinary Art'. I will massage the ears, the eyes, the stomach and the pride of all my eaters. In the end, it's always the pride of the customers that's the most difficult to satisfy. And I'll write a cookbook teaching many things more useful than all of those cookbooks that I read in Hanoi's library on Sundays before going to see Grandma to make my weekly menu report.

★   ★   ★

Just as our cyclo-driver food stall began to prosper, just as my mother's culinary talents began to reach their peak and just as

I was about to finish all the cookbooks in the Hanoi library, the police arrived in great numbers and raided our eatery as a part of their 'Keep the City Clean and Beautiful' campaign. They took everything to the police station. I came out of the kitchen and saw mother throwing herself on the ground, rolling over the broken bowls among the puddles of grey and green crab soup, the reddish crab eggs stuck in her hair like sequins. It was quite early and no customers were around. Thai picked up a hose and began to hose down the mess of spilled food on the ground as if he was washing a motorbike, each spray accompanied by a curse – 'Bloody Clean City', 'Bloody Beautiful City'. The whole street turned into a huge pot of combination soup. Mother picked herself up laughing hysterically, the crab eggs that were embedded in her hair quivering in rhythm with her laughter.

With nothing to do that day, I went to see Grandma. She used me as a calendar so she said, 'I just blinked my eyes and it's Sunday again.' It was actually Wednesday. I didn't correct her, letting her think she had lived longer than she had, and proceeded to make my usual Sunday menu report. 'Last week we had White Cranes Saluting Flags, Orchid Chicken, Snow Flakes of Beef Balls…' Usually after each item she would just acknowledge 'Uh-huh.' I guessed she wouldn't know any of them. The books I used were recent editions, most of them written by southerners, more modern in their approach to cooking (they use mushrooms, bacon and coriander in every dish).

In his book *Customs of Vietnam,* Phan Ke Binh, a turn-of-the-century scholar, said that 'We don't lack the rare and precious ingredients, but our ways of cooking are still very clumsy, our cooks are mostly servants who simply copy what has been done before, as long as it's edible it's Okay, none of us can really be bothered to learn the high art of cooking.' Mother also said 'I don't know about her repertoire. I can whip something up from whatever is there, but her repertoire is quite limited really: a couple of stir-fry dishes, shark fins and braised ducks, that'd be the lot.' So on Sundays, each time grandma said 'Uh-huh' I was happy, partly because I was helping to erase mother's crime, partly because my menu was appreciated by someone else besides me. In this matchbox of a room filled with incense smoke, with clouds floating past the ventilation hole, a dish that I lifted from somewhere was enough to nourish us for a week. Perhaps I was making her turn of the century more glorious than it actually was. Perhaps her turn-of-the century made my upcoming millennium look more crass than it actually is.

I'm not introspective, I'm not sad, just occasionally a little confused, because each person belongs to an era in a natural way, like every painting has its own frame, and I don't know which frame I belong to. I am always in between this frame and that frame, nothing is settled. That's all. I am not difficult like Grandma, not easy-going like Mother.

When I got to the dish of Steamed Quails in Holothurian Juice, Grandma didn't say 'Uh-huh.' I looked at her and an unusual smile on her face made me feel a little uneasy. What if she asked what a holothurian was? Then perhaps both of us would feel awkward, not knowing what to say. She didn't ask, but kept on smiling and said gently 'Holothurians, yes, those sea cucumbers, they should be soaked in the juice of field crabs before serving.'

I felt relieved, at least there would have been a holothurian in her black muslin-covered, red-lacquered tray. But I still didn't know what a holothurian was. I waited for her to elaborate but she said nothing further, so I bent down and looked closely at her face for a while and then fled outside and ran away. At the Hoan Kiem Lake I remembered that I hadn't locked the door, so I ran back. Grandma was still lying there, spread over her possessions, looking at the clouds floating outside. I hesitated for a while and then stepped inside and closed her eyes for her. Now she could close her eyes for a moment and in a blink it would be the end of the century. But that's not what was important. What was important was that this was Sunday, the next day was Sunday and so was the day after. I strained to lift a corner of one timber plank, removed a prayer book from underneath and placed it in her hand. The plank wobbled but that didn't matter. The prayer book now propped up her soul instead of her body. And her soul was also grand. I lit a whole big bunch of incense to keep her smelling nice and went home, locking the door after me.

At our stall Thai was sitting by himself singing 'Sad Autumn Afternoons'. Mother had probably gone to the local police station with a full packet of Triple Fives imported cigarettes. We didn't know what to do so we went inside the kitchen. Thai dropped many eggs down the neckline of my blouse. I let him help me catch the eggs for the whole sad afternoon. I will definitely get married one day. In devastating times like this if there was a smell of a man around, and if there was a bit of kissing, it'd make the day pass quickly.

Many days passed. Each day I went to visit grandma in the morning and played eggs with Thai in the afternoon. I'd gone through all the cookbooks and now I began to remove those polite 5,000-*dong* notes from Grandpa's altar to buy plates of specialty food for Grandma. Real specialty food. Each day a different dish. I went to those places where the young girls with tight skirts worked.

They were all similar, offering the same twenty or thirty dishes named in three languages, quite different to but not as richly varied as my Sino-Vietnamese Sunday menus. I conquered their deficiency by adding mushrooms, bacon and coriander to all of their dishes. 'Grandma, today there's Golden Chicken Happily Returning to Water.' 'Today's dish is

Five Coloured Spring Flowers.' 'Today there's Eight Precious Ingredients in Lotus Leaf.' She was always happy. When old people say nothing like that it means that they are happy, and I even ventured my unsolicited opinions. My view is that when people manipulate food so obviously, taking care so that the bright orange of the carrots is prominent in contrast with the green of the cucumbers, when the prawn crackers straddle nakedly over a bright white flower, I find it all a little under-dressed. My view is that to disembowel a duck to put a chicken inside it, a pigeon inside the chicken, all cooked inside a huge melon is madness, madness copied and exaggerated to the point of becoming clichéd. My view is that to love food doesn't mean carving minutiae on useless tomatoes, nor does it mean stuffing tiny bean sprouts with meat, and as for Mother's culinary art, it's nothing but pure violence. Destruction. To love food is a far cry from worshipping protein. Very different from giving it exaggerated names. To love food demands a great deal of genuine gentleness from both sides.

My view is that...

There's nothing much to my views anyhow. My brave and bold theory is based on cyclo-driver food wrapped in the pages of Hanoi Library's cookbooks and placed in a red-lacquered tray. That's all. I don't even know what a holothurian is.

But Grandma couldn't see my embarrassment. The incense smoke curled thick and the flies swarmed black. Each time I opened the door I stepped to one side to allow a thick black rain of flies out, taking with them a little bit of her and a little bit of my offerings. I lit a lot of incense, placed another specialty dish on the floor, by now covered by innumerable dishes, sat down and began my menu report. I couldn't see her clearly, she seemed a little more grandly bloated, bursting at the seams of her clothes, destined to disintegrate tomorrow, to be taken away by flies and ants on a trip back in time for a whole lifetime. She seemed to lean towards the colour of Buddha, with her white chiffon blouse having gone almost brown. On her smile there seemed to have blossomed a purple flower.

By the time the last of the 5,000-*dong* notes was spent, there was no more room on the floor to place another specialty dish. Grandma was lying on the floor. Her face was turned towards the door waiting for me, her mouth next to a bowl of shark-fin soup. A terrible flow of slime oozed from her mouth to the bowl, or was it rising from the bowl to her mouth? I couldn't tell. I tried not to panic, asking her to return to her old place, to turn around to watch the clouds floating past Grandpa. It's better that way. Lying down like this is no way to enjoy a banquet. But the two wobbly timber planks had collapsed onto her possessions. The feather-light goddesses of her fine china potty lay shattered. I closed my eyes tight. When I opened them again I saw millions of busy maggots.

I rushed outside and ran home. I ran to the kitchen looking for Thai but he wasn't there. There were only broken eggs, as the afternoon before we had been a little too vigorous in our play and eggs had broken all over my body. Mother took the opportunity to sack Thai and sent him back to Buoi village. Perhaps in the future he might take up driving a goods-cyclo. I told Mother that Grandma wished to have another mushroom in aspic dish. This time I would cook it for Mother to bring it to Grandma, so that Mother and Grandma could become a little closer. I had already completed the funeral banquet and now the final offering should be made by Mother and witnessed by Grandpa. What's more, Mother knew what to do with the two timber planks. I used a fine cloth as a sieve to drain the pork skin first; I roasted the peppers lightly – two shakes in a hot pan only; and I pared the mushrooms right to the base...

Mother went to see Grandma. With nothing to do I sat down and sang the song I had heard Thai sing, jumping from line to line at random. In empty times like this singing a half-remembered song helps make the day pass.

The following week the beautification campaign stopped and our cyclo-driver food stall opened again.

Translated into English by Ton-That Quynh-Du

Nguyen Ngoc Thuan

Her Schedule on Saturday

Imagine that on the weekend a splinter flies into your eye and you have to see the doctor. You are in danger of losing an eye. You will, of course, be able to see with the other eye. But, aesthetically, it won't look as good. As a man, you can accept that condition more easily than a woman.

That was the reason my wife was so sad this morning.

'I'll have to use a glass eye for my whole life,' she moaned.

Imagine that on the weekend you have a strange object inserted into your body: a glass eye. At first, you stare as usual with your two eyes, but then you suddenly find that you cannot see out of one of them. To be clearer, you no longer have two visual choices.

This will allow you to understand why my wife was depressed on Saturday morning. She couldn't accept her glass eye. She feared one day another splinter would pierce her other visual choice and so she would have no choice left at all.

On the weekend, surrounded by the dusty city, you will drop in to a sculptor's studio in order to make a marble bust which will be placed in your home garden. All beauty must be preserved whenever possible. In many modern, liberal countries, people may even take nude photographs to memorialise their youth. Now keep imagining. You go to a studio and meet a strange man, a photographer. He will ask you to take off your clothes. He will approach you, ask you to sit like this and lie like that and he will focus the camera from every corner, zoom in and out and make everything extremely clear. And finally you will have a photo of your youth taken from just the right angle. This thought will allow you to understand that to carve out a face from marble is reasonable and modest and fits suitably with East Asian traditions of wisdom.

So now you understand why my wife had come to the studio of Vy. Vy is a popular artist, well known for his ability to snatch one's spirit in a blink. My wife was sitting here and Vy sitting there, opposite each other, with a marble block in between. Thrice a week, two hours each session, I took her to the studio on my motorbike. Vy took out a big chisel and thud thud thud, he pounded away. And then came the Saturday when a splinter, separated suddenly from my wife's marble face, flew to her real face and pierced her eye.

What a bad Saturday! The bust had not been completed. She covered her eye with her hand, blood running through her fingers. In this way, the spirit of her beauty ended. She repented. If only she hadn't had the notion to immortalise her youth.

So on the weekend, you go on the internet to chat. Nowadays, such communication is meant to bring us closer to each other. But instead we have more solitude and live further apart. We go on the internet and manipulate some words and then send them out as conversation. What do we know about the other side of the world? Are the faces of the people there glad or sad? Are their noses aquiline or broad?

We don't know anything. For instance, on Saturday, you type: 'What can I do for fun today, please, please…tell me!' After you have sent it simultaneously to a hundred people, you wait and then read the directions of these invisible people, one by one. You select the one which is the most interesting and makes you happiest. Finally you'd find something you like: 'Meet sculptor Vy and hire him to carve your bust. In three weeks it will be yours to enjoy. Later, if you get bored, you'll at least be able to remember seeing an ugly artist at work.'

That is why on Saturday, my wife from Saigon left the rest of her crowd and all her trivial concerns behind and went up to Thu Duc district, into a dusty, suffocatingly hot studio, met a hairy and bearded Vy, and got a marble splinter in her eye.

'The doctor is insane,' she shouted, 'he said that even though the splinter is in this eye it may have a negative effect on the other!' She burst into tears. She'd been told she needed to return and be scanned to allow for a more thorough examination.

So your picture will be taken, but not for a portrait. Instead you'll be scanned through your cerebral cortex. And the splinter will be examined and evaluated as to its relationship to a certain nerve and your other eye. At last, they will get a true picture of the level of danger you are in. You will moan continuously until sundown that they have not told you the truth. The kind of truth known only among doctors, who lie because they don't believe that you are stable enough to deal with bad news.

'Poor me. If only that day I had read and listened to email number 74, I would have avoided the splinter. But I was stupid and went with email number 75.'

The 74th email had said: 'Go to X Mart, fifth floor, where you will find many beautiful things and the hope of happiness.'

What's that? Only when you ask yourself this question will you understand why I had to go to X Mart on Saturday when my wife was in the hospital getting X-rayed and the doctors were in their conspiracy against the truth. The Mart was too crowded that day and one had to slip through all the women looking for a weekend mystery. They all brought enormous baskets and could not imagine that in this world, at that very moment, billions of people were entering Marts at the same time and with the same questions in their mind of what to buy and what unique treasure they would find. They might also have got an email advising them to go upstairs to the fifth floor. What is available there? Nothing. Just a garish optician. Damn it. You had to come seven kilometres while your wife was in the hospital just to admire that spectacular scene — a gaudy kiosk full of glasses?

When you are about to leave, you hear a soft voice:

'I know you. Hi hi hi. You forgot me, didn't you?'

It is the soft and sweet voice of a girl shopkeeper.

'Have you come for glasses? Here's a pair that would suit you. Take a look.'

'No, I don't want glasses.'

But the girl looks down at the glass counter. When she straightens up, suddenly a pair of glasses is being pushed near your eyes.

'You see, perfect,' she says, holding a mirror up to your face.

'Why don't I remember you?' you ask.

'You don't remember anybody,' she says coquettishly. 'What do you think of these glasses?'

'They're rather nice.'

'Then that'll be the first sale of the day for me. I haven't managed to sell anything all day. I shouldn't have called you here, but I suddenly remembered that I owed you something.'

'What do you mean?'

'Shall I wrap these up? Think it over; it was three years ago, in the Seventh district. Here you are. Is the wrapping nice?'

'It's okay. But how can I remember?'

'So it goes,' the girl says sulkily, 'Then I suppose I won't be able to pay what I owe you. Just assume that I welched on it.'

Yes, just assume she welched on her debt. But how could it be true that you got to know such a pretty girl and then forgot her? It's Saturday, your wife is in the hospital with a marble splinter in her eye, and you make your way to this silly market, climb upstairs to the fifth floor, worm your way through a flock of women, and buy a pair of colourful glasses for your wife, even though you know she won't be able to wear them now.

Your wife will scream: 'It would have been much better if I had followed the advice in email number 4.'

Would you have wanted to follow the fourth piece of advice? Probably not.

Fitted with your artificial eye, you will, once you stand before the mirror, comprehend that human beings have limitations. Men try to imitate the truth, but no imitation can take the place of your eyes. You don't want to look at yourself any more. You will go back to sculptor Vy, shower curses on him. You ask your husband to accompany you. Beat him up, you tell your husband, he has caused this. And if you are her husband, you have only one of two choices: to beat or not to beat that sculptor. If you don't beat him, you'll have to spend more depressing days and months continually forced to answer the questions: Won't you sacrifice yourself for me? Don't you love me?

That is the reason that on Saturday, a marble chisel in your head, your body twisted in painful humiliation, you run for life from the studio of the sculptor named Vy. There, a barrel of plaster threatened you horribly and you knew that if you fell into it you wouldn't be able to breathe any more. Your body would be stiff as if you'd been moulded in a cast. There are many kinds of artists and you should not think that they are weak and sick just because they think too much. Some are as big and strong as a blacksmith. So you will come to understand that one should not provoke a sculptor, especially an expert in marble.

Today is Friday, and you don't know what to do. Do you want to surf the web and send a sad message to everybody: 'What to do for fun today, please, please, please tell me?' My advice to you is: stop it. Are you sure that next Saturday you won't fight with a marble sculptor fellow, drag yourself seven kilometres to cram yourself in with women on the fifth floor of the X Mart to buy sunglasses? And when you leave, will you wonder why you have forgotten a pretty girl from your past? Or will you suddenly realise that your life is flowing without form and some splinters will fly into your eyes and you'll hate Saturdays? But it doesn't just have to be a Saturday. What if the splinters fly on Wednesday, Thursday or Sunday? You can't hate all the week.

However, you should remember the most important thing, which you may forget when you are fighting: go to Thu Duc district to get the bust. It belongs to you. Your wife paid for it. A bit extravagantly. Remember to ask two big sturdy boys to accompany you there. That's your life...

Translated by Ho Anh Thai and Wayne Karlin

Catherine Cole

Long Live Peace

The old man pours hot milk into his cup, his hands trembling with the weight of the tiny jug. An offer of help would not be appreciated. He is ninety-two, he has told me proudly, a very good age for a man who's seen too many comrades die young. On greeting him I bowed awkwardly, then led him to this table. The waiter deferred with a nervous smile as the old man waved the menu away. This old man is famous, has given lectures on television about his friend, Ho Chi Minh and the garnering of supplies for the fighters of Dien Bien Phu. He has written about the strategies used to secure victory in Doc Lac and the Him Lam hills. A revolutionary hero, beloved of his people, old now, so old, his steps have shortened and a milk jug weighs a ton.

Our meeting has a complex genesis. Like so many Hanoi introductions it relied on connections. A friend of a friend of Thuy, a woman who works in the publishing house which has hosted my trip to Vietnam, has another friend who knows the old patriot well. My nervous phone call expecting a general's voice led me to this table opposite the tiny, pink-cheeked man.

Thuy had driven me to the meeting and in the traffic I'd closed my eyes against the chaos, the children, their heads as unprotected and vulnerable as chicken's eggs.

'This isn't a communist country,' I said. 'It's the most capitalistic county I've ever seen. *Laissez faire*. People can do anything they like. No regulations. No safety procedures. Children begging. People paying for schools, medical care, university.'

Thuy let me rave.

'And the motor scooters!'

The shift in her expression alerted me to the fact that I'd overstepped some mark there on Pho Phung Hu'ng, a street lined with vintage Russian Minsk motorbikes, all of them awaiting the loving attention of a Minsk restorer. Criticise the social, political, all you like. Just don't do the boring Western tourist rave about the traffic.

'You can't cross the street. No one stops at the traffic lights, such as they are. No one wears crash helmets. They go the wrong way up one-way streets. Drive on footpaths or the wrong side of the road.'

Thuy's face closed. She twiddled the handlebar of her own love, the Chinese motor scooter on which she had pillioned me. The subject is boring. Say what you like, her expression said, but I'm not listening.

'What ever happened to all the pushbikes? The cyclos? Safe. Quiet. Bells, not beeping horns.'

She revved her bike, drowning out my words. Then a train passed on the track across the road and people peered out, their faces curious through the street's petrol fumes.

★ ★ ★

With a little cough, the old man lets me know he's happy to answer questions about Dien Bien Phu. Milk poured, he asks me to begin. Despite his encouragement there is an awkward sensitivity about the meeting. I'm unsure whether his reluctance to talk about war is because it's all too painful or is just a victor's reticence at crowing about victory. I tell him that the history I learned at school left out too much. It didn't capture any of the street battles, the rice paddies, the slaughtered water buffaloes, the anger and determination of the Viet Minh. I had no idea there were people like him organising bicycles packed so high and wide with supplies they supported 300 kilograms of rice and other goods, resembling strange sculptures as they were wheeled through the jungle.

I have a book of quotes I've collected and I open it and read one by France's Colonel Brosjean: 'You're going to comb a sector infected with Viets. Destroy everything. Kill everything that moves. Destroy every living thing.'

'Aaah, that was 1946,' the man says when I've finished. 'We were at war.'

He listens politely as I say that all history is duplicity. His old hands warming against the cup, he nods, smiles, his teeth pale yellow with age and the cigarettes given up long ago but the nicotine still staining.

Since I arrived in Hanoi, I say, I have learned a lot about buffaloes and their importance to a rice-growing nation. I'm reminded of this every day as I walk the streets of the Old Quarter past wooden water puppets, the little puppet boys playing flutes on their charges' wide backs, on sale for the tourists.

'Ah, buffaloes,' he says.

He slowly tells a story I have already heard about the French killing or capturing water buffaloes so the peasants couldn't provide enough rice for the resistance. It is a sad tale of starvation and buffaloes impounded in barbed wire compounds, yearning no doubt, if buffaloes yearn, for the soft mud and water of the paddies, dragonflies and little children playing. And the dangerous night raids to release them.

When I murmur the names Morliere, de Castres, Delinares he smiles and repeats them. Old foes in war, old friends in defeat, their battles forgiven but not forgotten.

He tells me to go to a spot near Tho Nhuen Street where there are still vestiges of a sign daubed by the French in the late 1940s: *Long live France. Down with the Viet Minh.* Then slowly he recites: '"Sticks and grenades/ Grenades and rifles/ We'll kill the French/ Come on Brothers." It's by Nguyen Huy Tuong,' he explains.

The hands on the coffee cup seem too neatly manicured, too tiny to have killed anyone. Behind his back the waiter waits nervously, shifting from one foot to the other on the cold marble floor. A little nod, a movement of my fingers would bring service to our table.

'Another coffee?' I ask. The old man has barely answered before the waiter is serving it.

'And now we have peace,' he smiles, the milk jug quivering again as it is slowly raised and poured. 'Where do you live?'

'Here or Paris?' I ask, knowing he knows where I live in Hanoi, that he is influential enough to know my movements and the purpose of my visit. 'Paris. In the Tenth. Near République.'

He studied at the Sorbonne, he says. A long, long time ago. 'Danyers?' He thinks he remembers my uncle's name on the Law School honour board. Himself? Well, he lost two sons in the war with America but two daughters live in Hanoi. There is family in France too, in Tours where another daughter is a well-known physicist. He asks about my family. Knows the family's company name, long defunct in Hanoi but remembered for its work before the war with Japan. He nods at the mention of my Uncle Simon and Aunt Lily, so that for just a brief moment I think he might have met them too, but no.

'Lily is a pretty name,' he says. 'I have a grand daughter who shares it.'

I am impatient now, to ask him more about war, not the niceties of family names, but about Hanoi as it resisted the French. 'Do you know the poem by Nguyen Dinh Thi?' I ask, pushing my notebook across the table towards him.

His eyes narrow as he reads. 'Hanoi is burning with a raging fire.'

I read along with him, 'Hanoi is rocking/ The Red River is seething, wrath is boiling/ Our streets are burning.'

He closes the book and passes it back. I take it, embarrassed by my enthusiasm for the poem. 'It's beautiful,' I add.

'So Hanoi has found its way into your soul too. Do you know the saying, "a revolutionary fighter struggles for peace even if he doesn't live to enjoy it himself?" He watches my reaction, a wry smile on his face. 'You like Vietnamese poetry, Miss? Then you must learn this one by Vu Cao:

"You live forever beside other patriots
    under white gravestones in the rice fields
    from my heart's depth I call you 'comrade'
Loving heart among so many hearts."'

I glance around the café. It is filling with people eager for lunch. More waiters have appeared to cope with the crowd.

'Would you like to eat here?' I ask.

He lifts his hands in apology. 'Another time. I will take you to lunch another day.' As he rises from the table shakily he takes my hands in his. '*Hoa binh muon nam,*' he says kissing them. 'Long live peace.'

Pham Duy Khiem

Tu Uyên or The Portrait of a *Tiên*

One night in Paris I told the story of Tu Uyên to a friend, almost a compatriot, my 'half-brother' as he said.

He was born in America. His father was Vietnamese, his mother a foreigner. Orphaned at an early age, he had come to France on a scholarship to finish his studies. He knew almost nothing about the land of our ancestors, which he had never seen. However, certain nuances of his manner made him seem profoundly Vietnamese. I even found in him the fine flower of imagination and of dreaming which, in its delicacy, was characteristic of our fathers, and which, I believe, disappeared with them.

★　★　★

One evening in spring I arrived unexpectedly at his house. It was not a cold night but, to my astonishment, he had closed his window. I noticed that he had cleared the books from his table and placed a vase of flowers there.

'I bought them a moment ago,' he said. 'They are not for me. They are not even for anyone whom you have ever seen, or for anyone that I know…I have closed the window to create complete silence. And now I am waiting. A fairy will come, just like in the legends. It is not the first time that I have waited for her…She will knock softly. I will open the window, ready. You have already come, you, my friend: isn't that a happy sign of what is to come?'

His eyes smiled, the eyes in which, at the same time, determination burned and dreams floated.

★ ★ ★

Shortly afterwards, I met him as he was leaving the Luxembourg Gardens, not far from the Fountain of the Medici's. We walked a few steps together. Suddenly I saw a young girl in front of us. She stopped at the corner of the street, calmly turned around and waited for us. Dressed in black, she stood very erect, but she was also very frail. I was struck by her extreme slenderness, and by the delicate oval shape of her face. The freshness of her childlike lips contrasted with the paleness of her face and with her mourning clothes. She aroused vague memories in me of someone I already knew. Altogether, I had never seen anyone so pure, so severe, and yet so fresh at the same time. She was a mixture of decisiveness, of barely contained nervousness, and of an almost timid grace.

But as we approached her, my friend realised that she wanted to talk with him. He excused himself, left me. She said something, completely seriously. He politely accompanied her, two shy and very young people, like two children playing a serious game, in the first surprised meeting with their fate.

Soon their silhouettes had disappeared into the crowd on the street. I never saw the young girl again. My friend never spoke of her and I respected his silence in this matter.

★ ★ ★

A little over a year later, he knocked on my door after a short visit to England.

'You know how I usually travel; always on the move, trying to see as many things as I can in the shortest possible time: cities, the countryside, the landscape, museums, historical monuments, and humble scenes of everyday life.

'This time I did not leave London, and I saw very little in London...And there was a thick fog over the city for the whole seven days that I was there...'

My friend stopped. He had a look on his face that I knew well, a way of gazing into the distance that somehow still seemed turned in upon himself. I asked him: 'What did you do in London?'

'I searched all the galleries for paintings by Rossetti.'

His response surprised me because I hadn't known that he was interested in pre-Raphaelite art. Then he continued, slowly: 'Do you remember the young woman who stopped at the corner of the Rue de Medicis and turned to look at us? I had seen her somewhere else, we knew each other but I had no recollection of ever having spoken to her before. On that particular day, she had come to the Sorbonne for the first time and not been able to find her way out again: usually she travelled in the company of an old woman.

'I only ever saw her once again after that...We sat down and people passed in the distance in front of us...She asked me to never speak of that evening...For a year, I had no idea what had become of her. I never wanted to look for her again. I did not want to tarnish the purity of our destiny.

'But I have never been able to forget her. That is why I went to London. I don't know whether you noticed that her lips were like the lips of women in Rosetti's paintings.'

* * *

It was on that particular night that I told my friend the story
of Tu Uyên.

* * *

Tu Uyên was a student. One day after he had helped at a
festival at a pagoda, he was returning home alone, when he
saw a leaf fall to the ground in front of him. There were
characters written on the leaf. He bent over. The letters
formed a verse, inviting him to a poetic duel, which was a
romantic custom in days gone past.

Raising his eyes he saw a young girl of astonishing beauty
standing a little way off, at the foot of the tree. He replied to
her verse, and as they walked they engaged in a competition,
exchanging verses with each other. After a short while, the
young woman disappeared. Tu Uyên realised that he had
met a *tiên*. For a long time he remained in a dream, unable to
decide where he should go next.

At the end of the day, he was still thinking about their
meeting. 'He forgot to sleep during the five divisions of the
night, or to eat during the six divisions of the day.' In a word,
he was love-sick, an illness that nothing can cure.

But Tu Uyên remembered the famous oracles of the
Temple of the White Messenger, which was dedicated to
the genie of the river Tô Lich. He went there one night,
prostrated himself and offered his prayers. He slept in the
temple. An old man, with long white hair that floated in the
wind, leaning on a bamboo pole, appeared to him in a dream
and said: 'Tomorrow morning, go to the Eastern Bridge and
you will find what you are looking for.'

Tu Uyên was overjoyed and woke up. Dawn had already
come. He ran to the place where he had been told to go,
found no one there, waited a long time. Just as he was about

to leave, he saw an old man selling pictures. Tu Uyên looked at the pictures and saw that one was a faithful portrait of the young girl whom he had met then lost.

Tu Uyên bought the picture of the *tiên*, and hung it up in his room. He was eventually able to get rid of his incurable sorrow by doing some work. At each meal, he set out two bowls, produced two pairs of chopsticks, and did not serve himself until he had invited the young woman in the picture to eat with him, just like a husband with his wife.

One day, he was sure that he saw her smile in response to his invitation. The next day, when he returned home from his lesson with his teacher, his meal had already been served. When he tasted it, the food was exquisite. On the following day he pretended to leave home in the usual way but then suddenly returned home again. He surprised the young *tiên* who had left the picture and was busy adorning herself.

Without raising her eyes to look at him, she said: 'My name is Giang Kiêu and I live in the palace of the *tiên*. My family has been favoured with a great story of predestined good fortune, which allowed us to meet for the first time. Then, when the queen of the *tiên* saw that you could not forget me, she allowed me to come down in order to look after your house.'

To keep her with him, Tu Uyên took the picture and tore it to pieces.

Giang Kiêu removed a pin from her hair and a palace appeared, with sumptuous furniture and a crowd of servants. They arranged a great feast and the *tiên* came down to assist at their marriage.

Tu Uyên and Giang Kiêu lived a simple life. They had a son who succeeded brilliantly in his studies. When he was almost fully mature, Giang Kiêu said to her husband: 'In this lower world, people only live for a hundred years. Your name has been inscribed in the Book of the Immortals. Let us ascend to the Kingdom on High.'

She gave Tu Uyên an amulet. Two cranes flew down from heaven to take them away. Before they flew away, they went to their son and said 'Wait for us here. We will come back down and find you.'

The residents of that village have built a temple on the spot where Tu Uyên's house was located, so they could worship him.

★ ★ ★

My dear brother, you have never known Hanoi, the town of your father. It doesn't matter. No one remembers the temples dedicated to Tu Uyên. The Eastern Bridge no longer exists (it used to be, so it is said, between Sugar Road and Copper Road) and the Tô Lich River no longer runs near this area.

On the site of the Southern Gate, near where the couple met, stands the Nyeret city square. There you can see grocery shops, shops that rent bicycles and a police station. But it seems that the *tiên* no longer come down there to write poetry.

Translated from the French by Harry Aveling

Viet Lê

Hot Dogs for Dinner

It was almost Christmas and my older brother, Bui, his wife, My Lanh, and their twins were over for dinner. Our apartment is small but there was enough room for the six of us at the glass and metal dining table bought at the local Salvation Army, tucked in the far end of the living room. I made *cha do*, and *goi cuong* with fish sauce. The youngsters, the twins Trang and Tran – known as Tina and Tony at their school – and my son Luc had hot dogs and rice. Rice because we had run out of hot dog buns. Luc had loved hot dogs ever since he started kindergarten and the young blonde teacher Miss Margarine – no Miss Marjorie – fed the kids hot dogs for lunch one day. It was a school barbecue, Luc told me afterwards. In the supermarket, he'd pointed out the wrapped packages in plastic. They didn't look very tasty but I bought some anyway. 'Nothing more American than hot dogs and hamburgers,' as Vinh would say.

'He's gonna grow up to be as big as an American, give him milk, cheese, pizza, hot dogs, everything they eat! You're gonna be a football star, right Luc?'

Luc gave his father a thumbs-up while munching away at the hot dog sliced like pepperoni on a bed of rice.

'Us Vietnamese, we're so small because of all the fish paste and rice we eat. You know why we eat so much rice with everything? Not because we love it. Because it's cheap! A little fish, a little meat, some lettuce, a lot of rice, and you feel full. Now look at a hamburger. That's a big piece of meat. More meat than I could eat in a week. I'm just starting to eat hamburgers. I want to go to sleep after a Double Double. That's why Americans have so much meat on their bones. They eat so much meat. You know that saying, "you are what you eat"? It's true! Ha ha!'

Vinh was on his sixth can of beer already. Before our company came, he'd had some cheap wine. He was shy and never really liked company unless he had his drinks.

'I'm working my son up slowly. He's not ready for a big hamburger so, since he loves hot dogs so much, we give him hot dogs for dinner.'

Bui grinned 'Hot dogs, huh?' he asked. 'I thought eating dogs was illegal here. Ha ha.'

They were both getting red with booze. My Lanh rolled her eyes as if she'd heard that one before. She said, 'You know, dogs and cats are in paradise in this country. They don't do any work here. Humans are their servants. Everything is backwards! Back home, cats have to catch mice and earn their living. Dogs have to work in the fields with their masters. I wonder if it's also backwards with parents and children. My neighbour, Cuc's teenage son is talking back to her, missing school. Can you imagine if our children were to grow up like that?'

'That boy needs to know who's boss, a good spanking, that's all,' Bui answered.

Vinh added, 'You know, they call it child abuse. Give a kid a good spanking because they are bad and your own child can turn you in to the cops. Now that's backwards.'

'I don't believe in hurting your own flesh and blood,' My Lanh said.

'Dinner's getting cold,' I warned. 'Have some more *cha goi*. I went to the market and bought all the ingredients. Remember how mother used to cook this dish and I learned how to make it? I was fourteen. This is Bui's favourite dish. One day after he came home from work from the Embassy in Hanoi, I surprised him with it. It was nice and crisp on the outside but the stuffing was raw on the inside! Mother had to save the day and recook it.'

Bui smiled vacantly. Our children would grow up without knowing their grandmother.

'So how do the twins like first grade?' I asked.

'Well, Trang – she's quiet but faster than a fox. Tran, I'm not sure about him,' replied Bui. 'He's a little prankster. He can never really sit still. Mr. Elsworth called us at home and said that he was worried about Tran, that maybe he needs to stay in second grade for another year. We're thinking of getting him a tutor. I heard at church that they have after-school programs.'

'You know, they say brains run in the family,' my husband said, reaching for the sauce.

Bui glared. Vinh did not return his gaze but munched happily on his *cha goi*, his face blank like a water buffalo chewing grass.

'Not all of us can have four eyes like Vinh.' My Lanh shot Bui a disapproving look.

'Not all of us can have stupid twins.'

They are both drunk. 'We're all family here, let's act like adults for the kids to look up to,' I tried to smooth things over.

'At least my twins are not troublemakers like your son who can't eat Vietnamese food.'

'At least my wife's not a bar whore.'

My Lanh did not respond. I worked in a bar during the war too. We both sat there mute.

'Remember, *your* wife is my sister.'

'She's the only brains in that family.'

'I told her not to marry an arrogant son of a bitch like you!'

'Remember you're a guest in my house.'

Bui has always had a temper and a quick mouth. Even though he's a small man, he always beat up the neighbourhood kids when we were little. I could tell he was trying to calm down. He clenched his fist.

'The twins look tired,' I interrupted.

My Lanh agreed, 'It's past their bedtime. We should go home and tuck them in, Bui. We have to get up early for mass tomorrow.'

The twins and Luc were sitting amidst Legos scattered across the living room coffee table and floor, unaware of the adult chatter.

As I opened the door for Bui and My Lanh to leave with the twins, the cold night air penetrated my silk blouse. I'd bought it just for this dinner, it looked brand new. My Lanh had noticed how beautiful the embroidery was earlier in the evening. Their eyes met mine as we hugged goodbye. *I'm sorry,* they seemed to say. 'I'll call you tomorrow, little sis.' I closed the door slowly, watching them descend the apartment steps.

Vinh was sitting at the dinner table, all the food still half-eaten. I'd prepared all week for this meal. Made an extra trip to Little Saigon to get the right thyme and basil to go with the *guoi cuong*. It was supposed to be like the family dinners when I was little, with my mother and my brothers, everyone laughing.

Just a dumb look on his face.

'How could you? You know that Bui won't stand for that kind of talk.' I cleared away the food, wrapping up the leftovers.

'How could he? Just because he's the eldest one doesn't mean he can be a bad guest.'

'You cannot be rude to my guests, my family!'

'I'm your family too. I'm the one who sponsored them here, they should be grateful.'

'Not when you're rude.'

'It's my house. I don't want to be a stranger in my own house.'

'You look like you need sleep. Look, Luc's already asleep.' Luc was sprawled on the couch in a foetal position.

'I'm not a six-year-old kid. Don't tell me what to do!'

'Your eyes are red. You look tired.'

'I feel fine. Your brother was an asshole.'

'I think you had too much to drink.'

'I'm perfectly sober.'

I ignored him. He'd been drinking every day since he got home from the parts factory. Lately instead of just one or two beers, it had increased to six or even eight bottles a night. Sometimes he even picked up whiskey or a bottle of vodka from the liquor store on the corner. Sometimes he pretended that the glass he was drinking from was water, not vodka. I didn't like to see him like that, passed out on the couch night after night in front of the blue light of the unblinking television.

Now he was asleep at the small dining table, head cocked to one side, resting on his arm which was spread across the table. His glasses were still on. Saliva glistened on the corner of his mouth, tracing its way down his shirt sleeve. I stacked up the dirty dishes – red, yellow, purple Fiesta Ware stained with food left on the table. The lamp hanging over the table made it look like a scene from a movie – a bar scene or something where some actor was hung-over in the background. Luc cannot grow up with a father like this. There have been too many fights over the last year, too many misunderstandings.

I stacked more dishes, placed them one on top of another, layers of food sandwiched between orange, blue, yellow ceramic. Carrying it waist-high to the kitchen, some food dropped off the top plate onto the linoleum floor. Yellow mess like paint splatter. I let them all drop. *Crash!*

'What the fuck are you doing!' Vinh was bright red.

'What are *you* doing?'

'Don't talk to me like that, bitch!'

'I am a lady. I had more schooling than you ever will!'

'Who's paying the bills?' He got out of the wooden chair and headed towards the kitchen.

'Clean that up!' he demanded.

'I am not your servant!' I picked up a plate shard and threw it in his direction. It hit the wall and exploded into smaller fragments. I threw another and another as he approached. One hit him in the stomach, bounced off softly.

Vinh lunged towards me, grabbing my left wrist. My right hand yanked his glasses off his face. I threw them in the air. He is blind without them.

'Let go!' I twisted from his strong grasp.

Our shouts had already woken Luc and he'd run like a frightened rabbit into the bedroom we all shared.

On the kitchen floor with Vinh on top of me, still grabbing my wrist.

Plates crunched underneath me. Food, moist and slimy seeping through my blouse and skirt. 'Mommee!' I heard Luc sob from the bedroom. Now Vinh had both wrists as I tried to kick him off me. He pinned my arms back above my head with one hand.

'Get off me!'

'Get *me off* bitch!' He lowered his body. I screamed, trying to kick his balls. I missed.

'Get off me!'

'Shut up!' He covered my mouth. I bit his hand and screamed louder, squirming under his weight.

With one hand, he grabbed my throat. I tried to push him off with my hands. His grip tightened. I choked.

Suddenly he froze, let go, withdrew wordlessly. I scrambled to grab the cordless phone as I ran outside. He looked at me, almost pleading. His eyes blood shot, no longer hidden by the glare of his glasses. He looked as though he'd slammed his face against a brick wall.

I screamed, 'Don't mess with me!' as I hit 9-1-1 and ran for the front door.

Outside on the front steps of the apartment giving the details to the young female operator, I repeated myself sometimes because she could not understand what I was saying. I was calm. It was cold and I realised that somehow my blouse was gone and I was sitting on the steps in just my cream bra. I wrapped both arms around myself waiting for the police to arrive.

'My son is in there!'

'Okay ma' am. Do you know where he is?'

'I don't know.' I scrambled up the steps into the apartment. Vinh was inside, sitting on the old brown couch, hands on his face, the living room half-lit by the large brass lamp. It looked worse than the earthquake-damaged homes they showed on television. Everything knocked over, plate splinters. Luc was nowhere in sight, not in the living room, dining area, kitchen. I held the receiver to my left ear, the operator said, 'Let me know what is happening.' Vinh looked up when he heard me enter.

'Did you call the police?'

I didn't answer.

His voice was soft, pleading like a small child when scolded. 'Lemme talk to them, let me explain what happened.'

'Don't talk to me. They're coming soon so don't get any ideas.' I talked into the receiver, scanning the bedroom. The street lamp outside shed a blue cast on everything. I heard a ruffling from the small sliding closet.

'I am sober, let me explain to them,' Vinh's voice echoed from the other room.

Luc was on the closet floor, frozen like a frightened rabbit. I grabbed him by the arm. We shuffled into the living room.

'I found my son.'

The operator's static voice instructed, 'Tell your husband to stay inside until the police come.' I relayed the message to Vinh, still sitting on the couch as I left the apartment with our son. He didn't look up this time.

The blue and red swirling light on top of the police car was visible as I came down the steps. 'Police are here,' I told both Luc and the operator. Sitting on the curb of the parking lot in front of the apartment clutching Luc to my chest, I answered the brown-haired policeman's questions. He took pictures of the bruises on my neck, arm, torso. Flash, flash, flash. Another policeman climbed the stairs to the apartment, a hand on his pistol.

The brown-haired policeman jotted down the answers to my height, age, weight. He asked me to explain exactly what happened as I remembered it. Cold air hit my bare back. An hour had passed. Luc slept in my arms and I looked up at the full moon, the officer still in front of me.

Vinh came down the stairs, staring at his feet, wet hair over his forehead, hands behind his back, followed closely by a policeman. Glint of chrome. He looked like my brother Bui when they caught him at home in Saigon, tied his hands with rope, and sent him to a re-education camp for seven years. He looked like he was going to his execution.

'Don't say anything to him,' the policeman ordered. Vinh had been crying. They drove him away in the back of the police car.

'It's okay for you to enter your home. Your husband will spend the night in jail. We will be contacting you in the morning.' I grabbed Luc's hand, ready to clean up the glass and spilt trash waiting for us inside.

*   *   *

The next morning I woke up late, having forgotten to set the alarm clock since Vinh usually does that. Ten-thirty. Luc's class started at nine. I did not shower. Must get Luc to school. Looking in the bathroom mirror, purple-blue spots here and there like the mould on bread. I must wear a high-collared blouse so no one will know. Thank God he didn't give me a black eye.

Every morning I walked Luc to school before I caught a bus to the garment factory. I liked the cool air, the grey sky, the smell of damp grass. Today was the same but as I walked past the other apartments, I wondered how many arguments took place behind the curtains. Today I would have to wait an hour to take the 45 bus to Westminster. I would arrive around noon. Luc had not said a word to me this morning, even when I tried to tell him everything was okay. I dressed him in blue corduroy pants and a Sesame Street sweater, his favourite outfit. I packed him a hot dog in tin foil, an apple, some milk for lunch in his plastic red Superman lunch box. I added an extra Christmas tree-shaped chocolate.

Opening the door to Classroom 4, Miss Marjorie and Luc's classmates were sitting with their hands folded, listening to a phonograph. I held Luc's hand more tightly.

'Is everything alright, you're usually early,' the young school teacher came to greet us, large blue eyes like a spring lake.

'Everything's fine,' I smiled. I let go of Luc's hand and he sat down at his desk like a robot. *If that man ever thinks of hitting my child, he will not live to be sorry.*

'If you have some time, maybe you'd like to hear what the kids have been practising. It's something for the holiday pageant. It's a song that they can sing everyday of the year, not just around Christmas.' Miss Marjorie glided back towards the centre of the tidy classroom decorated with bright cut-out shapes and student projects: finger painting, butterflies, glittering alphabet letters.

'Class, we have a guest today, Luc's mom, who you can practise singing for. Ready? Okay! One, two, three!' She put on the phonograph. At the right moment, she gestured upwards for the class to sing.

'Good morning to you, good morning to you!' the class sang. 'Good morning to you. Our day is just beginning, there's so much to do.'

I looked at the familiar faces: Alicia (the girl in the apartment down the street), Jose (I heard that his older brother is in jail), Ben (Luc's best friend), Hong. My hand checked the top button on my blouse to make sure that it was hiding my bruises. I smiled at them and at their teacher. Luc was singing too.

The second refrain began, 'Good morning to you, our day is just beginning, there's so much to do.' *They are all so beautiful. What will happen to them, when they grow up?* Kept smiling, for they were singing for me. My grin crumbled at the edges of my mouth. I looked at each blissful face. *Which one will drop out of school? Which one will be hurt? Which one will die young? They will live their ordinary lives, live out unseen dramas, the stuff of every day. No more rocket ships and palaces. They are young and unknowing.*

'...there's so much to do...'

Andrew Lam

The Palmist

The palmist closed up early because of the pains. He felt as if he was being roasted, slowly, inside out. By noon he could no longer focus on his customers' palms, their life and love lines having all failed to point to any significant future, merging instead with the rivers and streams of his memories.

Outside, the weather had turned. Dark clouds hung low, and the wind was heavy with moisture. He reached the bus stop's tiny shelter when it began to pour. He didn't have to wait long, however. The good old 38 Geary pulled up in a few minutes, and he felt mildly consoled, though sharp pains flared and blossomed from deep inside his bowels like tiny geysers and made each of his three steps up the bus laborious and breathless.

It was warm and humid on the crowded bus, and a fine mist covered all windows. The palmist sat on the front bench facing the aisle, the one reserved for the handicapped and the elderly. A fat woman who had rosy cheeks and who did not take the seat gave him a dirty look. It was true: his hair was still mostly black, and he appeared to be a few years short of senior citizenship. The palmist pretended not to notice her. Contemptuously, he leaned back against the worn and cracked vinyl and smiled to himself. He closed his eyes.

A faint odour of turned earth reached his nostrils. He inhaled deeply and saw again a golden rice field, a beatific smile, a face long gone: his first kiss.

The rain pounded the roof as the bus rumbled toward the sea.

At the next stop, a teenager got on. Caught in the downpour without an umbrella, he was soaking wet, and his extra-large t-shirt, which said 'play hard...stay hard', clung to him. It occurred to the palmist that this was the face of someone who hadn't yet learned to be fearful of the weather. The teenager stood towering above the palmist, blocking him from seeing the fat woman, who, from time to time, continued to glance disapprovingly at him.

So young, the palmist thought: the age of my youngest son, maybe, had he lived. The palmist tried to conjure up his son's face, but could not. It had been some years since the little boy drowned in the South China Sea, along with his two older sisters and their mother. The palmist had escaped on a different boat, a smaller one that had left a day after his family's boat, and, as a result, reached America alone.

Alone, thought the palmist and sighed. Alone.

It was then that his gaze fell upon the teenager's hand and he saw something. He leaned forward and did what he had never done before on the 38 Geary. He spoke up loudly, excitedly.

'You,' he said in his heavy accent. 'I see wonderful life!'

The teenager looked down at the old man and arched his eyebrows.

'I'm a palmist. Maybe you give me your hand?' he said.

The teenager did nothing. No one had ever asked to see his hand on the bus. The fat woman snickered. Oh, she'd seen it all on the 38 Geary. She wasn't surprised. 'This my last reading: no money, free, gift for you,' the palmist pressed on. 'Give me your hand.'

'You know,' the teenager said, scratching his chin. He was nervous. 'I don't know.' He felt as if he'd been caught inside a moving glasshouse and that, with the passengers looking on, he had somehow turned into one of its most conspicuous plants.

'What – what you don't know?' asked the palmist. 'Maybe I know. Maybe I answer.'

'Dude,' the teenager said, 'I don't know if I believe in all that hocus-pocus stuff.' Though he didn't say it, he didn't know whether he wanted to be touched by the old man with wrinkled, bony hands and a nauseating tobacco breath. To stall, the teenager said, 'I have a question, though. Can you read your own future? Can you, like, tell when you're gonna die and stuff?' Then he thought about it and said, 'Nah, forget it. Sorry, that was stupid.'

The bus driver braked abruptly at the next stop, and the people standing struggled to stay on their feet. But those near the front of the bus were also struggling to listen to the conversation. 'No, no, not stupid,' said the palmist. 'Good question. Long ago, I asked same thing, you know. I read same story in many hands of my people: story that said something bad will happen. Disaster. But in my hand here, I read only good thing. This line here, see, say I have happy family, happy future. No problem. So I think: me, my family, no problem. Now I know better: all hands effect each other, all lines run into each other, tell a big story. When the war ended in my country, you know, it was so bad for everybody. And my family? Gone, gone under the sea. You know, reading palm not like reading map.' He touched his chest. 'You feel and see here in heart also, in guts here also, not just here in your head. It is – how d'you say – atuition?'

'Intuition,' the teenager corrected him, stifling a giggle.

'Yes,' nodded the palmist. 'Intuition.'

The teenager liked the sound of the old man's voice. Its timbre reminded him of the voice of his long dead grandfather, who also came from another country, one whose name had changed several times as a result of wars.

'My stop not far away now,' the palmist continued. 'This your last chance. Free. No charge.'

'Go on, kiddo,' the fat woman said, nudging the boy with her elbow and smiling. She wanted to hear his future. 'I've been listening. It's all right. He's for real, I can tell now.' That was what the boy needed. 'Okay,' he said, then opened his right fist like a flower and presented it to the palmist. The old man's face burned with seriousness as he leaned down and traced the various lines and contours and fleshy knolls on the teenager's palm. He bent the boy's wrist this way and that, kneaded and poked the fingers and knuckles as if to measure the strength of his resolve. In his own language, he made mysterious calculations and mumbled a few singsong words to himself.

Finally, the palmist looked up and, in a solemn voice, spoke. 'You will become artist. When twenty-five, twenty-six, you're going to change very much. If you don't choose right, oh, so many regrets. But don't be afraid. Never be afraid. Move forward. Always. You have help. These squares here, right here, see, they're spirits and mentors, they come protect, guide you. When you reach mountain top, people everywhere will hear you, know you, see you. Your art, what you see, others will see. Oh, so much love. You number one someday.'

The palmist went on like this for some time. Despite his pains, which flared up intermittently, the man went on to speak of the ordinary palms and sad faces he had read, the misfortunes he had seen coming and the wondrous opportunities squandered as a result of fear and distrust.

Divorces, marriages, and deaths in families – of these, he had read too many. Broken vows, betrayals and adulteries – too pedestrian to remember. Twice, however, he held hands that committed unspeakable evil, and each time, he was sick for a week. And once, he held the hand of a reincarnated saint. How many palms had he read since his arrival in America? 'Oh, so many,' he said, laughing, 'too many. Thousands. Who care now? Not me.'

When the palmist finished talking, the teenager retrieved his hand and looked at it. It seemed heavy and foreign. Most of what the palmist had said made no sense to him. Sure he loved reading a good book now and then – reading was like being inside a cartoon – but he loved cartoons even more. And even if he got good grades, he hated his stupid English classes, though it's true that he did write poetry – but only for himself. He also played the piano. A singer? Maybe a graphic artist? Maybe a movie star? He didn't know. Everything was still possible. Besides, turning twenty-five was so far away – almost a decade.

Before she got off the bus, the fat lady touched the teenager lightly on the shoulder. 'Lots of luck, kiddo,' she said with a smile.

Nearing his stop, the palmist struggled to get up, wincing as he did. The teenager helped him and wanted to say something, but he did not. When the bus stopped, he flashed a smile instead and waved to the palmist, who, in turn, gave him a look that he would later interpret as that of impossible longing. Later he would also perceive the palmist as the first of many true seers in his life and realise that, in the cosmic sense of things, their encounter was inevitable. At that moment, however, all he saw was a small and sad-looking old man who nodded before stepping off the bus and into the downpour.

★　★　★

The teenager lived near the end of the line, past the park. As usual, the bus was nearly empty on this stretch, and he moved to the bench the palmist had occupied. He could still feel the warmth of the vinyl and felt insulated by it somehow.

With nearly everyone gone, he grew bored. He turned to the befogged window behind him and drew a sailor standing on a sloop and holding a bottle. The ocean was full of dangerous waves. The boat, it seemed, was headed toward a girl who had large round breasts and danced in a hula skirt on a distant shore. He drew a few tall mountains and swaying palm trees behind her. He hesitated before mischievously giving her two, three more heads and eight or nine more arms than she needed to entice the drunken sailor to her island. And then he pulled back to look at what he had done: the scene made him chuckle to himself.

Through his drawing, the teenager saw a rushing world of men, women, and children under black, green, red, blue, polka-dotted umbrellas and plastic ponchos. He watched until the people and storefront windows streaked into green: green pine trees, fern groves, placid lakes and well-tended grass meadows. The park…beyond which was the sea.

The rain tapered off, and a few columns of sunlight pierced the grey clouds, setting the road aglow like a golden river. The boy couldn't wait to get off the bus and run or do something – soar above the clouds if he could. In the sky, jumbo jets and satellites gleamed. People were talking across borders, time zones, oceans, continents. People were flying to marvellous countries, to mysterious destinies.

With repeated circular movements of his hand, he wiped away sailor, boat, waves and girl. Where the palmist's thumbnail had dug into the middle of his palm and made a crescent moon, he could still feel a tingling sensation. 'A poet…not!' he said to himself and giggled. Then he shook his head and looked at his cool, wet palm before wiping it clean on his faded Levi's.

Jane Gibian

Carp

Though the painting
on the postcard is titled in english
Carp looking at the moon

it can't be so simple, for the verb
in this language isn't *look*
but perhaps *contemplate the moon*

or *direct one's eyes and think
of one's home country*: that
sorrowful carp, beside a mirror

image of herself, stares longingly
at the moon's watery reflection
in a complex sea, her majestic

frilled tail breaking the surface
to curve towards the moon
itself, and now a few small fish

join her gazing and yearning
for wherever the homeland
of fish may be

planted

On this slate-grey
autumn morning
the lake is
a churning sea
choppy & clouded,
the tortoise tower
rising still & ghostly
in the distant centre;
too cold now
for embraces
on the concrete
benches, but
starkly beautiful:
branches bend
to flutter
their leafy fingers
through the soupy
green water. In this
chilling greyness
ask yourself: if
your heart
was planted
what would it grow?

You imagine
exquisite blossoms;
a verdant tree,
but before you
can stop it,
your heart has
grown a plant
of strange flowers,
obliquely alluring
but covered in
thorns that wound
at a touch: the lake
stills completely
glassy like worn
stone & almost
unreflective.

Footpath (Hanoi)

1.
Two young men
        place an expressionless

white shop dummy
on the footpath
        and begin
           spray painting

her elegant crossed legs
gold

2.
Squatting by the road
three women bent

         soaping

              and combing

their long hair
over the drain

        untangling modest

               sorrows

into the busy evening
of the old quarter

Vietnam Haiku

garbage collector's bell,
barely wilted roses in each
pile of rubbish

tiny winter apples –
she hands me dipping salt
in a scrap of maths homework

cyclo parked in the night,
one playing card face down
on the hood

on the street of hairclips
buckets of pink crabs
boil in their shells

sidesaddle on the bicycle
one plastic shoe not quite
    slipping off

at dawn
each rosebud wrapped
in damp twists of newspaper

traffic jam:
revving the bike
in your white high heels

squashed rat on the road:
a group of boys
tug at the tail

police siren:
a row of bread sellers
sprint across the highway

each girl riding
with a single white flower:
teenager's funeral

late harvest
stretching towards the horizon
terraces of wet rice

long shadows
the birds in hanging cages
quiet under coloured cloth

Further Haiku

afternoon peak hour
     flashing kotex ads
          at each crossroad

crowded streets at dusk
a single shirt dances
on the rooftop

rowing to the temple
red dragonflies hover
on the shallow water

Vincent Lam

A Long Migration

My grandfather was an orphan. Either he never knew the identity of his biological parents, or he was never willing to reveal this information. For the Chinese, heritage is of great importance, but being adopted forms a new and legitimate lineage. Thus my name, Chen, as a grandson descended of an orphan, is from my grandfather's adoptive merchant family in the province of Guangdong. At sixteen years of age, my grandfather suddenly left Guangdong for Vietnam. He says there was a plot against him which had to do with jealousy over grades at school. My uncle Will says he was told that my grandfather had an affair with the school-master's young wife. Others say that the school-master warned my grandfather to leave, because the concubine of a local warlord had eyes for him.

The family matriarch in Vietnam sent my grandfather to Hong Kong for school. My grandmother says that this is because he was a difficult person whom the matriarch didn't want to deal with, and my grandfather says that he pleaded with her, and begged for a higher education until she sent him to Hong Kong.

In Hong Kong my grandfather, my Yeh Yeh, finished high school. He became a partner in a shipping venture. Yeh Yeh met my grandmother, my Ma Ma. The Japanese invaded Hong Kong, and Yeh Yeh said that he was persuaded to marry my Ma Ma in order to save her from the occupation. Yeh Yeh had papers which would allow him to return to Vietnam. My grandmother asserted that he took advantage of this situation at a time when her family's power was thin, to induce her to marry. Both agreed that he was promising though not wealthy, and she was the princess daughter of her father's dying empire. Ma Ma contended that Yeh Yeh thought she still had money and married her for this. Yeh Yeh said that he married her because he loved her. Also, he says, it was out of goodwill towards her older brother who had helped Yeh Yeh enter business, and who was worried for Ma Ma's safety in Hong Kong.

I was sorting through these histories in that last winter in Brisbane. I had only met my grandfather on one previous occasion which I was too small to remember, when he was spending the last of his money touring North America. He was both the heroic and tragic figure of many family stories – at once shameful, legendary and safely exiled in Brisbane. Now that I was to be Yeh Yeh's companion in the summer preceding his anticipated death, I was anxious to find out what was true and what were the exaggerations of memory.

The accounts always changed a little depending upon who explained them, and my Yeh Yeh's versions could shift from morning to evening. Rarely did a new version of a story require the old one to be untrue, but it was as if the new telling washed it all in a different colour, filling in gaps and loose ends so as to invert my previous understanding of the plot.

During those months, Yeh Yeh pissed blood every morning. Sometimes it would be just a little pink-tinged trickle, but often it would be flecks of clot-like red sequins swirling in the toilet bowl. Yeh Yeh had me inspect the toilet daily to give my opinion. One day it was liquid red like ink.

This was the summer after my first year of medical school. My family expected that I would use my wealth of clinical knowledge firstly to care for grandfather, and secondly to alert them when things neared an end. I would pronounce his impending death, and this would set in motion a flurry of rushed phone calls to travel agents. On jets from around the world, my relatives would rush to Australia to be with grandfather as he died. I felt obliged to forecast correctly. It would be awkward if all of Yeh Yeh's children flew to his bedside only to find him recovering from some brief crisis and not dying. Then they would wait, their workplaces would hound them, and they would finally be obliged to depart with grandfather still alive. Alternately, if I called too late, my aunts and uncles would make a frenetic dash hoping to see the last living moments, and only be able to attend Yeh Yeh's funeral.

★ ★ ★

In my luggage which was packed in Toronto, my grandmother sent an oblong wooden box which contained a series of small brown bottles held in felt indentations. Each thumb-sized bottle was capped with a tight cork, and tied around with string. There were two straight rows of these healing extracts. A paper label in Chinese was pasted on each bottle, and the strings were different colours. Each morning, after his urination, grandfather dressed himself while his tea was steeping. Always suspenders on last. He lifted this box from a drawer, removed the next in the series of bottles, and drank its contents. Then he poured a mug of tea for himself, and one for me. Yeh Yeh never said anything about this box of medicines. He was good at talking but had difficulty speaking about what was most important. My grandmother, Yeh Yeh's first wife, had divorced him forty-three years ago, and she now lived in Toronto, at the geographical other side of the world. Yeh Yeh put the empty bottle back in its little slot, and the box back in the drawer. He was quiet for a while as he drank his tea. Every morning he told me to thank my grandmother for this gift, as if forgetting that he had told me to do so the day before.

★ ★ ★

Seeing the toilet bowl dark with the red ink urine, I said to my grandfather, 'These things can happen. Let's see if it settles tomorrow. Drink lots of tea today.' I wanted to sound knowledgeable about the issue of bloody pee.

The next morning, it was a happy rose-colored stream with clots like coarse sand. I felt certain that I would forecast the end accurately. I gazed into it, looking deep through the urine into the drain, asking the liquid what it foretold. I also peed into the toilet, and the red swirled up like an eddy. Alive for a moment. I flushed the toilet, and it funnelled out almost clean, with a little bit of staining at the water line.

'You're very smart,' said my grandfather. 'It is better today.'

Renal cell carcinoma. They had operated once. My Yeh Yeh had refused a second operation. Just as well, said Dr. Spiros, it would only prolong things.

My grandfather lived in a cottage at Glenn Hill Retirement Village. There was a long cinder-block building fronted by a watered lawn. This building was divided into individual units, all accessible from a walkway. These were called cottages. The residents of the cottages ate in the main dining room along with the residents of the dormitories. The main difference was that the cottage-dwellers were able to walk and dress themselves, while many of the dormitory residents were wheeled to meals. Yeh Yeh did not participate

VINCENT LAM

in conversation at Glenn Hill meals. If asked a direct question at his dinner table, he would pause, raise his head as if unsure that he had been addressed, and say with a sad wave of his hand, 'No speakie Englis.'

In Vietnam, Yeh Yeh had been the proprietor, headmaster and star lecturer of the Percival Chen English Academy. Early in the morning, my uncle Will – who was finishing high school at that time, would find his father sleeping on the couch in the front room. Yeh Yeh would still be wearing his tuxedo from his previous night of drinking, gambling and bedding prostitutes. My uncle would help his father upstairs into bed. He would sleep in the morning, and would look fresh again by afternoon to go to the school. Yeh Yeh had no fixed teaching schedule, but would appear in classrooms of the English Academy intermittently. Star lectures. That's what they paid for, to be in his school, to be taught by Percival Chen. Decades later, there were alumnus reunions in California. Many credited my grandfather with teaching them both English and an attitude for success. At that time, the Americans were sending platoons and money into Vietnam. English was a language of opportunity. Yeh Yeh's fortune was made but never accumulated. It was quickly gambled, vigorously turned into cognac, and enthusiastically given away in late night transactions. There was a plaque from the Saigon Rotary Club on the wall next to his mirror. *'To Percival Chen – For Exemplary Generosity and Community Involvement'.*

On the telephone to Canada, I asked my dad whether grandfather really had forgotten all his English, or whether he just pretended to have lost it. My father said that when they were children, they all thought their father was a master of this language. Yeh Yeh told me that he had always faked it, that at the British school in Hong Kong he had learned that the British display great confidence when they don't

133

know something. Later at his own school, when he couldn't spell something that he was teaching, he simply avoided writing it down. He claimed that he never really spoke English properly, but had convinced people that he did. The hired teachers were Canadians, Brits and Australians. These people corrected spelling mistakes for the students, so he didn't need to. I suspect my grandfather understood more English than he admitted, but that he could not take interest in conversations at Glenn Hill. *Aren't the potatoes salty today?* In his cottage, Yeh Yeh kept a bottle of Rémy Martin XO Cognac in the cupboard above the sink.

★ ★ ★

My grandmother claimed that grandfather ruined her life by gambling and womanising. She said that his behaviour led her to nag and fight him, and this created bitterness in her. It was this wound which had made her such an admittedly difficult woman, she said. Sometimes, she explained this after yelling at me or another family member. My grandfather said my grandmother ruined his life, because early in their married life her nagging and fighting compelled him to seek solace outside the home. For a Chinese man in Saigon when Vietnam was still Indochine under the French, this meant mah jong houses. They would bring hot dim sum late into the night, and smiling compliant women at any hour. There was nowhere else to go, he said. Yeh Yeh admitted that it was wrong of him to spend so much time and money in unfaithful ways. He recognised that this would anger any wife, but said that he sought these comforts initially because there was no peace at home. My father told me that although the school was lucrative, Yeh Yeh never had any money. The school fees went directly to loan sharks. Yeh Yeh bought a new Peugeot with push-button gears, but once they had to sleep in the school for several months since they could not afford to rent a house.

★ ★ ★

In Brisbane, my grandfather had many friends. Enough of the Chinese in Vietnam had emigrated to Australia that he still had social standing in this new, hot, white country. We were often invited to dinner. One couple who took us out were younger than my grandfather, but older than my parents. Dr. Wong was a retired orthopaedic surgeon who had graduated from the Percival Chen Academy before studying medicine in Glasgow. After retiring, Dr. Wong had become an Anglican minister. He and his wife, with the encouragement of uncle Will, were trying to convert my grandfather to Christianity before he died. Grandfather was a prime candidate. He was previously sinful and glamorous, now reduced to near-poverty although still drinking XO cognac and gambling once a week (I had become the chauffeur for these outings, which my uncle was not to be told about). We were having a dinner of scallops, delicate oysters, and the lobsters without claws that they catch in Australia. My grandfather produced his flask, and asked the waiter to fill a glass with ice. He poured cognac for himself and offered it around the table, but no one took any. The minister and his wife were teetotallers. Yeh Yeh poured some for me. We talked about Jesus.

My grandfather was receptive and interested, although during years of friendship with Dr. Wong, he had been politely and charismatically sidestepping the issue of faith. He questioned Dr. Wong about the parable of the sower. Yeh Yeh asked whether God would mind if he had sowed seeds which lay ignored for a long time before sprouting. Dr. Wong said that it was all the same as long as there was faith at the time of judgement. I imagined my grandfather weighing the odds. Death was an awaiting certainty, and beyond that the odds were unknown, but there was nothing to lose by laying a few bets on the Bible. What was in the past could be repented for, and the future was short.

They set a date for the baptism.

My grandfather didn't drink tea in restaurants, because he didn't want to fill his bladder and have to pee blood during dinner. He sipped cognac on ice. There was a great deal of food on the table when everyone stopped eating, mindful of their cholesterol and their diabetes. They counted on me to eat everything, which I tried to do.

★ ★ ★

After Ma Ma divorced Yeh Yeh, she married a man whose business was mostly in Taiwan. This was daring at that time, for a Chinese woman to divorce her husband and then remarry. It was in newspapers. While reading in his garden one day, her new husband was assassinated. The bullet travelled expertly through the back of his neck and out his throat. He would not have suffered. He was thought to be a prime candidate for leading a secession movement. My father says this was a political ambition only imagined by others, and that it was unfortunate because he was kind to my grandmother. This had helped to calm her down. She was still excitable, and this was the last point in her life that her beauty could, at least superficially, compensate for her temper and vindictiveness.

Yeh Yeh had no excuse anymore not to marry his mistress, and so he did. She became Second Wife. Second Wife did not get along with grandfather's new mistress, who became Third Wife although they were never legally married. Both lived in the same household. Third Wife was docile, and tried to submit to the will of Second Wife, who nonetheless continued to be unhappy with the situation. Second Wife tried to kill herself with a gun, but managed only to shatter her arm, which then had to be amputated. With the shame of the disabled upon her, my grandfather bought her a house and sent her money periodically. No one is able to tell me what happened to her after this. Third Wife was kind to Fourth Wife. Fourth Wife was sixteen years old when she married my then middle-aged grandfather. Fourth Wife was more cunning than Third Wife, and insisted on a legal marriage. Soon after this, the Viet Cong changed Saigon to Ho Chi Minh City, the Americans were suddenly gone, and those who had links to the capitalist economy were being imprisoned or shot. My grandfather convinced the High Commission that he was a British subject by virtue of his having once lived in Hong Kong. When he fled Vietnam, Fourth Wife went with him because she had the marriage papers, while Third Wife remained in Ho Chi Minh City with her child.

★ ★ ★

One day, my grandfather woke, peed in the toilet, and then went back to bed. He did not dress. He told me that he didn't want to get up that day. He felt tired, and the thing in his side was growing.

'Come and feel it. See what you think,' he said in Cantonese.

His left flank bulged out like a balloon that was being inflated under the skin.

'*Mo toong*,' he said, there is no pain. He felt his side delicately, and pulled up his shirt so that I could see it. I pressed the tumour gently with the tips of my fingers. It was firm, hard like cold plasticine. What did I think?

'*Ho choy mo toong*,' I said. It was fortunate that it wasn't painful.

'*Hai*,' he agreed.

Yeh yeh explained that he always wore suspenders in these past few months. If he wore a belt, he pointed out, it would rub his side where the tumour was growing under the skin. His biggest fear was that the skin would split over the growing lump. He wore his pants slightly loose – held up by suspenders to avoid friction on this area. The thought of the cancer escaping from the confines of his body and making itself public in a wet, bloody way horrified him. He said he wouldn't be able to care for himself if the thing broke through. They would move him to the dormitories. Go look at the toilet, he told me.

I looked in the toilet. It was thick blood. It seemed to have a surface to it, clotting as if there was enough blood that it had become independent of the urine. Experimentally, I flushed it and saw the thickness of it break up and swirl. It was not as viscous as it initially appeared, but this was a deep and serious tone of red.

'Yeh Yeh,' I said. 'We should go to the hospital.'

'No hospital.'

'But you look pale. You are weak. Dr. Spiros said that this might happen, that you might lose blood and need a transfusion.'

'No more hospital. Your grandfather dies here.'

'Yes, but if we go to the hospital, they may be able to help you live longer. We'll come back here, and you won't have to go to the dormitory.'

'Who needs hospitals? Besides, you're a doctor. You're here.'

I was early in my training and wanted to pretend to be a doctor. I suggested that we call Dr. Spiros.

'Bring me my medicine,' said grandfather. He wanted the box of little brown bottles. I went to get them. There were eight left in the box. I pried the tight little cork out of a bottle, gave it to Yeh Yeh, and made him a cup of tea. In Toronto, I had gone with my grandmother to the herbalist on Dundas Street to buy these medicines. I had been surprised by her concern for his wellbeing, and her desire to purchase medicines. She had questioned the herbalist vigorously in purchasing these herbal concentrates which were reputed to invigorate the kidneys. She had insisted that the medicine must be of the best quality – nothing fake, nothing second rate. Before buying them, she produced her trump card, and told the herbalist that I, her grandson, was a brilliant doctor and I would smell each vial before she would buy them. The herbalist smiled obligingly, I sniffed them each in turn – their odour both bitter and heady, and told my grandmother that they smelled very strong. She was satisfied, and paid for them.

Dr. Spiros was not in the office. His registrar was there, but said that he couldn't assess anything without seeing the patient. We should bring him to the emergency department, and if the emergency department wanted to involve urology, they would page them. Yeh Yeh refused to go. I called Dr. Wong, who came to the cottage and spoke to my grandfather. He felt the mass, and then told him that as an orthopaedic surgeon he didn't have much expertise here. Yeh Yeh should see his specialist, he said. I realised that real physicians, when called upon in awkward family situations, try to pretend not to be doctors. Grandfather said he was ready to die. Dr. Wong said he could bring elders from the church for a bedside baptism. Yeh Yeh agreed.

The two of us walked down the little walkway in the bright warm afternoon of the Brisbane winter to Dr. Wong's car. He said to me,

'You know he's going to die?'

'That's why I'm here.'

'*Nay ho gwai*,' he said, patting my shoulder. This means that you are very obedient and well behaved, a Chinese compliment.

That night, I asked grandfather if he knew who his real parents were. He told me it doesn't matter, that one has to always move forward, otherwise the past holds too much pain.

* * *

After two years in Hong Kong, my grandfather and Fourth Wife moved to Australia. Towards the end of the Vietnam War, my aunts and uncles had been sent to different countries. The idea was that

someone, somewhere would land on their feet. Uncle Will went to Sydney, and later sponsored Yeh Yeh from Hong Kong. After several months, my aunt Alice told Uncle Will that if Yeh Yeh continued to live with them, she would leave. He was drinking and gambling heavily. Fourth Wife was younger than all of Yeh Yeh's children.

My uncle helped Yeh Yeh and Fourth Wife buy a house in Brisbane. Yeh Yeh told me he had never wanted to stay in Sydney. Too cold. Brisbane is tropical. Fourth Wife started a restaurant, and began an affair with the cook. She divorced my grandfather but continued to visit him weekly in the retirement home which they found for him. That was twelve years before the cancer. He told me that it's understandable. A younger woman wants a younger man. Yeh Yeh relied on Fourth Wife to bring him cigarettes weekly. While smoking these cigarettes, he spoke sadly about the early arguments, poisoned misunderstandings that he had with my Ma Ma. At that time they were younger than I was now, he told me.

★ ★ ★

The next day, Yeh Yeh was too weak to stand. His forehead was pale and sweaty. The toilet bowl was thickly stained with blood. I had to lift him under the arms to get him to the washroom. He wouldn't eat. I called my aunt Alice and uncle Will to ask what I should do. Should I take him to the hospital? They asked me what they should do, should they fly from Sydney? Everyone else was in New York, Los Angeles, Toronto. With the time difference I didn't want to wake them. In the evening, against my grandfather's wishes, I called an ambulance. The spinning red siren lights turned on the wall of the cottage, making it look like it was in constant motion. They took him out, wrapped in an orange tube of blanket. I tried to be medical, and tell the paramedics about his condition, but I couldn't remember any of the details.

Two days and eight units of transfused blood later, my grandfather was in the hospital complaining to Dr. Spiros that he should be discharged. Dr. Wong had come to baptise him, and brought fried noodles in white styrofoam boxes. The Wongs had a place on Stradbroke Island, and suggested that I go there for a rest. Grandfather was more stable now.

On Stradbroke, I stayed across from the headlands beach. In the morning I woke early to watch the humpback whales migrating north. As the sun streaked low across the water, their spouts were small torches in the grey shadowless tide. The light became full and round. I saw dolphins diving out of the crests of waves to hunt the fish that were driven into the cove. The sun lifted higher and burned through the day. From the payphone at the side of the road, I called grandfather at the hospital. He was doing alright, he said. He had sent Dr. Wong to the cottage for the bottles of Chinese medicine. There were two bottles left, he said. I should stay at the beach and enjoy myself, he said, and see if they have fresh crab in the restaurants. Yeh Yeh advised me to have them sauté it in cognac, that's what he would do. He said that I should remember to always move forward, to not allow the past to become hurtful, although this was sometimes a difficult thing to do. Yeh Yeh reminded me to thank my grandmother for the medicines, when I would soon return home and speak with her.

Viet Lê

Haunting

(Tiger, tiger, burning bright)

Ghosts are not what you imagine,
they don't take forms, inhabit their dispossessed,
aren't recognisable, nor loved.

Not the naked girl burning burning bones,
concave skin running running sweating Napalm glory
screaming in your memory
(Do I look like her? She's still alive, you know);

not the grass and wire and skeletal piles,
Tuol Sleng, clumps of dirt, weeds, night forests, bright fires;
not the small teeth, high cheekbones

black gun blasting VC –

none of these things.

The afterlife
of trauma, the image's aura: stereotypical, stereoscopic,
grainy black and white – atomic, indelible, spectral.

I have been looking for the uncanny
in daylight, afraid of the dark's secrets (the night)

mother was raped on the way to Thailand,
years before my birth; she never told me,
(I always knew). Marrow guided, I have been searching
for glimpses, hunting for my parents' ghosts
in imaginary countries.

Haunting is mute, barely
perceptible, your breaths heave and sigh.

It comes as this: small coincidences, signs,
a candle flaring at noon, obscure headlines, blood
in water, slight chills.

Strawberries for Sale

for Phieu and Ngan

I.
My chalky fingers bled
picking them my eighth summer: the taste
of blood-copper and strawberries.

Come summer time
second through sixth grade
my parents shared a rusty
blue van with my best friend's family
on road trips: San Fernando, Van Nuys, San Bernardino…
to pluck whatever harvest we could.

Asleep in the rhythm of diesel,
cities, highways, hills floated
till we were up in the blue mountains.

This must be where Buddha lives.

II.
Uncles, wives, daughters, sons:
other families, other migrant workers.

Decaying sweetness, gummy sweat,
waves of heat ripple upward like a stream.

Should be used to it, gook
with your rice paddies and cone hats

At night we catch crickets, feed them
leaves, braid our hair in the pale light.

Stiff spine cold to the cabin floor
we huddle with other families.

Your real father must be a black man,
cousins tease at the end of my summers in Nirvana.

They're jealous:
they're stuck in ESL summer school.

III.
I don't know what happened to Lori,
last I heard
from a friend of a friend of the family
her parents live in the hills.

If she saw me in the supermarket,
would she recognize my mole?

Biting a stolen strawberry
in the produce aisle:
copper and blood.

Pham Thi Hoai

Vision Impaired

For the first session I put on three layers of clothes above and two layers below the waist. My husband said this *tam quat* master wasn't a master of martial arts with wall-piercing fingers, so there was no need to protect myself with so much armour. The master, who wore dark glasses, might have been unsure if I was a woman or a man, if he hadn't been told. But I thought otherwise, that clothes were not just to shield or to conceal your body, as even in coffins bodies are fully clothed. I wanted to be tactful to show my good will the first time a stranger's hands were to touch my body. Not all men are as progressive as my husband, and the blind men that I know all seem to be behind the times, as if they lived in a far away world or their own, a world where the sun neither rises nor sets. I was fearful that if I was not careful I might cause offence to a person with a disability. Feeling the brassiere beneath the thick layers of my full set of clothes, surely he would understand that I regarded him as a person of good will. Then both of us could trust each other more easily, as not only was this my first time, but he had never worked on a woman before either.

Tam quat is not for women. My husband had to go through a great deal of trouble to bring him home. What kind of a world are we living in, my husband complained, that it's easier to hire someone to beat up your wife than to find someone to give her a thumping back rub. Everywhere he went, they all thought he was making mischief and found polite excuses to turn him down. Women bring bad luck, they would say. Only this master answered my husband in full. 'Wouldn't it be better for you to buy your wife some of those machines? Machines that massage, vibrate, suck and slap, machines that work on your feet, massage your belly, tickle your armpits, that use infra-red technology, everything under the sun is available these days. Those Chinese machines with plastic nibs and sticks that rub and beat you simultaneously, they are a penny a dozen and they last you a lifetime. I don't know why you bother with us, who have nothing but our humble bare hands. We aren't worth your trouble.'

My husband liked the mocking acerbic tone of this master, he persisted in asking and the master gave him a further blast 'And if you're after a genuine experience then take your wife to a hotel. There real people give you real services. A massage to freshen your skin on your way in, a sauna to warm your flesh on your way out, it's entertaining, gentle and elegant. All we can do here is twisting your neck and cracking your back, quite savage and beastly really, not at all suitable for women.'

My husband became even more interested. He has a natural affinity with the eccentric. He would spare no effort to entertain anyone with a reputation of being an eccentric. For a long time our house was full of artistic guests, but after a while he came to the conclusion that they were just pretending to be eccentric, because if one harbours the wish to be celebrated by others then one cannot disdain society from a distance. In any case, these artists proved to be thorny and unique only in pure talk, their artistic creations as smooth and conformist as the next, their sense of abrasive individualism nowhere to be seen. In the end my husband didn't quite know what to do with them. For a while he regretted the missed chance to make friends with a famous non-artist, a former official of the French time, who claimed to follow what he called *thank-you excuse-me ism*, who declared himself the last person in the world who still knew how to use these two endangered words, so as long as he was alive, those were the only words he ever uttered.

But unfortunately my husband came a little too late, the man's tongue had frozen stiff but my husband got there just in time to take his body to Van Dien Cemetery for burial. So for the whole of this year, my husband has been feeling sorry for himself and for the rest of mankind. To him, the young have lots of front but not much flair, the old are out of touch but not outstanding. This *tam quat* master, although young, spoke with the maturity and depth of an independent thinker who held his own considered opinions. My husband turned on all his charm, taking the master out to have a few drinks of sparkling wine at a place where the owner had a reputation for being arrogant, serving only a select few. In the end the master accepted my husband's request out of a sense of obligation, but adding that he had never worked on a woman before, so if something went wrong he would count on our magnanimity.

At first my husband told me to lie down on a divan to be within easy reach of the master. But the master said 'We're more used to sitting down on a mat. I hear that at the Institute of Traditional Medicine they offer a training course for masseurs where the patients lie on a table and the practitioners stand up, dressed in white blouses. But *tam quat* is a tradition of the common people. Let's remain informal, it suits our style better.'

My husband quickly rolled out a mat, saying that he was in total agreement with the master, this is our intimate space, not a public arena, we are here to enjoy ourselves in comfort, not to endure stiff formality, and the master should also feel at ease here. The master sat down on the mat. I climbed down from the divan and lay myself down. My husband said 'Her head is to your left and her feet your right, master.' He had tidied up our house with care, as usually our home was full of haphazard furniture, books, pot plants, bric-a-brac, gifts from our onetime artistic friends and curiosities collected by my husband. This master did not have a walking stick, nor a dog or a child to guide his way, as if he expected things to get out of his way and not the other way round.

I lay down rigid. I felt restricted no matter which position I took, on my stomach, on my side or my back, as if lying down was something I'd never done before in my life. Lying on my stomach my buttocks felt protrusive, the more I pressed my thighs together the more prominent the buttocks felt. But if I relaxed my thighs it felt a little revealing. Lying on my side showed even more. On my back it felt wide open. As soon as the master's hand touched me my body tensed up, a mass of watchful hypersensitive flesh.

The master said 'Your wife's not comfortable.'

My husband asked 'How come my wife is not comfortable? What do you mean, not comfortable?'

The master replied 'When we were young, on the occasions when we got a caning, we usually tensed up like this.'

My husband laughed out loud, gave a long commentary on love delivered through the cane, and said 'That's why I love this form of traditional massage. It's physical and unrestrained, every blow as memorable as the next, unlike the so-called massages of modern times. I hate pretentious fakes. Give her the real experience, you must not pull your punches.'

I like whatever my husband likes and detest what he hates, from the very beginning to the very end. To be a wife is to entrust your fate to someone else's hands, to give him all you've got, body and soul, holding nothing back as your own. My husband regards that attitude as too passive, taking the end point, obligation, as the starting point of the relationship. So I alter my position a little, saying that I trust him with my body and soul, that I entwine my fate with his, because we share our hearts. I don't see what difference it makes to have a common heart or a fateful obligation as a starting point. But if it pleases him then so be it.

The master said 'Oh yes, we like to use a bit of force too. Clients who get a real pummelling feel that they get their money's worth. Today we'll work free of charge on the hands and the feet, the marginal extremities that aren't worth charging. If you feel that does no harm then the next time we won't hold anything back, Mr Teacher.' My husband agreed, but stressed 'You'll hold back only this first time, yes? From the next time we must dispense with all these silly formalities. It wouldn't be a genuine experience of *tam quat* if we hid behind these qualifications and hedges.'

Each hand is less than twenty centimetres square but the master took the whole fifteen minutes to finish. What grabbed my attention most was the care with which he rolled my fingers, caressing every millimetre. After half an hour my husband joked 'By now you probably know my wife's hands better than I do,' and the master replied 'You've got a point there, Mr Teacher. It's quite common for people to know a face or a voice. To recognise someone by their smell is less common, and rarer still, by the sounds of their footsteps. But most uncommon is to know somebody by their hands. That wasn't not surprising in the old days when we weren't accustomed to shaking hands, but even in these modern hand-shaking times we still don't know each other's hands. Even those who spend all day wringing their obsequious hands don't know their own hands either.'

My husband broke in, 'So you must really know other people's hands.'

The master said 'No, not really. We know only the backs usually. Our customers aren't concerned with hands, it's the back that's most important. All we need to do for their hands is to crack the knuckles, making ten sharp sounds, which takes ten seconds. That's all it takes to keep them happy. With some customers only nine joints would crack, taking nine seconds — less than the time it takes for a perfunctory handshake, Mr Teacher.'

My husband said he'd like to hear the ten cracking sounds, just to see what it was like. The master placed one of my hands, with its palm open, inside his palm — closing it. His thumb moved smoothly along the knuckles of my hand as though they were the ivory of a piano. Four neat cracking sounds. Then his thumb moved quickly to the lower knuckles at the base of my fingers. Another four sounds, four notes lower than the previous, then his thumb and his index finger closed in around my thumb and neatly cupped it, making a low muffled cracking sound. The tenth note came from somewhere deep below the base of my thumb. My other hand also sang ten notes. My husband was impressed. The master said 'It's a simple little trick really, anyone with a little dexterity can do it. If you practised it you'd master it in no time, Mr Teacher.'

Then it was my feet's turn and my husband was visibly moved. When the master massaged the mound of my foot, rubbing each toe and between the toes, massaging the ankle, then placing my foot, which also measured less than twenty centimetres square, in the palm of one hand, the other hand covering my foot from above, gently nursing my foot in the way one would protect a fragile little bird, my husband smiled at me. I smiled back. When unsure what my husband might be thinking, I always smile. The master's warm hand closed around my ankle. His other hand chopped, knocked, and slapped unceasingly on the sole of my foot. He tickled me lightly and my foot jerked back in a movement that jolted from heel to knee. My husband said 'And you said that *tam quat* was barbaric.'

'Yes,' the master said. He yanked hard and my ankle sang a low snapping note. 'Or you could say it's common, Mr Teacher,' he added. Again he yanked hard and my other ankle cracked with the same low, sharp sound. My feet remained attached to my legs, yet they felt so light and so weightless, soft and lazy like two large wilting leaves, and so comfortable; all they wanted to do was to remain forever in this blissful state, so that they could continue to be so nursed, tickled and indulged. They'd become spoiled rotten.

'You know, nowadays modern pleasures are too easily available but ephemeral, and people with depth like you, Mr Teacher, feel unsatisfied and turn to the simplicity of traditional practices. It doesn't take much to learn, otherwise people of darkness like us couldn't get a grasp of it to practise. There is no basis for it really. We simply copy from others, the whole lot, the good and the bad. We don't know what to discard or what is of real value, so we adopt everything in the hope that it might do the trick. Outsiders don't see how it works and think it's mysterious, a bit like thinking that snakes must have legs to move so fast. Acupuncture or acupressure may have some scientific basis, but just to give a rub and a thump like this orang-utans can do just as good a job. It's a way for us to eke out a living. We would love to have another way to make a living but as fate has dictated it to be this way, we have no choice...'

My husband didn't know what to say. We have had many eccentric visitors to our home, and sometimes they speak in profound ways that border on insanity, but no one was quite as ambiguous and difficult to pin down as this master. All day long he spoke in a mocking but humorous tone. We didn't know if he wanted to keep a distance from us or to get closer to us. Did he regard us with contempt, or did he think of us highly? Was he honest with us or was he testing the water with his circular style of talk? But one thing was clear, professionally he knew what he was doing, and my husband insisted on ordering a cyclo to take him home, and to bring him back the following day. My husband did not say it out loud, but I knew this enigmatic master was to be a welcome visitor to our home for quite a while.

★　★　★

On the second day my husband was even more on tenterhooks than I was. He urged me to go and lie down on the mat before the master arrived. I lay down on my stomach, closed my eyes and let my mind roam. The master didn't know my face. His hands sometimes felt warm and sometimes refreshingly cool. He spoke with a mocking voice full of barbs. The way he spoke yesterday he was probably having fun at my husband's expense. Perhaps he was also contemptuous of me. But if that was true then how come he caressed my feet with such loving care. Even the most dedicated and indulgent pedicurist would be no comparison. I now know that I have two feet, not just for walking, but also for making demands, to be spoiled rotten and even for daydreaming. Of our body the feet are the hardest working, yet I brush my hair several times a day and never brush my feet. Every night my husband seeks out my breasts several times but ignores my feet. But last night, all of a sudden, he gave my feet a long and wet kiss with more passion and urgency than the kiss on my lips, and it felt deliciously fresh and unfamiliar, just like our wedding night. I was moved to tears. There couldn't be that many women who have had their toes sucked by their husband. Today he told me to wear a silk blouse and a pair of silk pants. That's sufficient, he said, men usually wear only a pair of shorts at *tam quat*. I didn't go to all the trouble to bring him here to massage your layers of sartorial resistance, he added. This is all about your skin and flesh which I love and indulge, he said. I am doing this for you, as you would never have sought these pleasures for yourself. What's more, too much protection might seem that we suspect the other party of ill intent. My wife is not like those girls who sit with legs crossed into knots and walk with joined knees. Too much protection is just like an invitation to invade.

The silk made me feel soft, or maybe the master's touch had become familiar. Or had I already begun to feel in tune with his hands? First came the circular movements, rubbing gently, moving from the shoulder blades along the back, spreading across the small of the back, down towards my buttocks. Again I smiled at my husband. The master said 'The back is alright, but the shoulders and buttocks will take quite a bit of work.' My husband looked perplexed. The master explained 'It will take only two sessions to loosen the muscles of the back, that's no problem. The shoulders and the neck are so stiff and knotted, they'll take at least a week. But the sides seem a little bit misaligned. We aren't sure yet. If it's a curved spine, then there's nothing we can do, Mr. Teacher, you'll have to get a doctor, *tam quat* masters can make no difference whatsoever.' My husband begged the master to examine his wife more closely. The master insisted that his ability was limited. While this conversation was happening my husband's hands moved to one of my buttocks and began to massage it, and the master's hands the other one, the stiff formality of the day before was well and truly discarded, as agreed. In the end my husband conceded to the master's wish, and praised the master's remarkable humility, so different from the boastful quacks, who were equipped with only cheap sticky medicated patches but claiming to be able to treat all kinds of illness. He also quietly congratulated himself for having a keen eye and a good judgement of people.

For the whole duration of the session the master took his time, leisurely explaining to my husband every move and every trick. 'This is punching, fluid and shallow punches only, withdraw as soon as the blows connect, the force coming from the wrist and not the arm. A good pummelling must sing cracking pleasure to the ears. I've said *tam quat* is for the common folk. Our folks like noisy crowds. That's why we fear solitary confinement more than execution. At executions at least there's gunfire and yelling spectators. This is called patting, your hand forming the dome shape of the tortoise's shell, cupping air and slapping down. You must also make a nice slapping sound. This is the chop, this is a friction rub, this is pinching, pulling, hacking, squeezing, pressing, rolling, they all sound like torture. I've said *tam quat* is not an art of gentle caressing. This is called catching the mouse. Along the back, here and here, under each side of the ridge, there hides a mouse, you have to flush it out to make it run like this, that's called catching a mouse. This is called the march of a thousand ants. Use the tips of your fingers lightly, but the customer must feel the goose pimples rising if you're any good at it. But many customers have backs that are as broad and thick as a divan, and marching ants are nothing, in which case we have to resort to using our fingernails to dig into the flesh like a cricket burrowing its nest and then maybe they'll feel something. Those people love nothing more than a good pummelling. Now this is called the wading stork, your fingers walk like the deliberate and rhythmic feet of a stork, take your time and don't rush. You can also call it the pecking stork, pecking in single strokes, in a leisurely and unhurried manner. A flurry of typist finger strokes may cause the customer to feel he's reaching the height of pleasure, but that'll be no good. The height of pleasure must be when it hurts the most, the waves of pain followed by a moment of feeling faint, and a few seconds later, pleasure hits at its most extreme. And this is called the horizontal snake roll. I've told you, *tam quat* is savage and beastly. Marching ants and pecking storks, catching the mouse and rolling the snakes, no dragons and phoenix here, these terms are down to earth but they grate on your ears the first time you hear them. Snake rolls are just the ways we roll the skin. There are five places on our body where you can do this, the elbows, the knees and the back. A good roll is when the skin rolls along, one spot chasing another like waves. And now, the height of pleasure, it's simply called plucking. You start plucking here at this spot of the back, and move down, all the way to the coccyx, like this.'

The master changed his position so fast I didn't have time to panic. By now he was bent over me completely, his fingers feeling my backbone from my waist, gripping the skin and plucking hard. With each pluck my back made a cracking sound and it sang a series of notes as his hands moved further and further down. I trembled in silence. Another sound, another and another then he would reach that mole. It took months of intimacy for my husband to discover the existence of this mole, right there at the hidden spot at the base of my spine, the coccyx. It's a matter known only between the two of us, it's private and strictly forbidden territory.

By now my husband was so captivated, almost hypnotised, that if the master had mounted his wife he would have found it OK. They probably call this riding a buffalo to pluck rice seedlings. The master actually climbed over me. I have seen *tam quat* practitioners sitting astride their customers' buttocks like this before. So these moves and positions all followed a certain script. I know my husband likes to act cool, but surely he was going to intervene, he surely was not going to allow his wife to go the whole hog, where my thighs would end up on the master's shoulders like I've seen at some kerbside *tam quat*.

But the two men were engrossed in their task, with one patiently explaining everything and the other listening with such intensity, drinking in every word. For almost a year now my husband had not listened to anyone like this. I almost passed out when the master's four fingers circled the pea-sized mole and the last sound cracked in a low soft tone.

In the middle of the night I woke up to find my husband straddling my back, loving and gentle, passionate and crazy, a gigantic crawling ant, a pecking stork and a slithering snake all at once. So I had worried unnecessarily over a little mole the size of a pea.

On the day that I shed my silk blouse, but keeping the brassiere on, an idea occurred to my husband and he replaced the electric lights with candles. This was on my account, to provide me with a sense of privacy, because as far as the poor master was concerned light or no light made no difference. And he was right. The master calmly took hold of my naked back, taking minute care of it like all the other times, giving my neck and shoulders his every attention. As for me, my pleasure seemed to permeate even more deeply and my husband probably enjoyed watching the beautiful curves of his wife's body bathed in the soft flickering candlelight.

Many days later, my husband asked me to remove the brassiere as well because the straps around the neck and the middle of the back got in the way of the master's hands, spoiling his smooth movements. In addition, by now my back was smooth and my neck was almost tension-free, but my chest and abdomen had yet to feel the touch of his hands. My husband feared that if we didn't remind him the master might gloss over them, so he insisted that the master show him the manoeuvres for the front half of the body. The master firmly refused. My husband resorted to sulking 'So I see you're bound by social taboos like everyone else, hey! Or do you regard us with contempt?' The master replied 'No, I wouldn't say that. You are one in a million, Mr Teacher, who dares to live your own way. Nobody would treat you with contempt, and even if they did, it wouldn't worry you. The simple truth is that we have had no experience in handling women, and we don't want our inexperience to give us a reputation of clumsiness.'

My husband tried a provocative tact, 'Oh, men or women, aren't we all humans? If even a person like you would discriminate then what hope is there for equality…I had thought that you and I had agreed on this at the beginning.' My husband was so insistent, the master reluctantly agreed, but on one condition. 'Okay, but if we mishandle things a bit, you must forgive us, Mr Teacher.'

How can the master's sure hands mishandle things? These are the hands that rolled my fingers, caressed my feet neglecting not a square millimetre, fingers that never actually touched my sacred spot, always just surrounding it and letting it go, circling and teasing, those fingers that pulled bunches of my hair to make a ticking sound off the scalp, grabbing exactly twenty-nine, my age, strands of hair at a time, the hands that pulled my ears so hard and crisply that they made such a sharp cracking sound, never making a mistake at any of the seventy-eight spots of my body capable of making a sound, those hands that each time sliding under my armpits always stopped so marvellously close to the base of my bulging breasts. Hands are the eyes of the blind. Ten fingers the ten eyes. Now those hands are hugging my abdomen, then spreading themselves over my belly, fanning across my sides, investigating and probing before determinedly circumventing my navel. Then with one hand in pursuit of the other, he began a circular rubbing motion that became an ever widening circular divergent motion, with one hand veering towards the lower abdomen while the other waded up towards the chest area. Then they sweetly rubbed hard against my skin with a lot of friction along the bones of the ribcage. Then again and again they rubbed along that narrow strip from the neck to the sternum, taking care to avoid the breasts, squeezing their way in between. My husband thought they were in the master's way, so he took hold of the nipples and parted them to make more space. Then I couldn't tell which hands were whose anymore.

*　★　*

One day my husband told me to discard the pants so that the master could show him with clarity the misalignment of the curved spine. If left untreated, this condition can cause backaches in mild cases, and in severe cases can cause disruptions to periods and even early menopause, my husband said, having looked this up in a book. Now the diagnosis of my condition was confirmed, the slackness of my left side causing tension on my right side. My husband confirmed that his wife had exhibited all the symptoms, especially the tendency to be picky with food, constipation, being prone to colds and flus, sleeping with difficulty. If the master did not have the courage to treat his wife, he would do that himself. But the master must advise him. Must give a demonstration for him to follow.

The master hesitated 'You are a book person, Mr Teacher, everything you do is underpinned by theories you read in books, you can attribute success or failure to theory. We, as mere practitioners, can only base our practice on our own experiences, our success or failure depends on lucky chances. We really wouldn't dare invading the territory of the sciences. We would like to retreat.' But by now my husband was quite used to this game of verbal tug-of-war. He knew he would prevail in the end no matter how complex and ambiguous the master's arguments may be. Deep down he had even begun to feel a certain kind of disdain for the master, dismissing the way he crafted his circular arguments and the way he pretended to be humble, which served to accentuate his virtues, as typical traits of the useless Asian style of discourse, yet taking delight in catching the master out and gaining the upper hand. This time my husband replied quite brusquely 'Look, master, if you were the type who would be happy to work the street, I wouldn't have bothered to ask you home. You and I have a common problem. We are ambitious and secretive. We hold others in contempt but we fear being laughed at by the people we despise. If you allow a small task of re-aligning a curved spine to defeat you then what are the chances of realigning the stars of fate, realigning the affairs of the world?' The master protested 'Aya, to realign the stars you'll have to ask someone else, Mr Teacher.' My husband grasped at the master's words 'Okay, but for straightening a curved back, you've got to help me, okay?' The master nodded in agreement. By now the two men knew each other very well. They talked to each other in this manner because they liked to hear each other's words, and the more they could anticipate the other's arguments and ideas, the more pleasure they derived from the conversation.

The master took the lead and my husband followed. He was clumsy. The master's knees felt soft when pressed against my back. In contrast, my husband's knees felt like a pair of heavy pestles. The master had finished my thigh on this side quite some time before, but my husband was still struggling,

not quite finished, my leg placed over his shoulder had gone
a little numb. And how could he finish? He had insisted that
I wore the pair of underpants embossed with our initials.
Maybe the master could decipher our initials by touch and feel.
The master showed him the difficult manoeuvres. Massaging
the muscles of the pelvic floor, rotating the joints of the hips.
My husband grasped very quickly all those moves that were
complex, even putting forward his own propositions that
sounded quite scientific about collapsed discs, arthritic hips
and pelvic floor exercises.

But as to simple moves such as cracking the back he
was hopeless. He held on to my waist, bit at the nape of my
neck, mauled my breasts but my back did not make a sound.
The master, on the other hand, simply sat firmly behind my
back, supporting me with his knees, his chin resting lightly
on the nape of my neck, his arms circling under my armpits
around the shoulders, fingers firmly locked together. Then
the master gave a gentle push and my back sang a series of
beautiful notes. My body arched backwards, my feet in the air
hovering above but not quite touching the mat, and my head
falling to rest on his chest. The master bent down forward, his
cheek touching my cheek for a moment, his mouth mine for
a second. His hands slowly and quietly let go of the shoulders,
catching the falling breasts in the process. Slowly my breasts
swelled, the two nipples perked up shamefully. The master
said 'Tam quat is quite tactless and inelegant, please forgive my
clumsiness, Mr Teacher.' Then he calmly massaged on with
circular, deliberate and slow movements. Gradually I sank
into his chest, and I could hear the calm, even beats of his
heart. Could he visualise what I looked like? Or maybe he
could only feel that women's bodies are just like men's, with a
few extra curves? Does he feel any affection towards me, and
how can his heart beat so calmly? Is he doing this to give me
pleasure or to please my husband?

For over a month, *tam quat* became our passionate ritual, with my husband diligently tidying up the house, rolling out the mat, burning incense and lighting candles. I'd take a bath, spray a little perfume on myself and then the master would arrive at eight o'clock on the dot. In October it was dark at eight o'clock. In the soft candle light the three of us became one. My husband was badly hooked, an addict, it was never enough for him. He even felt that the underpants, embossed with our initials, were in the way. 'Every other area of your body has enjoyed this pleasure unhindered, why does this part of your anatomy have to be deprived?' he asked me. How a piece of clothing could hinder the pleasure to a part of my body I didn't know, but if taking it off pleased my husband then take if off I would. Again I closed my eyes and rested my shoulders on the master's chest like all the other times, but the master's hands came to a sudden stop halfway through. The master gave an involuntary start, I sensed, followed by a sudden but reluctant release of his grip, half wanting to let go, half wanting to hold firm. I held my breath. Did the master feel uneasy because my breasts had swollen too much? Are they spoiled too much today? Or did the master forget for a moment that he was sitting on a mat in the middle of a *tam quat* session? The *tam quat* mat is a place for torture, where my body is to be given a pummelling and then to be left alone. Brutal and barbaric. Or sophisticated? But the master paused a little too long and when I opened my eyes I could see my husband looming between my thighs.

I don't know whether I sat up or the master pushed me off. Or did my husband yank me away from the master's grip? It happened so quickly and crazily that I am still not sure what took place. What can I say to put my husband's mind at peace? The master gave a start, what did he sense? What did he hear, what did he smell? Or what did he see that changed his attitude? How come he stopped so suddenly midway through a session? How come he turned his head away for a fleeting moment when my husband began to love me? My husband is a very tactful man, even at the moment of release he's quiet as if nothing has happened. If the master had not seen, heard or felt something, how come he became a little rattled? He left in a huff like a man with an injured pride. Left while the candles were still burning, saying not a word.

The following day my husband decided to light no candle. It got dark. My husband said, if he was really in the realm of darkness then to him darkness is light. Let's find out if this master of *tam quat* is just sharp of wits or also sharp of eyes.

I lay there, safely cocooned in the comforting darkness, feeling compassion for my husband but unease for the master. I prayed that the master's world was truly darkness, darkness unlimited to the point of hopelessness, and that way my husband would be spared his pains. Spared of having to trace in his mind the master's moves, every one of which now caused my husband acute pain. Didn't the master avoid our secret mole a little too adroitly? Didn't he give the pubic bone just so much attention? Didn't he get to know my body, from head to toe, like the back of his hand? No need to retrace the words that the master used, words that my husband drank hungrily with a mixture of anticipation and emotion, but were now coming back to haunt him. Didn't the master say one day 'One spot chasing another like waves'? Waves are the things you cannot describe without seeing. Didn't he also say 'Your hand should be cupped like the shell of a tortoise'? Has the master ever seen a tortoise? What about ants? Storks? Snakes? But didn't he say 'Fate had dictated us to be like this and we have to oblige'? What did he mean? 'To be like this' is to be like what? True, he did say 'people of darkness like us'. But he said people of darkness and he didn't say blind people. This bastard chose his words so cleverly, full of double meanings laden with ambiguities and impossible to pin down. He was not leery but tactless and clumsy. He did not grope your wife's breasts, but mishandled them. Each day he 'accidentally' pushed against your wife's buttocks and spread your wife's thighs wide open a couple of times. And the curved spine! He could see through every millimetre of your wife's body and yet he said 'Not so sure'. Accusing him of deception would be like calling public attention to our stupidity. Asking around would simply make people laugh, they'd say out of ten of those who wear dark glasses and work at *tam quat*, fortune telling, busking or begging, nine are faking their blindness. Real blind people usually pursue wholesome lines of work such as making toothpicks, basket weaving, shelling peanuts, paring onions, things like that. Nobody would know who he was from our description. No names. With such a difficult temperament, he could have been an out of work portrait artist wandering around speaking in that disdainful manner. Once the bastard even hinted that he wanted to follow a different line of work. What kind of work? Sketching realist charcoal portraits? That line of work requires an eye for detail. Now my husband is in an impossible quandary. That's what you get for becoming familiar with the common people. His vision impairment was fake but your judgment impairment was real. You poured your heart out and your wife bared all her flesh. Darkness descended and enveloped both of us. In the dark, the blind can see better than the sighted.

The master did not arrive at eight o'clock. Neither at nine o'clock. The darkness was tense. My husband said nothing. The house was untidy, furniture lay haphazardly, anyone who tripped would fall over the bottles and jars on the tables. I lay there in tense anticipation, just like in those nights of my childhood waiting to catch sight of ghosts. This time I will not fall asleep waiting. In November the nights are long.

Nine out of ten may well be fakes, but I don't care. I count on the master being the one out of ten who is genuinely blind. Usually my husband possesses a healthy scepticism about the opinion held by the majority, preferring the perspicacity of the visionary minority, but on this occasion he seemed to have gone along with the nine out of ten majority. The night is still young and I still invest my trust in a pair of eyes worthy of impairment. I pray that the master is blind. Blind in a clear, perceptive and proud manner. A blindness that would make things easier for the master and bring relief for everyone else involved. Genuinely blind, permanently blind, without any hope of regaining sight. Blind as though the eyes had been gouged out. Blind so that my husband could be grateful for a special friendship, so that the master can continue to be a special guest to our home. He can even be blind from this day onward, it's never too late. I will act as his guide taking him anywhere he needs to go. I know my way around. I have waited to the point of ripeness. But why is the master not coming, stepping around things with his easy gait like every other day, so that I can again sink my head into his chest?

I can't remember how many days I waited. I can't remember how much torture was dished out to me in the *tam quat* sessions that my husband continued to give me until my body became a bag of bloody bruises and swollen flesh. And when there was nowhere left unbruised on the misshapen bag of flesh that was me, my husband did not touch me anymore. Then he also left, without a word, just like the *tam quat* master.

Translated into English by Ton-That Quynh-Du

Pam Brown

The Hanoi Cycle

This road begins in dust and noise. A crazy man in a threadbare shirt throws a broken brick onto the bonnet of this rusting Russian car. I am the blonde foreign devil sitting alone in the back seat.

★ ★ ★

I remember a book by Edward Said in which I discovered the theory that a culture defines itself in contrast with some alien and fanciful entity. I redefine my culture every time I leave it, and, here, in Hanoi, I become the alien and fanciful entity, briefly.

★ ★ ★

In preparation, I have learnt to count in Vietnamese, to say 'thank you, hello' and 'excuse me'. I know something about the modern history of this place and I admire Ho Chi Minh. Also, I have a letter from Sue, who lives here, which says 'In Vietnam, everything and anything can happen.'

★ ★ ★

The first morning. From the window I watch the lone fisherman squatting in a tiny boat working with a net. From dawn until nightfall he moves around the little lake beating the sides of the boat to drive any fish towards the net. In the drizzling rain, in the breeze, on the humid days, he is there. Every day except Sunday.

* * *

At the State Department Store there are few customers and not many bicycles for sale. I buy a durable bike – *Thong Nhat* – Reunification Brand.

Sue buys a basket for the bicycle. Then, after some discussion, she learns that it cannot be attached to the bike as there are no screws, nor are there any screws for sale anywhere in the State Department Store. Sue returns the basket and gets the money back.

* * *

Geckos run across the walls, attracted by the fluorescent light. Mosquitoes float silently around my deep, deep dreams. Cycling and cycling all night long.

* * *

At the Foreign Languages Teachers College when I am introduced as a 'poet' the whole class bursts into enthusiastic applause. This cheerful spontaneity is almost overwhelming.

In Sydney, they laugh and snigger and you have to work incredibly hard to find their hidden hearts.

* * *

Poetry here is a positive tradition, even if, at times, didactic.

Ly Thuong Kiet, who repelled the Chinese invasion in the eleventh century, and Ho Chi Minh, who repelled the French and the Americans and founded the Vietnamese state

last century, were both poets who used their poems to rouse
the people to join the armed struggle.

These days, one of the teachers tells me, young men
write poems to their sweethearts.

★ ★ ★

Fleshy green nymphaea bob at the edge of the little lake into
which we sometimes throw organic scraps. This morning I
take some stale baguettes down to the lake and I am stopped
by a woman who asks to have them.

★ ★ ★

No one talks about *doi moi* – the government's new program
of renovation. When I mention these musical little words to
a local teacher she throws her hands up to her cheeks and
laughs at me.

Here, life is lived by a combination of Confucianism
and communism which to my alien and fanciful perception,
operates in an unpredictable, joyous chaos.

★ ★ ★

One night, while we sleep under diaphanous mosquito nets, a
rat throws peanuts around the flat. In the morning we find a
red carnation which the rat has picked from its stem without
overturning the vase. Selected for its beauty, we decide.

★ ★ ★

At the Evening College an older student, who lectures
in Politics at Hanoi University, says that he was once an
interpreter for Ho Chi Minh. We conduct a conversation
about this revelation with twenty other students listening, as
is the way of language classes.

And he concludes with a statement, 'All that and the war
against the United States of America is in the past now.'

This is it − it is chronological. History, here, is literal. There is no analytical interpretation, no parataxis in the narrative. Probably, you could live here for many, many years in the absence of what Europeans know as cynicism.

★ ★ ★

After work, the college director takes a small group to dinner. We sit on low wooden stools drinking, smoking, talking, laughing and eating tough pieces of chicken in aromatic noodle soup. I feel that everyone is brimming with life. I toss the chicken bones onto the floor, as is the custom.

★ ★ ★

There is a day for everything.

The days which favour me are the day for being careful of what one says and the day for expecting nothing.

There is an animal for every day.

My experience is that small events go haywire on monkey day. On pig day there is a sense of great integration and on goat day I am able to solve perplexities.

★ ★ ★

In Hanoi, everyone calls a rat a mouse.

I am an alien and fanciful entity, born in the Year of the Rat.

★ ★ ★

At the Women's Publishing House I am presented with a bunch of pale, fragrant roses.

At the Writers' Association my colleague and I are described as 'two swallows who come in the Spring'.

When we ask about censorship they answer that there is none.

★ ★ ★

Back in Sydney, I will receive a letter telling me that one of the women 'writers of despair', Duong Thu Huong, has been arrested but there is little information about her misdemeanour.

* * *

I have learned to say 'I am not a Russian', the names of streets and lakes, herbs and various foods. I have learned 'sold out' and 'the globe is round' – '*qua dat thi tron*' – a proverb which means 'we will see each other again'.

* * *

I take some photographs of the wreckage of the huge B52 bomber shot down near the big lake in Lenin Park.

Nearby I eat sweet and delicious frog legs. A dirty, skinny dog hangs around my feet for the tiny frog bones.

After lunch I cycle to the beautiful banyan tree planted in memory of Ho and pose for a photograph under it.

* * *

At the Temple of Literature I light joss sticks and pray for good poetry for myself and for my friends.

I visit the Temple of Literature every few days. It is the only place I have found where solitude is possible.

This beautiful temple was built in 1070 as a school dedicated to Confucianism. The teaching is that a person is essentially a social being bound by social obligations. Farewell Buddhism. Farewell transcendence.

* * *

We have run out of rubbish bags. Sue selects *Oscar and Lucinda* from her bookshelves. She demonstrates the method of bag making by tearing up the book and gluing the pages together, in the local manner. This is one of the many Vietnamese solutions.

* * *

On the roadsides there are small groups of women whose hands and arms are blackened. They have cotton scarves masking their faces from the fumes. Every day they work the pitch, make the bitumen, fill in the holes.

At night, I avoid piles of wet, filthy rubbish as I cycle along without a light. Women with huge grass brooms sweep the rubbish from the gutters onto the road. It is shovelled into an ancient Russian truck.

Women are Vietnamese technology.

* * *

Before leaving Sydney, I had been asked to investigate the eighteenth-century poet Ho Xuan Huong. I find that she is well known to the Vietnamese. She was a popular poet who wrote boldly spicy poems castigating hypocritical monks and she dared to defend unmarried mothers in the face of the rigorous and punitive moralism of the time.

However, Sue and I are puzzled by the so-called 'suggestive eroticism' of her famous poem *The Fan*, which ends with a joke on phallocentrism: 'Kings and lords just adore that little thing'.

* * *

Vietnam needs a clean water supply, electricity, better housing and a cash flow. But, I suppose, it will get 'progress' sooner or later.

* * *

In particular streets every stall sells the same goods. Silk Street, Banner Street, Bicycle Seat Street, Scissor Street, Bathroom Street, Grave Street, Thermos Street, Wood Street. And a street which Sue fondly calls 'Filth Street' – narrow and muddy and busy.

★ ★ ★

Up in Paper Street lurid pink paper stencils hang everywhere, everything is gold and red for the temples. And in this tiny street in the old quarter many old and rickety blind people wander up and down with their sticks and their begging tins. At night they crouch around in small cooking groups like silhouettes of monkeys or scrawny cats on the footpath in the dark.

Up in Paper Street you can buy fake money to offer the Buddha. The money you use to buy it is just as worthless outside this country, in the rest of the world.

★ ★ ★

Early morning, still dark. I lie awake and listen to the terrible sound of pig slaughter. Loud, deep howling moans of pain and distress pour into the darkness as the pig is bled alive and slowly dies. This is the only sound at this time of day.

Each day there are pieces of fresh pork on the wooden slabs at the nearby market. And often I eat the salty pork which is served at the 'Rice for the People' kitchen at the little lake.

★ ★ ★

At the theatre there are five hundred locals and no other Europeans in the audience. Everyone cracks sunflower seeds, chews cucumbers and talks throughout the performance, displaying an irreverent appreciation.

The play, called *Bitter Journey*, is about dispossession and corruption during the war against the United States.

Next week, at the Youth Theatre, there will be a production of Xechspia's *Oteno*.

★ ★ ★

A Molotov cocktail kills the Russian embalmer. Uncle Ho lies in a refrigerated glass box, all pink and ethereal and wise. The Russian custom.

In his will, Uncle Ho requested cremation so that his ashes might blend with Vietnamese earth.

★ ★ ★

Apart from visiting my friend, I am not certain of why I have come to this beautiful, broken-down, mouldering old city. I do know that it's not for information.

★ ★ ★

In Hanoi, a French film crew is making a movie about the battle of Dien Bien Phu.

In Ho Chi Minh City, a French film crew is making a movie of Marguerite Duras' book *The Lover*.

Another French film crew is making a movie called *Indochine*.

The film makers say it is a daily combat. The producers complain of extortionate demands for funds made by rapacious bureaucrats. The Vietnamese technicians and extras frequently threaten strikes, so bad are their living conditions.

Catherine Deneuve, the film star, refuses to confide her impressions of her film or of Vietnam to the press.

Ooh là là. Ce n'est pas bon!

★ ★ ★

In the misty rain, I wait at the gate for Hoa, the interpreter from the Writers' Association. After about ten minutes, I see her coming, zooming along the slippery road by the lake. She is bringing a copy of the huge and now out-of-print book, *Vietnamese Literature*. It is tied with string and dangles from the Honda handlebars.

* * *

Xechspia's *Oteno* seems high camp, and again, the audience is entirely Vietnamese.

There is a spirited dance scene with Iago's soldiers and their sweethearts which we cannot recall having read or seen before.

I persuade my companion to leave and we cycle off into the night in search of Bulgarian wine.

We share the wine on his balcony and I ask him about his family. The topic makes no difference but the experience of talking late into the night is familiar and causes me to lose sense of this foreign city, so that I experience ambiguous feelings of enjoyment and resentment.

* * *

On West Lake the paddle-boats are made from war debris. Old aircraft hulls have become painted swans and roses floating along on spent bomb casings.

* * *

In Herb Street, the big brown paper sacks stacked around the footpaths are folded back to reveal many shades of beige and brown and ochre and red powders and chips and bits of bark and dried leaves and flowers. The sensational air is loaded with palpable congeries of scent.

* * *

The boy in the partisan's hat and worn jungle green cottons leans against the little tree waiting for a customer to buy the snake he has trapped in a wire basket. He is reading a dog-eared book. He looks up and when our gaze connects I realise I am looking too intensely at his beauty.

* * *

Twice each day the small flat fills with the gushing and splashing sounds of water being pumped up through five flights of rusty pipe into a big metal vat. Today I celebrate the event by running to the fountaining tap with the plastic jug and tin basins to catch as much water as possible.

★ ★ ★

The ponderous smoky exhaust from the battered old Volgas and buses is tangible. Hundreds of bicycles, scooters, carts pulled by buffalo, the newer cars of embassies and foreign agencies, old military trucks. Women with poles bouncing and balanced on their bony shoulders, men and women carrying buckets of water, cyclos loaded with live chickens in rattan baskets and pipes and parcels and huge rolls of paper, bicycles with live pigs tied onto the back, scooters carrying three or four people – whole families on a Honda. And everyone with a horn or a bell is hooting and ringing. Each intersection is a thrilling and horrible challenge through which I wobble or glide. The only rule is to keep riding – if I stop I will collect the teeming traffic behind. And, somehow, in the midst of this noisy chaos there is the slightly insane sensation of an inexplicable and confident stability.

★ ★ ★

We rise in the middle of the night and make a necessary cup of Russian coffee. As we leave the little flat I stand on the balcony and listen to the terrible screaming of the pig slaughter. The lake is still. There is no breeze. The last morning.

★ ★ ★

In the early morning darkness, on the way out of town, we cross the wide Red River. We pass the market gardeners cycling in towards the city with fresh produce - herbs and vegetables and fruits and grain – ready for the day's trading. They will still be working late into the night.

★ ★ ★

We sit in rows in the dim gloom of the run-down Noi Bai Airport. It is just before dawn. We each hold a boarding pass in one of three colours printed on the usual recycled paper with the ink not quite fast. After an hour or so an airport worker calls out '*mau vang, mau vang*' and holds up a yellow card. Mine is blue. When the time comes I board the second plane to Ho Chi Minh City.

Nguyen Ngoc Thuan

The Watchman

The store had been empty since the last monsoon, but because the boy's contract didn't expire until the end of the year, he kept his job as a watchman. Half a dozen times each day he did his rounds, and every night he stayed awake and alert. No one told him that only mosquitoes patronised the store during the day, and rats were the only customers at night. The building was nothing more than an empty husk. But his boss made the boy believe it still contained treasures that needed to be guarded.

So each day he made his appointed rounds, and each night he drank more and more coffee to stay awake. He even got a dog. The boy had a real talent for the job. He could hear every faint sound and analyse it. For him, each sound had two potential meanings – a mosquito's buzz might be just that, or it might be a thief's signal. Thieves always knew how to imitate seemingly innocent sounds – a falling leaf, a window's creak, a mouse's squeak.

The store used to be quite prosperous, dealing as it did in smuggled goods. However, after the goods were shipped off, and confiscated along the way during the last monsoon season, the establishment was abandoned, even though the owner was still hopeful of restoring it to its former condition. It was because of this hope that the young watchman had to remain vigilant.

'A good watchman is like a treasure-god who permanently stands guard over one's house,' the owner would say.

I began to play Chinese chess with the boy whenever I stopped over there to catch a nap in my truck. I usually took such breaks from three to four in the morning, when one's only companion is darkness. There was one more reason, though: the boy was very skilful at chess. He was both sharper and more honest than most others. As for me, sometimes one needs to relax with trivial pursuits, and the game was a way to kill time. A good game of chess would usually get me to the morning, when the porters would load up my truck. Once my boss told me that the store had been vacant for years and the presence of the boy was just to let people believe it was full of goods. In another words, it was only a boss's tactic.

However, the boy had faith in humanity. I had told him several times that he should just open the store and check out what was inside, so he would not have to make his rounds any more. But he wouldn't listen. He was stubborn as a donkey in sticking to his timetable - two times patrolling around the store at 8 pm and then watching the premises from 10 pm to dawn.

Our chess games had to be deferred whenever he did his patrol. Since it was cold at night, I became accustomed to making his rounds with him, just so I could keep warm. It also gave me someone to talk with. Any sleepless night gives you the ability to perceive time – it crawls as slow and long as a snake which drags itself over your heavy eyelids. In that kind of darkness, sometimes the eyes become paralysed, from waiting to see something, from the slowness of the snake.

But I sometimes thought that the boy and I were just caught up in a hopeless game. What were we doing? Were we guarding the empty frame of a building or the rats inside or the ghosts of the goods in the store? No, we were not guarding anything. We were just meaningless motes flitting in and out on the margin of contradictory laws. To be a driver like me was to waste my life on the roads. To be a watchman like him was to waste himself on meaningless rounds, to waste his energy and youth for a building which housed only rats and mosquitoes.

On the road, I would drive at 100 kilometres an hour and at times needed to take a break and play a game of chess. Other times, while I was driving, I'd puzzle out chess positions in my mind. It was a bad omen that during my games with the boy, we had one chess piece, the *xe* (chariot), which had the ghostly quality of always getting lost. Whenever I found it, it would disappear again, every three or four days. We replaced it with a beer bottle cap on which a tiger head was imprinted. We played so often that soon the tiger faded and then disappeared. But in our minds, that tiger was still on the beer cap, charging and retreating every night, taking the place of the *xe*.

Then one night a new player joined us. He was very cunning, attacking us from all angles. The *phao* (cannon) became a devil in his fingers. Energetic, dreadful and sly. We often fell in his traps, which were so complicated that later I wondered that we hadn't gotten any insight from them into that player's real nature. A chess game can reveal the human being who plays it. Whimsy, foolishness, slyness, honesty or treachery can be read from a man's play as if one was reading a secret diary whose pages exposed his true heart. But the boy and I were blind to his nature. The three of us drank tea together every night, like three good friends, while the boy and I wracked our brains trying to figure out the magic that seemed contained in the *phao* chess piece, when it was in our opponent's hands. What we didn't realise was that we had sheltered a damned common thief. We were so entranced by the power with which he wielded his *phao* that we forgot we had a store full of treasure behind us.

As it was with the man, so it was with the boy's dog. He was also taken in. He no longer barked as he did the first time he'd seen the man. Instead he would greet him exuberantly, his tail wagging. Soon, he became accustomed to our little group of peaceful and innocent chess players. As for us, we gaped in admiration at our opponent's trickery and his fierce chess strategies.

During our games, we had inadvertently revealed both the timetable of the boy's rounds and my driving schedule. We'd also had let our opponent know about the door on the other side of the store: the most vulnerable place in the building. We had given him knowledge that he could use like a knife to stab us. To top it all, we let him know how the store was left unwatched for twenty minutes at three in the morning. Only the dog was left on watch at that time, alone – and the dog had become so friendly to him that it only took a bone to keep him quiet. So what other obstacles were there for the man?

That thief came at midnight to play chess with us. I drank a bottle of beer and was about to start on a second bottle. I was stunned as usual at his brilliant use of the *phao*. It is hard to imagine now that while he was playing so brilliantly, he was preparing to break into the building. But what he did not realise was that no matter how talented a human being can be, talent cannot divert destiny. With talent can also come the kind of luck which cannot be predicted or perceived but remains hidden somewhere until it erases most clever and cunning calculations and exposes one's error.

So, at 2.30 am, after our General had died a shameful death on the chess board, the thief left. But at 3 am, he made a careless noise which revealed himself. He was so confused that he underestimated what might happen; in other words, he was confused about his own fate. What we had forgotten to tell him, was that above the door there was a large log that would fall on the head of anyone who opened the door. A bucket of paint was also placed there so that it would drop when the door opened, and the would-be thief would be painted in the darkest and most garish colours. Besides those safeguards, a ring of small bells would be dropped over the head of any thief. This garland of bells would chime when he ran away, until he managed to take it off much later, unless he was deaf, in which case the bells would continue to ring even in his house.

But as I said earlier, nothing happens without an exception. Hearing the heavy log fall, the boy and I sprang up. But the garland of bells did not fall on target. The stupid dog was satisfied with the big bone he was given, and wagged his tail at the enemy. The thief rushed further into the store. He probably did not think that we could chase him so fast and figured he might be safer inside. He was battered, left dazed by the falling log, blinded from the falling paint. His fate smirked and led him into the store that was his last refuge; it gave him no choice.

It was pitch-black. Nothing could have been darker. We crept in after him. The chess piece I clutched in my hand seemed to thicken and vibrate, as if it was struggling to make its last move. I suddenly discovered that there was nothing worse than having a chess piece in your hand when you had to cope with a thief. I saw that the piece was my *phao* – my bad-luck cannon.

Suddenly the boy rushed in ahead of me.

'I can see you,' he shouted. But he was lying. As if he could see in that darkness! If we could do everything over again, I would have taught him that the most important aspect of a human being is the ability to know fear. And one should teach oneself to respect the fear for one's own life. But it was too late. There was a metallic flash and a blast of noise, the sound of gasping, and then of a body falling. The frightened rats ran off in all directions. Too long sheltered in this store, the rats had never been so terrified. They had bred peacefully until the thief appeared and raised his knife to murder their tranquillity.

Cornered and desperate, the thief stabbed out, trying to discourage the boy and make him run away. But destiny did not allow him to succeed. The two fought fiercely – until that knife ended his own life. From the beginning, he had been an ingrate. But later, after the passage of time, I gradually discovered an even greater meaninglessness in these events. The store was only full of mosquitoes and the boy had done a foolish thing – he had protected the rats. It was tragic. A man robbed an empty store and a boy gave his life to protect its emptiness. It turned out that the store was swarming only with frightened rats. They ran haphazardly over the two bodies wriggling in the pool of blood. The knife had completed its brutal circle.

By the time someone lit a lamp to see what had happened, the boy had died. God knows if he found out the store was empty before his death. I don't know. No one ever knew. And I pray that he didn't know.

Today, in front of the store, a notice was hung announcing a vacancy for the position of watchman.

Translated by Ho Anh Thai and Wayne Karlin

Adam Aitken

Beyond Khe Sanh

My father's proudest political act was to help organise anti Vietnam War demonstrations in the early seventies. He was an advertising executive by day, and a covert activist by night. His telephone was tapped by ASIO, the secret intelligence service. He spent many nights drinking cheap wine and planning with all manner of left-wing Australians opposed to conscription, opposed to the Liberal government, and opposed to the United States alliance. I was still a young boy whose interests were football, playing violin, painting, and reading. My mother hated the series of parties she had to cater for in those heady days of wine and rage.

He never talked about his early days in Asia, in the fifties. In Bangkok he met my mother, a young Thai graduate, and they fell in love after watching *Bridge over the River Kwai*. My father was always guilty about something that he could not explain. A secret about my mother and himself.

Forty years ago in a steamy Venice of the tropics, when Diem took power in Saigon, the Communists under 'Uncle'

Ho Chi Minh created the Liberation Front, and superpowers focused on the 'backward' nations of South East Asia. After Korea, a huge military-industrial machine, oiled up and on high alert. Spy missions began over the skies of Hanoi and through Laos and Cambodia. In 1957 my father left Melbourne with pride and nervous anticipation. He took a twin turbo prop to Singapore and enlisted with Cathay Ltd, a small advertising agency. He never went to university, like many young men of the fifties. He had trained in the art of winning minds, and would become a major player in the biggest legal international drug trade ever: the tobacco industry. His talent for persuading and winning customers would come in handy in the Moratorium.

I can't help comparing my father to other Australian men who'd fought in Vietnam or Laos or had ended up in the Philippines and had won trophy wives who could not wait to leave the place. The comparison made me feel better because my brother and I had drivers, gardeners and two Hakka servants or *ahmas*. We were driven to school in company cars. We spoke languid, relaxed, tropicalised English. My mother's commands were softened by politeness formulae. 'Would you mind...?', 'Would it be possible...?' Meanwhile the servants struggled to find a satisfactory balance. The first languages I heard were a mix of Tamil, Hakka and Malay. For them it was all orders, commands. My mother was the real commander-in-chief at home. But the servants liked her because she came between 'Tuan' and themselves. She softened his Western demands, his impatience. They received orders and passed them on to the Master's children. There was no way out of the evening bath and the scrubbing brush. 'Eh lah, you-can-or-not? What you mean cannot-do. Easy.'

Dad was descended from a long line of fortune seekers going back to the East India company. His boss would have heard about his marrying a local, the way he had gone 'troppo', driven insane by heat.

★ ★ ★

I think of my father as the orphaned child of a settler heritage, someone who stopped speaking to his father and two brothers in the 1960s. Perhaps his Asian wife had been a cause of such a traumatic split, the catalyst which cleaved his destiny from theirs.

My grandfather, who died of lung failure in the arms of his second wife in New Zealand in the early 1970s, was already a deserter from family life. He'd returned from an Army desk job in New Guinea during the war and announced that he was divorcing my father's mother. He was going to New Zealand with a new girlfriend, a nurse he'd met 'over there'.

As an abandoned son, my father never came to terms with this rejection. My father mentions the shame it brought. Melbourne still had a Victorian notion of divorce. What upsets the settler narrative – I mean my part in it, and my parents' part – is that the link between us and the original Aitken was lost – Thomas Aitken, son of a Scottish baker, arrived in Melbourne before the Gold Rush in the 1840s. He became a successful brewer of beer who married twice. His first wife Mary died giving birth to twins, who died a year later, within a day of each other. Six months later, when he was forty, he married Terza, the eighteen-year-old daughter of an East country artisan, and together they had eight children. Thomas built the Victoria Brewery (today's VB) and accumulated so much wealth that when he died, his will was over seventy pages.

There's some sort of glorious past my father thinks his father cheated him of. It could have been a matter of money. Yes, my father wanted compensation from the 'old bastard'.

And when Dad married an Asian woman, well, that was 'beyond the pale' in more ways than one.

So who am I? my father asked of himself when his company sent him to Hong Kong. He proceeded to go places, and partied hard around Singapore and then Bangkok. I am no settler, I'm no split consciousness of Australia, he thought to himself.

Look, I am not saying that my Dad's great uncles massacred Aborigines when they were in the Victorian Light Horse Brigade, but the way my Dad goes on about his horrible childhood, it just might be true that there are skeletons in that particular cupboard. My father loved to go up country to visit the great aunts – spinsters Beatrice and Mavis. They adored him and nursed him through the terrible asthma attacks he always got when he was near horses. I like to think that it was the horses taking revenge for being ridden around and whipped. Dad's least favourite aunt Peg was trampled to death in a stampede, a fact he relishes. The aunts kept Victorian daybooks, sketched West Country ruins copied from British post cards and painted flora and fauna. They knew about art and opera (they *loved* Dame Nelly Melba), and could explain the difference between Hayden and Beethoven.

Dad loved his childhood, in fact, when everything was what Melbourne expected it to be. He didn't have to wonder at its value then, he didn't have a clue about how much he was made by that city. But not made for it.

Did Melbourne give Dad a sense of what he aspired to? I hate to admit it, but Dad was in the same year at high school as Jeff Kennett. Dad was forced to be a Young Liberal by his father! I know, I saw the lapel pins. His father would take him to watch Bradman from the Members Pavilion at the MCG. Dad had a cricket bat signed by the great man himself, but it was lost or stolen after he'd gone to Hong

Kong. Playing golf at the Royal Melbourne? Driving a Bentley to the Melbourne Cup? Graduating from Melbourne University and joining a firm of accountants (that's what Granddad wanted).

(Dear Dr F. I am still having recurring dreams in which I am forced to play golf with right-handed clubs. I seem to be getting more accurate, however.)

I like to think my mother changed him, but to what extent? One thing she couldn't restore to my father was his lost past. She could not even begin to imagine what it was like, even if he had wished to discuss it. Dad had killed it off for good, or so he thought.

*   *   *

First contact

I am unable to stop these fantasies of how my parents met and fell in love. I want to believe that my father is really not a businessman at all, not colonial in any way, not sanctimonious and patronising about Asian women. But the truth is that he is a man of the Australia of the 1950s. Women exist to fulfil man's dreams of a good wife, mother, sexual servant. I want to imagine that the first encounter my parents had was romantic. My story goes backwards from those terrible times of conflict, separation and divorce, towards the redemptive possibilities of two young people in love. Fiction gives me some possible models:

Plot A) An Australian businessman wanders into a Saigon bar with a camera. Just starts snapping away. Getting the 'Real Orient'. A young starving Asian girl just walks into frame. They 'strike up a conversation'.

Plot B) The narrator is a jaded middle-aged male foreign correspondent who works for *Reuters*. He's married to a Catholic back in Australia, but hasn't seen her for two years. He enters a dance club in Saigon. On first spying the beautiful and vulnerable 'taxi dancer' with the catlike eyes, the journalist notes down in his diary: The way she does her hair, *'allowing it to fall back and straight over her shoulders'*. The correspondent is beginning to put on weight, his eyes are bloodshot, and worst of all, he is *ungraceful in love*. What saves him is his muse and the nostalgia and the erotic frisson that colour his memories of that first meeting:

> *...and I saw Phuong for a moment as I had seen her first, dancing past my table at the Grand Monde in a white ball-dress, eighteen years old, watched by an elder sister who had been determined on a good European marriage.*

The war and its cruelty, its bombings and its intrigues can be put aside merely by closing one's eyes and dreaming of her.

> *I shut my eyes and she was again the same as she used to be; she was the hiss of steam, the clink of a cup, she was a certain hour of the night and the promise of rest.*

The correspondent is tormented with the guilt that he has no commitments, no ethics, he takes no sides. All sides are abhorrent. But then he does. He takes sides. She is lovely enough and the promise of rest he craves. She is lovely enough to kill his rival for.

> *Sometimes she seemed invisible like peace.*
>
> ...
>
> *'Another pipe?' Phuong asked.*
> *'Yes.'*

I took off my tie and shoes; the interlude was over; the night was nearly the same as it had been. Phuong crouched at the end of the bed and lit the lamp. Mon enfant, ma soeur – skin the colour of amber. 'Sa douce langue natale.'

And then the journalist tells her that his competition, a handsome American Peace Corps volunteer and undercover CIA operative, Phuong's other lover, is dead. *'Assasiné.'* Poor Phuong! What shall she do? She can't be in love with a man who's dead!. *Phuong the fortune hunter, the taxi dancer, the courtesan. She settles for the journalist. He becomes a success reporting on the Vietnam War.* She keeps on filling his opium pipe. She grows old, gets fat, learns to have opinions, grieves.

'Another pipe?' Phuong asked.
'Yes.'

★ ★ ★

Plot C) Or is it this way? On a Sunday, at the Silom Road pier my father catches a ferry on the Chao Phraya River. He needs to get to the Chulalongkorn University to give a student an English lesson. My mother embarks also, as she regularly takes this ferry to get to her part-time job in the French Department. After observing her across the crowded ferry for the entire journey, the young Australian disembarks and walks straight into this poor young girl, who wears other people's oversize shoes, and just happens to be carrying a 'BOAC Airline Bag'. He courageously opens with the line, 'You know, I do their advertising account.' Luckily, the girl speaks English and is not at all shy. Perhaps the line impresses her. They strike up a conversation about the bag. My mother says 'It seems overly large for a girl like me.' No, these are not the exact words, but is slightly coquettish, this reference to her own body, her fine dimensions. My father is suspended in hope. *That* is the important word, *hope*.

'Would you care to join me in a glass of sugar cane juice?' he asks, in the formal way of Western gentlemen of the 1950s. It's a stupid second liner, but it suits the 1950s.

The young graduate feels like she has been 'discovered', that she had been waiting, as if in a fairy story, for the arrival of this man. He is the returned spirit of her dead father. He comes to provide the future, family, kids, wealth, sex. What more does a poor Asian girl need? She notices how the Australian has monogrammed luggage, 'PA' in Germanic Capitals on his briefcase. His shirts are tailored in Hong Kong. They get married, have some beautiful Eurasian boys. Years later, in the swinging sixties, she takes to wearing them with the collars cut off when she is repainting the living room in London.

* * *

A Letter to Phuong

My gentle Phuong,

I have been reading American novels about Vietnam. I think of you when I read Western male descriptions of their goddesses. *'Her Western presence was strong, and had a quality that was formidable rather than seductive. He saw this as non-Western; baffling.'*[1] Is that you, my gentle Phuong? Perhaps you too have a 'heart-shaped face' and your hair is extraordinarily black, long and straight and resembles a river or possibly a net for catching fish or men, or boys…Perhaps you 'shine with intelligence' and you are 'fragile like a bird' and you make grown men break down and weep, or perhaps you have a leg withered by malnutrition and you inspire the most romantic of soldier journalists to send you to a hospital in a European country and have it straightened out. You are a whole country that can't speak for itself and must be pitied and saved. Or you are more ambiguous and work as a double agent for both the enemy and friends and you look sexy in camouflage and a couple of captain's stripes and the journalists' bar goes wild with envy when they see me walking out with you.

And when I make love to you I 'forget everything, I forget death and pain' but as we lie together under the mosquito net listening to the distant gunfire across the river, know you will never belong to me. You explore my every muscle and infiltrate my heart. I lose all sense of reality, of course. I live in a swoon, a delirium of alcohol and opium and know that I will never leave your country. 'She touched the wound there, and the other, behind my ear; then her finger traced the mark left on my forehead by the butt of that VC's Kalashnikov, in the Delta.'[2]

Then we talk about having kids, of me being a father, if I don't get myself blown up by a landmine in the meantime. And you have children, Phuong, you might lose me and then the kids will be orphans. Eurasians condemned to a lifetime of looking for white father figures they can trust. Someone who won't get blown up or suffer from nightmares or hear helicopters hovering over their heads every time they go out to buy the milk.

'*Shall I fix you a pipe?*' you ask. You are the Phoenix in *The Quiet American*, French–Vietnamese mistress to 'Fowlair', the *London Times* correspondent. Phuong, did it ever occur to you that Graham Greene invented you so that his warrior men could die or disappear, but be changed by love. Love transforms them from brute killer to pussycat for about one night a month. Women don't rescue them or change them. Nobody possesses anybody's soul. Love gets lost in the din of bombardment, the rumble of collapsing rubble.

Another voyage, this time south to the driest city on earth

When my father left Australia, a few years after the stalemate in Korea, there was the volatile mix of paranoia about the Reds, and the ambivalent, perhaps unconscious desire for the Asian adventure, the *voyage en orient*. My father returns ten years later and everything is about to change. He attempts and succeeds in smuggling into the White citadel his 'banned goods', an Asian woman from somewhere vaguely near a war zone. But I like to think that he did a deal with the Customs Officer, who winked, and out of the corner of his mouth said, 'Ahh, she'll be right. She's white enough. Go through.' The war was just entering TV sets, invading living rooms, as someone said. One night, my mother fixed my father a drink and he found there were less romantic ways to lose one's soul or dissolve one's brain in unhappiness. Together they watched a young Vietnamese girl with no clothes and severely burnt by napalm, running down a road, into their living room.

I wrote this in Bangkok. It is 1982. April. The hot dry season, 36 degrees indoors and not even midday. I keep telling myself that writing can transcend weather, even a story of a love affair that never really was. I am beginning to believe the old race theory that tropical weather makes Asians lazy and lethargic, ergo: Western inventions like air conditioning.

I wrote a poem:

Colonialism

The slavegirl
folds away her fan

and turns on
the air conditioner

How did my father cope leaving Melbourne for Hong Kong, then Singapore, then Bangkok? Miranda, here's the updated synopsis: my father ran away from Menzie's Australia and in an act of restitution for his exile devoted twenty-four hours a day to establishing the British and American Tobacco business in South East Asia. He fell hopelessly in love with my mother Malee, Buddhist/Socialist intellectual and family misfit, a Bachelor of Arts graduate from Klong Toey port area of Bangkok, the City of Fallen Angels. She fell foul of the police after they raided her flat and found illegal copies of what they though were communist propaganda. In fact they were only French novels. My father was growing less and less keen on taking boring expats to clubs, and was failing to pay his bribes on time. They decided to marry, went to England, and got married when my mother was three months pregnant. My brother and I were born. We returned to the new Federation of Malaysia. We returned to Perth and Sydney. I returned to Bangkok to recover my 'Asian past' and write a book.

★   ★   ★

A retour

I came to Bangkok to write my first book of poetry. I came here after a break of twenty-two years. In 1964 I went to kindergarten with the sons and daughters of the Bangkok expatriate community. At first my aunts spoke to me in Thai: 'More to eat? Go for your bath now. What are you doing today?' My mother told her sisters, 'He doesn't need to learn Thai. He's English. He'll only get confused.' She and my father came here from London, and we were on route to Australia, where my father was born. After eight years away, working in Singapore, Hong Kong, Bangkok and London, he felt the urge to reconnect with the Lucky country.

I had a vague idea that a war was taking place two countries east of Bangkok. Perhaps it was the news images I saw on TV. Perhaps it was the bullying American kids who liked playing war games in the breaks. Perhaps it was my mother's anxieties. Perhaps it was the armed guards standing around Don Muang Airport, or the tall Westerners in khaki fatigues I saw riding in three-wheeler taxis.

I live in my uncle's library and sleep on a thin mattress. Having been a journalist and a translator of airport novels, his library contains Proust's *Swann's Way* (which he translated into Thai), the odd *Playboy* magazine, old Thai communist propaganda, Buddhist tracts. After another skim through for pictures, photographs, I find a dusty album in dark blue cloth binding. I open it. I see this house as it was twenty years ago, newly built, and my uncle and his wife standing before it like a young couple in an Asian version of *Time Life*. The only difference is they aren't holding a baby and there are no white paling fences, and instead of roses banana trees sprout in the distance.

I discover a copy of *The Quiet American*. Thanit thinks I am wasting my time writing poetry. No money in it. Thanit is investing in a massive historical theme park. It will show Thailand's history from before the time of Buddha to Now. Old houses from all over the country will be shipped in piece by piece and reassembled. Now that Thailand is basically a modern country, its time to recover its archaic charm. All he needs now is time to repay his debts and stop working so hard for the Sang Som liquor company. I imagine myself a privileged product of the sixties, a man with liberal-minded parents who transcends racism and bigotry. I was born on the right side of the bamboo curtain.

But back to the fifties and Graham Greene. What kind of male finds sexy that Greene mix of bargirls, whiskey, jaded journos and CIA agents? Compare my mother with Phuong, for instance, that herbaceous indigene, that bird of Fowler's imagination. Objects of Western desire for transcendent femininity, an innocence before the Fall. War goes on, Phuong prepares opium pipes for her lover and feeds the CIA agent's dog. Fowler cynically perceives her lack as an inability to love foreign men. Maybe she is spying for the other side. Fowler prepares himself for betrayal, and deep in his heart the old fear at the core of its paternalism that the West is humiliated, defeated, guilt-ridden, morally bankrupt, with no meaning, no reason, no religion. The West is a pimp chasing Asian tarts. At night Fowler's hand rests between her legs. She is all surface, soft and without hair.

Then things get serious. After two years of vaguely intimate fraternisations, the 'real thing' begins. Such a romance should begin with the only question that matters:

'Why did you **come** to Asia, mon cher?'

The question must be asked in the dimness of a neo-colonial mansion somewhere in the city's diplomatic heart. The evening is *lit from within in a golden glow.* There is a piano, sandalwood, soft fabrics swaying in a light breeze.

> *At first he thought she was unaware of him,*
> *but then she turned,*
> *and smiled over her shoulder —*
> *as though they had already met,*
> *and shared some intimate joke...*[3]

The warrior falls in love with the girl's hair, her silk blouse, a black slit skirt. He falls in love with the leisurely way she returns to her piano, after that one fatal smile.

That's how the novelists do it, even though they admit when they have staged it. One must be able to write a sentence awash with sensuousness:

She wore the strangest jewelry, and this had something to do with her ability to speak French with a Vietnamese accent.

Her eyes are hybrid, *Vietnamese almonds coloured French blue green. 'Do you like Chopin, Mr Langford?'* Stunning.

But my father was no Fowler, certainly and my mother was not Phuong. Nor was my father the dangerously well-intentioned American undercover CIA agent Pyle. He does share something with Christopher Koch's model for the war photographer/journalist, Mike Langford in *Highways to a War*. Dad loved photography and took a great pleasure in supervising television advertisements and magazine shoots. He wanted to be a glamorous photographer himself. They are both image hunters.

If my father hated war, Langford seems to have no existence beyond the front line. Langford grew up on a farm in Tasmania. My father was a businessman, a suit, a young Australian who didn't make it into Melbourne University, a young man whose father Clive wanted him to be an accountant. *To make money* (which he did for a while). His generation was born in the Depression and grew up without fathers, or with traumatised returned servicemen for fathers. My father grew into the Cold War, and managed to have enough money to buy a car. It was the start of the Coca-Cola swilling era, the decade of the mass-produced small transistor, John Glenn, monkeys in space, Kennedy's assassination, Sputnik, and the Playtex-Cross-and-Separate bra. My mother was an optimist and a modernist. She needed a Western man to reach her potential. She thought the West was marvellous and spelt freedom. That's shared background. Of a sort. The twinning of their destinies seemed logical, their desire determined by large forces.

My father's sense of himself as a man in Asia begins with the fall of Singapore and its retaking. The Empire gets a second chance. It finishes with Ravi Shankar playing sitar for a tripped out pop band called The Beatles. No, it finishes with the assassination of Lennon, and for my father, it finishes with the sacking of Whitlam and the end of the Labor Renaissance in swinging Sydney, 1975.

A lack of love in the world? When I was five my mother's teenage sister Vasanee played her favourite forty-five over and over on her new Japanese transistor – it was called 'Yesterday' but Vasanee was a cool modern Thai chick. She too made it to a university in the States. Now she's Thanit's patient wife, and I am the son she could never have.

What about rock and roll Thai style/Aussie style? David Bowie marries a Chinese model and sings about that. In the video clip the ageing pop star and Amazon environmentalist has his 'China Girl' rolling about in the surf, splaying her limbs like a beached starfish. It's no accident that Bowie looks like a left over from the British Raj, in khaki trousers. I have my mother running a Thai Restaurant in a small mountain town, a resort called Katoomba. The restaurant is next to the classic antique '20s clothing boutique.

After years of convincing myself that telling this story was not my game, I decide that it's about time. I'll get down to the bottom of it – what the Cold War and the Real War meant for two young lovers from East and West, what my mother and father saw in each other, what really made me who I am. If my mother really had, as she said, left her country of birth because she loved my father, would she have left with any other man? Was my father the special one? After all I was born in the sixties: I deserve to be the child of love! They seemed so confident of each other's company that they could leave their respective families and not see them for over a decade, apart from the odd visit on the way to somewhere else?

My concept of origins and return is a little mixed up: the London where I was born. I reconstructed it from the lyrics of my father's Beatles albums: *Rubber Soul*, *Revolver* and the *Magical Mystery Tour*. This was the first Return, to Australia, a country where neither of them ever seemed completely happy: as if their ideals of the future had become emaciated, sitting in front of the six o'clock news watching nightly bulletins on the Vietnam War. I hardly remember them laughing together. There were no amusing fillers those days at the end of a horrific half hour. My mother never saw the need for a colour TV until recently. The fact is the Vietnam War looked bad enough in black and white. Suffering of that scale doesn't need colour.

The fact is I don't look anything like my father. Unlike my brother, we seem utterly beyond a blood relation. Though I am used to people speculating on the genesis of my face: Spanish, Italian, Indonesian, Peruvian. Such pressure to explain *the face*, origins no one can guess first time. I like that. This seems to be the central preoccupation of a whole city at the moment. Sydney, the bride of the Pacific, no purer in heart and feeling than any semi-tropical entrepot, busy constructing its face, buying up stuff to build on to it – like makeup – with a taste for the manufactured goods of its neighbours: the old ports of South Asia, Singapore, Jakarta, Hong Kong. But Bangkok, not ever colonial, not quite.

Although we share one language, I speak to my father and brother through hints and clues to how we're are feeling.

We leave messages, we don't communicate. It's the Ancestry of Silence that came down to me via my father and to my father via his father, whom he has not seen or heard of since 1959. The Silence keeps on building its web. My father hasn't spoken to his father for twenty odd years. Clive never did 're-adjust' to Melbourne, a wife, three kids, a bungalow in the suburbs, after his return from World War II New Guinea. He was a head case so he escaped to New Zealand. I wonder what he thought of Vietnam when he watched the news – the same news we watched. Unable to press my father directly for information. I get the usual: 'I'll tell you one day,' or 'I hardly understand *myself*.' I try my mother. She replies, 'One day, you'll hear it all.' The silence embeds itself in every line of poetry I write – and in every line I cannot write. War means silence, secrets, paralinguistic gestures – groans, sighs, tears, pain. No words.

So often the silence dominates the day. Fowler confesses to no character in particular, just the silent *reader*. Fowler is trying not to get himself blown up, trying not to promise his pretty concubine marriage, security, predictability; his confession is a quilt of fictions.

Phuong, you are an Oriental body, an opium pipe, you are peace, and silence. You are the antidote to guilt.

Leaving again: Rayong, on the border with Kampuchea

At the sudden descent of dusk, you walk through the coconut grove and into the forest spreading up into the hills surrounding the bay. First you follow a power line that runs along a track, then wavers into and through the forest. You follow the line to a radar installation nestled on a spur that overlooks another stretch of beach, and the bay embraced at each end by high rocky headlands. You move along the track until you enter a small clearing and are confronted by a teenage navy recruit in a sandbagged checkpoint, caressing a large machine gun. He doesn't smile. Thanit whips out a packet of Marlboros. The twitchy teenager takes one but tension remains. No legendary Thai bonhomie here. You walk on. 'I told him you were my son, that we weren't tourists, we don't have cameras. You are the tourist, ambiguously foreign, and to the military mind, a potential terrorist. On the other hand you are allied to a cheerful "native".' Thanit is the citizen entitled to the protection of the military. You must respect each other, so that the military don't arrest you as spies, or worse though the signs are not clear at all, of you and the military. Are you a citizen? A half-citizen perhaps? Uncle is pleased with his diplomatic skill, his charm. He laughs at everything, even laughs into the barrel of a gun. He wears a bright shirt with Hawaiian-style tropical motifs. He'd make a good target, you think. You have watched too many war films set in the Pacific.

Dusk falls all too suddenly, and you walk back along the power line route, through the coconut grove and back out of the forest that spreads into the hills surrounding the bay. It is almost too dark to see the track. You exit the forest and round a spur. There is the hulk of a Vietnamese fishing boat, its black timbers half buried in beach sand. Even the sand here is a volcanic black. There are patches of congealed oil around the site of the abandoned boat. All that's left are the bulkheads and a rusty diesel engine. A broken umbrella juts out of the sand; its rusty spars remain above the high tide mark. The boat was an unwelcome visitor. It had no doubt been commandeered and pirated. The passengers taken away to be raped or dismembered like the planks of this boat, burnt perhaps, stripped of precious metals, cursed. Even the nails have been removed.

I am sorry Phuong, if this had been your boat. I am sorry for what my countrymen did to you.

Whatever moves and dies finds its place, transformed into what its Karma deems is right. Oh for a cheerful cremation, assets distributed to deserving relatives and loved ones. Phuong, I hope you had left a 'next of kin', another life. Now the exiles are leaving the forest, and coming back to your wretched beach. Now every beach is haunted, no longer welcoming. The sun exits the sky and is tinged with iridescence, sunset clouds in the tropics. As the time of rest approaches so does the fearfulness of the night in a country that you haven't yet learned to love or call your own. But the tireless navy sees everything, like some fearless God. From a tower high on its mountain radar sweeps through the dark as it watches out for its citizens and its enemies. Somehow, it will find you, the most native of natives, who knows there's nowhere left to yearn for.

1   Christopher Koch, *Highways to a War*, Penguin, 1995, p. 129.

2   ibid., p. 186.

3   ibid., pp. 124–5.

Vo Chuong Dai

The Remains of the Dead

what remains
        always and away
between the cracks
        rhythms of life
between the bricks
        buildings close by close
the remains of you
        and me and we
            always and away
what remains
        in the broken pebbles
in the layers of pavement
        dust flying dry
between the fibres of your clothes
        the letters frail with pale

you and me and we
                    in the air on our skin
in the air we breathe
what remains
                    in the photographs
taken in the spring
                    stained with bomb shells and nerves
reconnaissance and flight
                    broken bodies and strained tears
                              you   you   you
what remains
          what remains

                                                            away
                                                            always

After the War

After the war
After they took over the city
After they sent your husband
to jail for fighting
After you lost
your home
and furniture shop
After you had to sell pickles
and coffee
for a living
After your children
said Uncle Hô died for you
After your husband returned
with a head of leftover hair
and your daughter didn't recognise him

After you sold the earrings
your husband gave you
on your wedding day
After you bought
passage for him
to escape
on a fishing boat
After you
your parents
your children
escaped
on a fishing boat

Did you look back?

Andrew Lam

Saigon in Our Prayers

He touched the woman lightly on her arm, barely a tap and she turned, startled. She had been looking down at the ocean below, and failed to hear the stewardess' solicitation. In business class drinks were flowing, and hers was near empty.

'Ah, yes! Please, a little more Chablis.'

When he had boarded at Narita airport and sat down next to her, she simply nodded then continued to leaf through an old issue of *National Geographic*. Between them a laconic concord, and it might have lasted the duration, all the way to Saigon had he not touched her. Since the tap, however, their truce had been altered.

'I assume you're from Vietnam,' he said.

'Yes,' she replied with a sociable smile, 'originally.' Her accent not quite American, not quite French, but he recognised it. She offered nothing more. He wasn't about to let the conversation die, however, the closer they got to Saigon. Besides, it would be a minor defeat for his profession as corporate dealmaker. '*Co la nguoi Viet Kieu?*' he said, a gambit that had never failed – You're a Vietnamese expat?

She was reaching for the *National Geographic* once more but turned, eyes wide. 'Wow, you speak Vietnamese!' Then with the proper enunciation, she said: '*Viet Kieu,*' and chuckled as if she hadn't thought about it herself. 'A *Viet Kieu.*'

'Your first time back?' He asked.

'First time?' she said hesitantly. 'Yes, it is. My oldest son invited me. He's already in Saigon working on an investment project.' She leaned forward and, with long, elegant fingers, straightened the back of her silk blouse. Her shoulder-length hair was streaked with grey. Her perfume, the smell of intricate oils, water lilies and lady apple, sent his childhood memories surging – summer afternoons in the garden, a misty spray from a garden hose, the cheerful melody from an ice cream truck, and the long, forgotten sounds of his father's laughter.

Here was someone he imagined Thuy-Linh would eventually grow into. The grey hair came but the beauty stayed, or rather, it was taking its own time to fade. He could easily see his seating companion as a young woman riding her bicycle along tree-lined boulevards in her white *ao dai* dress on the way to school. With her elegant features – almond shaped eyes and dimples – she must have caused the heat to rise in the classroom.

'And you?' she asked. 'Where are you from? Your Vietnamese is good, by the way. Even got a Hanoi accent.'

'Boston. Born and bred, but not the stuck up, blueblood kind,' he said.

'Boston?' she said. 'My second son is at Harvard right now. Political science major. He's thinking of going into law.'

'Harvard man. I'm impressed. Only made it to Yale myself.'

'Oh,' her voice became more animated. 'Tommy, the one inviting me, he goes there! I mean, went there. He works now with Merrill Lynch. You're alumni! I'll introduce you when we land.'

'Okay,' he said. He felt as if she were looking at him with new eyes, and certain warmth. He didn't go to Yale, and he didn't know why he told her that. 'I can't believe you're old enough to have children in college, let alone at Merrill Lynch.'

She gave a little laugh. 'Believe it, young man. I'm old. Like the sea.'

'Hardly,' he said. 'You must be very proud. I mean, with such smart children.'

She looked down at her wine glass. She hadn't touched it since the second pouring, but she was drinking now. 'I'm sorry,' she said. 'I didn't mean to boast. What about you? What do you do? How'd someone from Boston learn Vietnamese?'

He looked at his gold Rolex. They were a good two hours or so from destination. 'Oh, it's too long a story,' he said.

'Oh, I don't mind, I love a good story,' she said encouragingly, and arranged herself so that she could better face him, a pillow at her back. 'You tell. I'll listen.'

'Okay,' he said, matching her enthusiasm. 'I'm not sure how good, but it's a sad one. And remember, don't say I didn't warn you.' Then he raised his near empty flute above his head and shook it lightly at the smiling stewardess.

'Years ago, I fell in love with a Vietnamese woman in Hanoi,' he began at length, and with that, memories of Hanoi's moss-covered villas and noisy motorbikes and old men with unfiltered cigarettes dangling from their mouths came flooding back. He saw Thuy-Linh's face again, and almost stopped talking. That misty morning, his first day as an English teacher, he watched in fascination as she rubbed her hands together – was it at that moment, when she raised her hands to her mouth and breathed warmed air between cupped fingers, that she stole his heart? 'I hadn't fallen in love with anyone in high school, nor in college, for that matter. Crushes, sure, and a few fell in love with me. But in Hanoi – well, how do the Vietnamese say it? In Hanoi, love wrestled and pinned me to the ground.'

'*Bi ai tinh vat,*' the woman confirmed with a quiet nod, but he barely heard her.

'I always wanted to visit the place that haunted my father. You know, he was a paratrooper in the late '60s. I was born after he came back and my entire life, I probably heard him talk about it twice, each time, he was drunk and incoherent. So after the country opened up, I went in, backpacking. My father experienced horror in Nam, but well, I guess I found romance instead.'

'She must have been very beautiful,' said the woman.

'Oh yeah, probably still is,' he said. 'All the boys and, I think, some of the teachers, too, had crushes on her. But I courted her, and she picked me. She was so different than all the girls I knew. There was, I don't know, a certain inner peace about her, a certain grace. Plus, she laughed at all my stupid jokes.'

The woman twirled the wine glass on her tray and laughed. 'Well, that's important.'

'For sure,' he smiled. 'There was also this quality to her voice, and it warmed me each time. But she was totally loyal to her conservative family as much as in love with me. Which caused her – caused *us* – a lot of problems.' For he was speaking now of their short life together, how, on and off, they managed to live together for over a year in his small apartment by Hoan Kiem Lake, hiding the fact from the authorities, her parents, and the other teachers, since it was illegal then to live with a foreigner. 'She was really afraid of what her parents would do if they found out, and that was our fight. I complained bitterly of the restrictive Vietnamese ways. I'm afraid I said some mean things.'

He wanted to tell the woman more: how memories of their tender love making – the way their shadows dance on the wall and mosquito net at night, as reflected by a flickering oil lamp – often played out in his head. So vivid were these flashbacks that he equated them on the same par as post-traumatic stress. Instead, he told her about the 'I love you' problem – how Thuy-Linh aggravated him by failing to reply, 'I love you' to him each time he said it to her. She often would just blush and turn away and say nothing. The last time he said this, she'd wept. Then she said it: 'I love you too, Mark, very much.' That was the only time she ever said it but the way she said it broke his heart. 'What's wrong?' he asked, but she hid her face in his chest and sobbed. He came home the next day to find all Thuy-Linh's belongings gone.

'I should have said I wanted to marry her,' he said presently, coming out of his trance. 'But after what happened with my parents, I wasn't too keen on it. I was too young, I guess, too hesitant. Didn't give her clear options.'

The woman said nothing but he could tell she was listening intently, as if she was permitting him to tell more. 'So after a few months my visa ran out. I came home, got an MBA. Now, I'm based in Tokyo. I go to Vietnam often but I've more or less stopped looking. And now, I have a Japanese girlfriend.'

Michiko, funny, artistic, brazen and eccentric Michiko, who wore ridiculous hats, which she designed herself, on practically every religious holiday, and who could outdrink him and most of her friends – young and rowdy writers, artists and singers – who, in time, became his. In the apartment they share in the chic Chuo district, his face staring out from practically every wall, though his friends could hardly recognise him – as woodblock prints, or as abstract in shades of blue or rendered bewildered by pointillism – and, in none of them, was he shown smiling. Maybe Michiko always knew what he wouldn't admit to himself: that though he adored her, his heart didn't belong to her.

'Then last week,' he said, then paused to drink and calm himself. 'Last week, the phone rang. It was Thuy-Linh. She said 'Mark?' and just like that, my heart nearly stopped. It felt like nothing had changed. I tell you, I was glad that I was already sitting down. My heart was going nuts; I could barely talk. She had been married in Paris but got divorced not long after. She said very little about it and I didn't want to push. She's back now in Saigon with her child. We didn't want to talk long. Except she wants to see me again.'

'You're still very much in love with her,' his seating companion said, but it was not a question.

He looked at her. 'I never stopped,' he said sadly. True, he no longer searched for her, but he couldn't help being reminded of Thuy-Linh each time he went to Saigon or Hanoi on business trips – the nape of a slender neck in an open window, the pealing laughter of a young woman in a candle lit restaurant, the silhouette of a devout worshipper burning incense in the Buddhist temple's hall. 'I think Thuy-Linh still loves me, too. But I don't know what to do. Michiko…As open as we are to one another, I never told Michiko about the phone call. Or that Thuy-Linh was waiting for me with her little boy at the airport.'

The woman nodded but said nothing, and silence reasserted itself. He lifted his flute but his hand was shaking, and the golden liquid tossed and pitched. He put the flute back down and smiled apologetically while the woman studied him. 'Well,' she said finally, her tone upbeat. 'It's a good story. I see now why you speak Vietnamese so well. But I can tell you that it's not a sad story. It's an unfinished story. And you deserve cold champagne, I think so.' She made a sign to the stewardess who was walking down the aisle with a tray of drinks. 'I'm having some too.'

'Thuy-Linh's little boy's almost nine. His name is Laurent. She wouldn't tell me much but I couldn't help wondering if...' he said before stopping himself. 'No,' he said quickly, 'better not get ahead of myself.'

She handed him a tissue from her purse. 'Thank you,' he said. 'You've been very kind to listen. I feel better. *Cam on co.*'

'*Hong co chi,*' she smiled and briefly rested her hand on his wrist. 'It makes me feel better too. I'm glad to know that a happy ending is waiting at our destination.'

He wanted to believe her. But he didn't dare envision it, didn't dare hope. He didn't want to think about how the story would end and what it entailed. 'Okay,' he said and pretended to be relaxed and stretched his arms above his shoulders. 'Enough about me. Now, we're getting to *your* story.'

'My story?'

They were flying toward a region of towering cumuli, a huge forest of luminous forms, and lights streaked and streamed in from the windows to set faces ablaze. A few passengers shut their window. 'I bet you left on the first wave,' he said, squinting a little to read her face.

'First wave? Ah, I see. Plane and helicopter people, right? Before the tanks rolled into Saigon? No. No such luck. Boat person, I'm afraid. More like second wave, or may be even third. It would have been...' She took a sideways glance out the window, her hand shading over her eyes. 'Do you mind if I tell you later, when I'm ready?'

'Of course,' he said quickly. It came to him then why she'd been studying that sea so intensely. He knew of Vietnam's troubles, of course, its past horrors – refugees, boat people, re-education camps. But the country he went to on regular business trips was one with shiny high rises and cyber cafes and neon-lit billboards selling Toyota and Coca-Cola and Tiger beer. It didn't occur to him, considering her comportment, her excellent English, that she was someone who might have experienced the worst of the old era. 'You don't have to, I mean if you don't feel comfortable, we can talk...'

'Thank you,' she said and he could see that she was trembling slightly. 'But it's alright. It's only fair. I'll tell an abbreviated version.' The stewardess placed two small plates of mixed nuts on their trays and he was glad he had something to munch on so as to not look at her.

'We left by boat,' she said. 'After the war ended, my husband and I stayed thinking that young, apolitical academics wouldn't be affected under the new regime. Like you, I taught English. My father also taught it. He practiced it with Graham Greene, in fact, when Greene was living in Saigon and working on that famous novel. My husband taught math. But we lost our jobs. The communists confiscated our house. They sent a few of our friends to prison. We would be next. So we left by boat. Two boats actually, because there wasn't enough space on the first.' She drank a little bit more champagne and gathered herself. 'So my husband took our daughter and left. It was my suggestion. 'Go first,' I told him, 'we'll catch up.' A week later I took Tommy. I was pregnant with Phillip, my second son. The whole time, I prayed and I prayed. We made it to the Philippines. They... didn't. No news. Nothing. An entire boat, over a hundred people, gone.'

He remained very quiet. He felt a little stupid, having gone on and on about his broken romance. 'I'm really sorry,' he said finally.

'It happened a long time ago,' she sighed. 'Even so, my mind plays tricks on me. I sometimes fantasise my husband is raising my daughter in another country. That he is mad at me. Isn't that insane?'

'No, not at all,' he said quietly. 'How else would we go on, I mean, if we didn't invent something to hope for?'

She looked out the window briefly. 'When we were drifting down there, I missed the simplest things: the sounds of children's laughter, a cold drink, anything on the radio besides static,' she said. But she straightened herself, then raised her well-manicured hand on which two diamond rings glittered. Her voice was lighter, upbeat. 'But,' she said, 'that's an old story. I survived. My sons survived. I remarried. We went on.'

'And now – now, you're coming home? After so many years?'

'Now I'm going for a visit after more than a quarter of a century,' she corrected him.

He'd flown over this ocean many times, but it had never before taken on an ominous aspect. With closed eyes, he could see the woman and her son jostling for space on one of those decrepit, crowded fishing boats bobbing on the water, no land in sight. Then he thought of Thuy-Linh, pregnant and alone. He saw her taking the place of the older woman on that boat. He clenched his fist and shut his eyes for fear of crying – it came to him as a shock that his grief had such depth. 'I didn't go to Yale,' he said through a groan. 'I don't know why I lied.'

'Oh,' said the woman. 'Hey! that's okay.' And as if to prove it, she reached out to touch his hand once more. He gripped it this time, then rested his face in his left palm and wept.

It was keeping his turmoil at bay. 'Listen,' she whispered. 'If there's one thing I understand well, it's how rare second chances really are. To fall in love with someone and have that love reciprocated, you're already blessed. To lose it and get another chance, well, you must act on it. It's no good for anyone involved if you don't.'

He nodded repeatedly with his eyes shut, lest he'd embarrass himself by crying again. He continued to grip the woman's hand, however, as she talked and only let go when he heard the sounds of a cart with its clinking bottles and squeaking wheels going down the aisle. It was near dusk out, and behind the clouds, the sun was crimson red. There was a warm glow inside the cabin, and the aromas of baked bread and grilled meat wafted in the air. His stomach growled.

'You okay now?' She asked and handed him another tissue.

'Yes,' he smiled meekly at her. 'You've been so kind. And you? Are *you* okay?'

'I'm fine,' the woman sniffed, wiping her eyes. He hadn't realised that she'd been crying, too. 'But a little drunk. Usually, I don't drink more than one or two glasses before dinner. I don't even know if it's breakfast or lunch or what back in San Francisco.'

'Well,' he deadpanned, 'I hate to tell you this, but San Francisco's pretty far behind.' She looked at him and laughed. 'And,' she quipped, 'so is Tokyo.'

The pilot's low, authoritative voice came on the loud speaker, announcing the remaining time of their flight. 'The humidity in Saigon – or Ho Chi Minh if you will – is 85 per cent and the temperature 30.5 degrees Celsius. That's a cool 87 degrees Fahrenheit…I'll update as we near destination.' There was a collective groan in the cabin, followed by sporadic laughter.

'God,' said the woman, shaking her head. 'I don't know if I can take that heat.' But her voice became sober. 'I'm not afraid of the past, you know. I made my peace. It's going back to a place that's gone on without me, that's a little scary. So many friends and relatives have scattered. I have more relatives in California than in Vietnam.'

'Well, I have more friends in Saigon and Hanoi than I do in Boston. We haven't been properly introduced. My name is Mark. Mark Alexander. And I can show you and Tommy around, if you want,' he offered. 'I know a great *pho* soup place on the old Pasteur Street.'

'I'm Phuong-Anh Harris. But call me Anne. It's easier on the tongue. And that's very sweet of you.' Her smile was warm, but he wasn't sure if she were entirely convinced of his sincerity.

'Seriously,' he said. He needed her to believe him. He wanted to make her happy, too. For he could now see what was at the destination: Amid the milling, sweating crowd at the arrival gate, a woman in a green *ao dai* dress holding the hand of a shy, brown haired boy in school uniform as she anxiously scanned the faces of arriving passengers. He felt breathless with anticipation. 'What can I tell you – what can I do to make you feel better?' he asked, preparing himself for the landing. 'Please – Please ask me anything.'

Nguyen The Hoang Linh

Gun and Flower

Need to have a pistol duel
between Good and Evil,
Will Evil weep
If it's presented with roses?

Need to slaughter
those who are full of blood,
Can the blood warm up
winter-cold souls?

Need to fight
for this life?
Yes, we need to, friend,
If you are to say NO.

Save and Delete

If love can be saved
Error won't be bothered when loading
If love can be deleted
Just a nose blow
to finish it
If you are fed up

I just want to tell you a small story

Once I wrote a poem on a computer
And named the file 'tinhyeu'*

Dissatisfied with it later, I was about to delete it
The computer, which I'd regarded as senseless asked me:
'Are you sure you want to delete 'tinhyeu'?'

And I shivered, friend.

About Vietnam

If my next incarnation is a Vietnamese
I will aspire to be born
right in a prison

Those who save me
Will be the Vietnamese.

Christopher Kremmer

The City of Darkness and Light

There is no staircase, only a rickety ladder that creaks as we climb towards the attic above where the artist awaits us. Looking down I see, a few rungs below me, Nguyet's radiant, slightly nervous smile urging me upwards and onwards.

'Keep going. His paintings are *really* good. You will enjoy. Be brave,' she coaxes.

Nguyet knows a few things about art and courage. Evacuated to the countryside during the war, she survived the American bombing of North Vietnam. She's also survived the equally challenging peace. Spurning easier options, she followed her heart into the sharky waters of Vietnam's emerging art market, building a small but steady client list that includes overseas buyers. She did well because she needed to. While her country was re-united, her marriage fell apart. She raised two children on her own. But in the fifteen years that I've known her, that smile has never dimmed, and now, on the hunt once more for a good painting, she is revitalised, ageless under a mop of jet black hair, tingling in her pale, unblemished skin.

At the top of the ladder I find myself level with the floor of the attic, my perspective transformed. So this is how mice see things. It's a garret all right, an appropriately oily mess of rags, palettes, ashtrays and spent paint tubes, cramped under a Mansard roof, with small balconies giving views across the rooftops of the thousand-year-old city. The windows frame the subject. Not the Left Bank, but Hanoi, the artist Co Chu Pin's Paris on the Red River.

From behind an easel a face jumps out. Not a startled yeti, but Pin, chunky cheeks with a bearded border, the artist lost and found in his own ecosystem. No wilderness here, though. No nudes, just the gnarled, sclerotic streets of the old city rendered in viscid paint globs. But the art, like the city it depicts, has changed greatly since I first saw both in the early 1990s, before *doi moi* – renovation – gained momentum. Pin's canvases in those days were grey, his streets tangled in power lines hanging from rusted French stanchions. The houses needed a fresh coat of paint. Now, most of them have had at least one, and Pin's paintings reflect the mood. Colour and light stream from his doorways. You can almost hear the chatter of the diners who overflow onto his pavements. His art, like Hanoi itself, is reborn.

Yet new Hanoi is no nirvana. The old problems – poverty, political control and isolation – have been replaced by new ones – over-population, insensitive development and conspicuous consumption.

Pin was born in this house. He has lived his entire life in this street. He's not moving, but the city is changing around him, and the only way to go is up. New buildings sprout amidst the old, narrow needles of reflective glass with concrete skeletons, squeezed onto tiny allotments. Pin fears his quaint vista of roofs will soon be replaced by tower blocks glowering over him. He has been cuckolded by modernity. 'I love old Hanoi, but it's all slowly going,' he says, resigned to melancholy, but then, suddenly urgent. 'I want to capture it while it still exists.'

In the nineteenth century Hanoi was the capital of French-occupied Indochina, a place where the baguettes were long and the coffee strong. But when the Imperial Japanese Army occupied Vietnam during World War II and requisitioned food, this fertile sliver of a nation bordering the South China Sea experienced famine. The Japanese left eventually, persuading the French to return, who in turn passed the baton of Western domination to the Americans, who, after trying to use an anvil to crush an ant, dropped it on their own collective foot and retired resentful and hurt. The idea then was to starve out the ant with an economic and diplomatic embargo. That worked, kind of. Vietnam still won, but its victory was bittersweet, almost Pyrrhic.

I remember how my heart sank the first time I saw Hanoi. It was 1993, decades since the war had ended, yet Gustave Eiffel's once graceful bridge over the Red River was still a patchwork of beams improvised in defiance of American bombing. From its deck, the city beyond looked like a sallow bean curd stew. Entering it, I found the shops moribund and most of the buildings derelict.

Hanoi still jealously guarded its role as fortress of Vietnamese political and cultural life, and dowager queen of its cities. Capitalistic, tropical Saigon may be forever young, and Danang as free as the breeze off the South China Sea, but the encrusted capital still crouched in the humid Red River Delta, ambiguously triumphant and reticent. Impoverished it was, but not at all humiliated. Its ruling commissars positively swaggered with self-satisfaction, even as the demobbed soldiers who won the war strained at the pedals of rickshaws. This was to be my home for the next two years.

Neil Sheehan, the *New York Times* reporter whose stories based on the leaked Pentagon Papers undermined public support for the Vietnam War, had visited Hanoi a few years earlier, in 1989. At the Temple of Literature, the city's first university, founded in 1076 AD, Sheehan found the names of the scholars of centuries past recorded on stone steles. Hanoi, he wrote, was a city 'caught in the warp of time, a place of history and icons, some still living to remind one that here the past never dies'.

In those days, the bicycle bell was more often heard than the car horn on Hanoi's quiet streets. There were no taxis, nor dance clubs, nor cinemas showing Western films, as there are today. Architectural triumphs like the ornate French opera house were in a parlous state, there being barely enough resources to feed the country's 70 million people. And the food was marginal in quality, a legacy of decades of war-induced poverty.

Art was Hanoi's saving grace. With nowhere else to go, my wife Janaki and I would spend our free time exploring the lakes and tree-lined streets of the French quarter, picking up cut-price masterpieces at the city's many galleries. Vietnam has a long and illustrious art history. At the Cham Museum in the coastal city of Danang you can view ancient stone sculptures of Ganesh carved when Hindu influence dominated the region from 200 AD onwards. The rise of Buddhism fostered more religious art, and a thousand years of Chinese rule fostered a rich tradition of lacquer painting and calligraphy.

French colonialism brought revolutionary change, putting Vietnamese painters and sculptors in touch with all the main European art movements, including Impressionism and Cubism. But later, under the communists, the Fine Arts Association enforced Socialist Realism, and prevented artists who failed to comply from exhibiting their work. Then, the American War as it's known in Hanoi, cut them off again, and the romantic flowering was replaced by the brutal, martial values of a people fighting for survival. Painters sowed rice sacks together to use them as canvases, or just painted on copies of the Communist Party daily newspaper *Nhan Dan*.

But in the early 1990s, despite all the obstacles, Hanoi's classically trained artists sensed a historic opening, a chance to create and exhibit more than just pictures of heroic workers and peasants. They were the first post-war generation, and seized the opportunities triggered by economic change to reconnect with the global art scene. Not only were members of the Hanoi-based 'Gang of Five' technically proficient, they were committed to finding a balance between the country's traditions and its new political reality. One 'gang' member, Tran Luong was boldly political, while others like Dang Xuan Hoa confined their rebellion to matters of style. As Joseph Hoff wrote in the Vietnamese-American magazine *Nha* 'To render a still life, abstraction, or nude was to engage in subversive activity.'

Today, a BMW stands parked in Hoa's driveway, where the artist greets me at the door of his rambling, architect-designed home. A wiry, catlike figure with trademark black goatee, he pads lightly across a broad expanse of polished stone floor calling to a helper to bring drinks.

'Life is good. I can do what I want to do,' he says. At forty-nine, his work hangs in Hanoi's Fine Arts Museum and is sold at auctions and galleries around the world. One painting can earn over ten times an average Vietnamese worker's yearly salary. Yet affluence seems not to have taken the edge off Hoa's art. His moody self-portraits open a door on Vietnamese introspection that is the antithesis of our image of a militant people. His new canvases are studies of family members, pensive, quizzical figures who turn their backs to each other. Their bodies seem to hang, suspended by invisible forces.

'People in Vietnam are forever waiting. They're worried, with many difficult decisions to make in order to achieve a good life. And there are still certain limits placed on us artists by government,' Hoa says. 'But there is a new wave, and they have good conditions in which to make art. They try to experiment. I hope they do better than we did. I'm optimistic about the future.'

Vietnam's has not just survived – it's risen from the fires of war like the proverbial phoenix. The country's luck has changed; for the first time in decades, it's out of the line of fire. It strikes me, cruising the streets on the back of friends' motor scooters, that while the rest of the world frets about terrorism, the main risk to life in Hanoi these days is a motoring accident. It's a city in which you can have your portrait painted on the pavement by an honours graduate in the morning, spend lunchtime at a restaurant that's survived three wars and two famines, learn lacquer painting in the afternoon, and party on after dinner at a bar that serves traditional rice wine spiked with medicinal essences of lizard and seahorse and goat's penis. In the autumn of 2007, the siren song of the past – Hanoi's and my own – took me down narrow alleys to houses where I'd once lived, and favourite soup stalls where I'd enjoyed many lunches. Passing the now splendidly restored Hanoi Opera House, I was cast back to a cold winter's night when the first performance in decades of Handel's *Messiah* woke the dead and sent the rats scampering across its creaking floorboards.

Some of the city's changes seemed truly revolutionary; the pumping, drug-enhanced dancing at the New Century nightclub, for example. Besieged by pimps and dealers offering girls, opium and ecstasy, I couldn't believe such a place could open in once staid, matronly, communist Hanoi. Neither could the authorities. They shut it down a few months later after some 500 police raided the place, detaining over a thousand patrons including foreigners.

Falling in love with Vietnam warts and all is not optional – it's compulsory; and yet, everyone falls for it in their own way. French tourists fantasise about their empire's lost glory, American and Australian veterans soul search about the horrors of war, and legions of backpackers explore the most remote corners of the country.

I'd been invited to give a reading of my work at Hanoi's only English language bookshop, The Bookworm, and found myself in the vicinity of a street named in honour of a Vietnamese poetess of the nineteenth century. Making my way to the short dogleg street that runs off stately Tien Quang Lake, I came to a French-period villa, number 10 Ho Xuan Huong. Janaki and I first saw it in 1994. We rented it for US$2,000 a month, renovated it, and spent the early years of our marriage there, living as you can only live in a city that dedicates its streets to artists and poets.

Today, a restaurant for Vietnam's well-off and well-connected crowds the font of the villa. Standing on the pavement, looking up at our old bedroom window, the wooden shutters closed, I am an outsider once more. Then suddenly, something strangely familiar graces my cheek. It's the air, soft, neither warm nor cool. And I am a Hanoian once more.

Next morning I awake to the sound of church bells issuing from St Joseph's Cathedral on Nha Tho. My temporary residence, the aptly named Church Hotel, stands on the shortest, but hippest street in the country, crammed with cafes like 'Moca', and Vietnam's top boutiques, places like 'Grace', where Japanese designer Nobuyuki Nogi and Vietnamese partner Anita Tran work natural Asian fabrics into stunning couture.

On the steps of the cathedral a bride stands resplendent in her virginal white wedding dress, awaiting her groom. A lank-limbed peasant toils past her in conical hat and flip flops, carrying a load of vegetables in two baskets slung from either end of a bamboo pole balanced on her shoulders. The farm — and the contradictions — are never far away.

Today I join forces with another of Hanoi's most successful and knowledgeable art dealers, Pho Hong Long, who runs Dong Phong gallery on Ngo Quyen Street. A misty Orientalism pervades many galleries where willowy Vietnamese maidens draped in the traditional *ao dai* grace the walls. Mr Long, however, is passionate about the edgy rising stars of the new generation. He's also concerned about the rampant fakery afflicting the country's art market.

'There are three types of fake,' he tells me, smiling incongruously. 'First, are painters who impersonate the greats, copying their work and even their signatures to the last detail. Second, are those who copy the style of the masters and sign their own names. Some dealers encourage young artists to do this because the famous artist is not doing business with them. The third kind of forgery is the well-known painter who copies himself, reproducing the style that made him famous over and over again. He no longer develops as an artist.'

Genuine fakes are produced in broad daylight on Hanoi's streets. Michaelangelos and Da Vincis fill the rip-off galleries that crowd Hang Trong, Hang Hanh and Nguyen Thai Hoc. You too can own a Brett Whiteley – albeit, not one painted by Brett Whiteley – thanks to Vietnam's lax copyright laws. Some copyists take overseas orders through their websites.

Vietnam's art market has had its ups and downs. The boom peaked around 1997, with rampant copying and an oversupply of decorative art keeping prices low since then for all but top artists. The market is still dominated by foreign buyers, rich Vietnamese preferring to buy cars and houses.

Once you've seen enough galleries and know what you like the next step is meeting the artists at their studios. This is not as daunting as it sounds. Hanoi's dealers are constantly roaming the city, seeking work by established and new artists for their galleries, and are happy to take you along. For the artists, it's a chance to sell and spell. Time wasting and tea drinking hold a place of honour in their craft.

I had taken a liking to the work of new generation artists like Ha Manh Thang and Ly Tran Quynh Giang, both in their twenties, and both of whom cite Francis Bacon as an influence. Accompanied by Mr Long, I made my way to the tiny studio where Thang, a native of Thai Nguyen province now resident in Hanoi, creates his explosively colourful images of people and things.

Thang's sculpted features and mischievous eyes are focused on the collision point where Vietnam's ornate culture collides with Western capitalism. On giant Chinese scrolls he paints dazzlingly colourful images of himself and his girlfriend seated on thrones and dressed in the robes of ancient Vietnamese royalty. But look closer and you notice that those exquisite robes are covered in Western designer labels like YSL and Gucci.

An artist since the age of ten, Thang rejected the classicism taught at the Fine Arts College in favour of a vividly individualistic style. Like many of Hanoi's top artists, he's trying to articulate a response to the cultural and economic churning all around.

'I want to find a mix of Western and Oriental culture,' he says, coyly running a hand over his closely cropped scalp. 'In this period you cannot look only at tradition, but you don't want to lose it either.'

Mr Long cannot contain his enthusiasm for his young protégé.

'He never repeats himself, that's why I love his work,' he chimes in. 'He's not copying himself or anybody for the market.'

In the early '90s, you could still find pieces by one of the 'Four Pillars' of modern Vietnamese art, Bui Xuan Pha, for reasonable prices. Nguyet had modelled for Phai in his twilight years, and been given many valuable works which she later sold to establish herself as a dealer. One day, as I browsed at her keyhole gallery, she pointed out two of her Phais. One was a good sized oil painting of Ha Long Bay, about 110 by 80 centimetres, priced at US$800, the other, a small sketch the master had made of one of his contemporaries, Kim Dong, priced at US$100. I bought the sketch, which now graces the walls of my home in New Delhi, little knowing I had made a big mistake.

It wasn't that the Phai was a fake. By pinching pennies and not buying the more expensive painting, I had shown a lack of courage and paid the price. Dealers in Hanoi in 2007 told me the sketch had appreciated twenty-fold to a couple of thousand dollars. But the oil painting had risen in value by a much more dramatic margin. Today it would fetch tens of thousands of dollars. So much for my budding career as an art collector.

While Vietnam's artists today enjoy more creative space, the government still maintains a share in most private galleries. Political artists like Le Quang Ha occasionally have their exhibitions shut down by cultural commissars who once adored gritty Socialist Realism, but now prefer happy capitalist art. Fortunately, thirty years of hardline communism hasn't been able to snuff out Vietnamese individuality.

The women painted by Ly Tran Quynh Giang glare defiantly at the viewer, obsessively frustrated and melancholy. It's not a revolution, more an obstinate refusal to be uncritically cheerful in the new Vietnam. At twenty-nine, she's a cool young woman wearing her jeans low on the hip with Calvin Klein underwear showing. At her parents' elegant home, furnished in dark lacquered pieces, she whiles away the days smoking Camels, drinking endless cups of green tea, and painting in a high-ceilinged room dominated by a huge ancestor altar. She learnt violin from the age of seven, and the instrument often pops up in her work, a counterpoint in her nudes. Hanoi gossip suggests she may have been more than close to one of her female models who died recently. When I ask this strident individualist what artists should do for their country, she answers in a voice soft as rustling leaves, 'Just paint. Create a lot. Artists can only control themselves.'

The time has come to leave Hanoi once more. I want to see Nguyet again before I depart, so arrange to meet up at one of Hanoi's – and Asia's – great hotels. Built by the French in 1911, the Sofitel Metropole on Ngo Quyen Street became a haven for the carpetbaggers who flooded into Vietnam after the country's opening to the West in the late 1980s. At the Metropole's well-lubricated Le Club bar you could meet oil men from Texas keen to exploit offshore fields in the South China Sea, or West Australian businessmen on the run from the law back home. The hotel has been progressively renovated and boasts ornate period furnishings and a phalanx of teak and wicker ceiling fans that set a tone of languid opulence, and the cocktails are named after its more famous guests, people like Graham Greene, who lodged at the hotel while reporting the war and writing his novel *The Quiet American*. The luxury of the place would be incongruous in any city, let alone a thrusting developing country capital like Hanoi.

Nguyet was waiting for me in the lobby when I arrived, her blazing smile caressing me at the end of a hard day's art hunting. I had invested again, this time more fulsomely in works by Thang and Ly. The fact that I'd gone through another dealer seemed not to phase her in the least, and she approved of my choices.

Over drinks we reminisced about the days when we made light in a dark city, when the future beckoned and seemed better, when, out of the blue, Nguyet revealed that her father, one of Ho Chi Minh's most trusted lieutenant's, had died recently. I was shocked that she hadn't mentioned it earlier, and worried that her hospitality on my account might have interfered with her grieving. She shrugged off my fears, and told me a story that in a few short sentences seems to encapsulate the modern history of Vietnam.

During the war, with bombs reigning down on the city, her father, a committed party member, had sent his daughter to the countryside where he had spent his own childhood. Nguyet would be looked after by his mother, her grandmother, in the rural heartland of the Red River Delta. For the young Vietnamese girl, it was a time full of adventures and marvellous stories told by her grandmother. But the one thing the elderly village woman shared that lingered longest was a nugget of homespun advice:

'To be good, a man must be rich,' said the old woman, whose own son had risen to the high echelons of the Communist Party. 'After all, who can a poor man help?'

It would take many years, but the party of Ho Chi Minh would eventually embrace the wisdom of a Vietnamese peasant woman.

Saying goodbye to Nguyet, I departed the Metropole's white-washed eminence and headed back for my last night at the Church Hotel. Walking the city's bustling streets, perhaps for the last time, I fancy I'm seeing Hanoi through fresh eyes; the crowded cafes, the restless trading and work; the materialism of the city's 3 million people, juxtaposed against billboards of Uncle Ho and community awareness messages about the threat of AIDS. Past, present and future merge like an abstract painting.

In the narrow lanes of the city, the people of Hanoi squat on low, plastic stools, hunched over bowls of steaming *pho*, much as they did in the old days. People smile more than they did when I lived here, are better fed and better dressed. They may even be happier, but not yet quite so happy as to forget the lesson of struggle – political, artistic and human – that is their inheritance.

Pham Thi Hoai

Saigon Tailor

Saigon Tailor's not in Saigon not in Cali. I was waiting for the train to pass at the Kham Thien Road railway crossing and the handlebars of my bicycle accidentally touched the basket of the cigarette vendor who turned around and called me a stupid bitch. I looked up and saw the huge sign behind her that said *Saigon Tailor – Dressmaking Classes for All Kinds of Fashions, Men's and Women's* – and in parentheses below, *(Including Suits, Jackets and Ao Dai)*.

That night I saw Dung and told him I was going to take dressmaking classes. He said, 'Please please you are always taking lessons, French lessons, English lessons, computer lessons, bridal make-up lessons...' We had a glass of sugarcane juice each. A flicker of thought crossed his face and he ordered a *Vina* cigarette for himself and a plate of sunflower seeds for me. After the cigarette he said, 'I'll tell you something. You ought to concentrate on one thing and one thing only and try to do it well. Better to be the master of one than a jack of all trades.' I said, 'Yes,

yes, this time I will.' He said, 'Please, please each time you say *this time.*'

When I went to the shop I saw twenty girls – all of them obviously from the countryside – sitting at their machines. None of them looked up at me. I wanted to turn back and leave the place but the cigarette vendor had taken up the space next to my bike. Asking her to leave would have invited another stream of invective and I didn't want to become a stupid bitch, and in any case right then someone called out to me, 'Hey you there, want to learn dressmaking?' It was the proprietor, a large woman who was squeezing her fat stomach and large hips past the girls towards me. Fiddling with the pages of a dog-eared exercise book she was holding in her hands, she said to me, '120 different styles, men's and women's, traditional and modern popular fashion. Basic course costs 250,000, Intermediate 400, combined Basic and Intermediate 600, a discount of 50, Advanced includes *ao dai* cutting directly onto real fabric, all teachers are reliable and trustworthy, and now what's your name?'

And now what's your name? She must be a very busy woman, I thought, so busy that my induction to the course ended with such brutal and forceful language. Later on I learnt that her name was Tuyet and I addressed her as Teacher Tuyet but sometimes I called her Mum like the rest of the girls. It was clear that I was a city girl – a real Hanoian – so all the girls deferred to me. On the second day I learnt that there were four instructors: two upstairs who taught cutting and two downstairs sewing. In addition there was Tuyet's daughter who took care of overlocking, the two daughters-in-law who did all kinds of odd jobs, and a woman cook from the countryside. I found nothing Saigonese about this Saigon Tailor. When I first sat down at the Chinese overlocking machine to learn to overlock in a straight line using the handles of a pair of scissors, I thought to myself it's not too late to leave. The

French, English and Computer classes were full of urbanites like me, educated and moneyed or pretending to be elegant and moneyed. The bridal make-up course at least dealt with appearance – a painted existence. But in comparison, this dressmaking course was truly a dark train carriage packed with dreams, and here I was buying an express ticket to a future lined with mass-produced shirts and jackets carrying South Korean labels. That evening Dung asked 'How did you go?' I said, 'Quite well, in three months' time I can open a dress-making business.' I thought the first thing I'd make would be a pair of *cullote* shorts. I would wrap them up in newspaper and tell him to open the package later at home.

The proprietor Tuyet, her daughter Xuyen, her daughters-in-law Phan and Duc, the instructors Quyet, Tuc, Chien, Thang and the twenty girls all had names with a rising tone which grated on the ears. And the place was noisy. All day long the room upstairs was filled with recitations of measurements and dressmaking formulas: hip divisions, chest additions, armpit reductions – always hip, chest and armpit. Downstairs the noise was even worse. Nobody could hear what the others were saying and even if you yelled, your words would be broken up into fragments by the overhead fan and sent in all directions. I thought I would end up in Trau Quy asylum before I learnt to make a pair of shorts for Dung. Therefore when the girl said her name was Lan I liked her instantly. Anywhere else such a name would be common. And she was truly different from the rest. She was sitting next to me, her tapered fingers teasing my uneven stitches, when her father came into the shop. Tuyet said, 'What do you want, a shirt, a pair of pants, or are you looking for a dressmaking class for your daughter?' He said, 'No, no,' and began sobbing. 'I am looking for my daughter. She left home to go to Hanoi to take up sewing classes. It's now six months and she has not returned.' Tuyet said, 'There are hundreds of tailors like this

in Hanoi.' He said, 'This is the nineteenth that I've been to.'
As he was leaving Tuyet called after him, 'And what's her
name, just in case.' 'Her name is Chut,' he replied. Lan came
out of her hiding-place underneath the table and said 'That's
my father.' So her real name also had a rising tone.

For the first few days I concentrated on the lessons as I
thought that I was behind everyone else. The order of the day
was practising sewing straight lines on offcuts of materials,
then making shirt collars and cuffs. On the third day Tuyet
told me to go upstairs to learn the basic cuts for shirts. The
two teachers, Quyet and Tuc, worked in a disorderly fashion,
attending to students only when called. Otherwise Teacher
Quyet would lie on the table singing to himself and Teacher
Tuc would sit and talk. Quyet was shirtless most of the time.
Tuc usually wore an unbuttoned shirt showing his fat gut.
Quyet was a handsome man. Tuc's real job was a teacher at
the College of Fine Arts and most of his talk went straight
over the girls' heads. Essentially Quyet taught us the basic
cuts and Tuc the artistic modifications. When I came upstairs
Lan was trying on a pink jacket, and Tuc was running his
hand over the front flap in the chest area, saying, 'This doesn't
hang right, it needs straightening a bit.' After that he said,
'Excuse me,' and put his hand underneath to check the lining.
Quyet was lying down listening to a *Cai Luong* song but got
up and said 'This jacket would look absolutely fabulous with
a seven-piece dress.' Tuc screwed up his nose, saying, 'Oh
no, not those cheap, kitsch seven-piece dresses. For a girl
like Lan, the thing to wear with this is a mini skirt, a short
skirt up to here,' his hand making a circle around her thighs
for illustration. He complained out loud, 'Pardon me, but in
this bloody place nobody has any idea about art.' I learnt the
basic cuts for shirts and blouses from Quyet. In his method
they were basically variations of the same cut. For women
you added a little at the front to allow for the chest, for men

you raised the front hemlines, and for children you didn't put tucks in the waistline. As a result, I managed to learn over ten styles in one day. At this rate a hundred and twenty styles would take just over ten days.

After the shirts and blouses came the basic pants designs. The usual colour scheme was a sickly blue for the tops and pale purple for the pants. Tuyet said these colours sold well to women from the countryside. Apart from this tailoring business she also presided over the Thang Long Poetry Club, of which the two downstairs teachers Chien and Thang were also members. They were elderly and serious men who told me that dressmaking required dedication – it was not something to be taken lightly. One day Tuyet was holding a copy of the *Ha Noi Moi* newspaper and reading aloud a couple of *luc bat* six-eight verses – something to do with green grass and a bridge – when she suddenly stopped and yelled, 'Bloody hell, they've mistyped *than tinh* instead of *an tinh*. Where are you Xuyen, Xuyen, quick, quick, get on your bike and go down to the bloody newspaper office and demand a correction and an apology. They can't get away with this. This is serious literature.' The two men nodded in agreement 'Yes, yes, *than tinh* makes no sense, it ruins the whole piece.' A commendation award from the Thang Long Poetry club hung on the wall, among shirt-collar samples. You had to look really closely to see it.

In any case I did not give up. Long afterwards, when this course had come to an end, like the other courses, after I had gone back to my work, travelling to the office everyday to diligently read the newspapers, and as I was thinking of enrolling in an Executive Secretary course, this tailor shop – this train carriage packed with dreams – remained etched in my memories. Sitting at the outermost machine nearest to the footpath I thought that when the Unification Express passed through, this dark carriage ought to be hitched onto it and towed all the way to Saigon. Real Saigon. In Saigon all the girls' names will lose their harsh rising tones. In Saigon, these girls who had left their villages chasing the dream of creating new fashions out of two colours – sickly washy blue and a meek mauve – would learn more than a hundred and twenty styles of cut, and I would be able to part with Dung from a position of strength. Here all I could hope for was to marry him and even that modest hope was a faint one. Dung was a practical man. He could see that two people reading newspapers at two different offices did not add up to a family. My demands were modest but Dung had his own needs. The tradition of our country is that women have to work their hardest and that's why I took these dressmaking classes.

After one week all the teachers agreed that I was bright. I could manage the hip divisions, chest additions and armpit reductions with ease and with accuracy, unlike the other girls, none of whom had completed Grade Four. Even Lan, who had only finished Year Ten, stood out from them. They were all interested in a similar kind of design, with frilled necks and puffed sleeves, which made them look like pumped-up balloons about to take off. I often had to stand as the model for their happy creations – frilled and hanging loose, bat wings and pleats, collar styles from Germany, from Japan. They all used my urbanite body as the standard on which to try their creations. Then they would try the dresses on themselves. All day long they were constantly taking clothes off or putting clothes on, right then and there, in broad daylight, in full view of the passing public from the busy streets, all their sense of decorum left at home with their mums and dads.

One day Lan told me that there was a dress in town priced at 900,000 *dong*. Its labour cost must have been 800,000. Where she came from, the most expensive dress was 20,000, of which the labour cost was 5,000, but that was better pay than toiling in the field. After the pink jacket she began to make a short white mini-skirt with a hemline that came right up to the thigh-lines marked by Teacher Tuc's fingers. Tuc said that Lan had good taste. Looking like a piece of pink chalk with a narrow white band around it, Lan came down the stairs, lingered a little for a bit of a show, then turned to leave to go downtown. Miss Tuyet called after her, 'Hey listen here, don't you think you should pay the rest of your course fee first?' Lan turned her head in an affected way – like an actress on stage – and said, 'Don't you worry Mum, I am not going to be run over by a train.' Turning to the other girls Tuyet said, 'If I had known I would have turned her in to her father. Bloody useless girl, never tries to learn and always worries about her appearance.'

From the machine nearest to the street I saw Lan bend down to crawl under the lowered boom gate and cross the railway lines. Her high heels got caught and she fell down spread-eagled across the rails, but she just lay there looking at the approaching train, her gleaming teeth flashing in a crazy grin. The following day she told me the train had to stop to avoid her, she didn't have to avoid it. I felt awed by her blind self-confidence, for after trying my luck with French, English, computer and bridal make-up courses, I did not have any confidence left in myself. This inauthentic Saigon Tailor was her starting point, but for me it could well be my final call.

Our friendship was as short and chancy as my average run of luck. For two months I gained nothing from her apart from the company of a girl with a sweet sounding name. She didn't gain much from me either. What she needed most was to have someone to pour her heart out to. But pouring her heart out to me was as difficult as threading cotton threads through the eye of the needle, a thread for each story line. So she mostly stayed upstairs and only came down on her way to town, each day wearing a different outfit. It was much easier for her to pour her heart out to Teacher Tuc, accompanied by the mouth

music of the handsome Teacher Quyet, and therefore the only
time she would sidle up to me, gently touching me with her
lovely fingers, was when she wanted to ask something like
'What does *improvisation* mean?' She poured her heart into
clothes and into wearing them to town.

I also tried to see what it felt like to cross the railway lines
when the boom gate was down. Afterwards in the evening I
told Dung that it was a strong and powerful sensation. 'The
train had to avoid me, I didn't have to avoid it,' I told him.
After the sugarcane juice Dung grabbed me and kissed me.
Our tongues tasted sweet, candy sweet, and our lips were
glued together. I disentangled my lips and said, 'If we got
married the gifts we received would be enough to buy a
sewing machine.' Dung said 'Please, please you are always
saying if this and if that.'

I felt that it was the right time to sew him a pair of shorts
so I took the material upstairs to ask Tuc to cut it for me. Just
plain material. But Tuc wasn't there, only Quyet lying on
the table right underneath the overhead fan, singing '*La Dieu
Bong*'. A few strands of his hair were swimming in a bowl of
vegetable soup served on a tray placed on the table next to his
head. He asked me what I wanted to make. I said a pair of
shorts. He said, 'Follow the basic cut for a pair of pants, just
cut off the legs.' I thought that wouldn't be quite right, that
this special present needed the artistic touch of Teacher Tuc,
so I tried to take leave, excusing myself by saying it was his
lunch break. But he got up and said, 'Give it to me,' and two
seconds later the material had been cut and he returned to his
lying position, his hair again swimming in the bowl of soup.

Downstairs Miss Tuyet was having a fit. The previous
month she had had a similar fit. One of her two grandchildren
– the one fourteen months old – usually crawled around under
our sewing machines. Occasionally we'd step on him by
accident and he would cry for a while – an ear-splitting kind

of cry, but he would soon stop. That day he picked up two needles from the floor and put them in his mouth. Nobody found out about the needles until Tuyet tried to give him a drink of soya-bean milk. She threw a fit. When Tuyet had a fit all the girls froze in the same spot – bad luck to those naked, in the middle of changing their clothes. The two daughters in-law, who occupied the two opposing mezzanine floors, one to our left and one to our right, would take turns answering their mother in-law back, but never missing a chance to have a dig at each other either. It was then, with a fit at ground level and verbal invectives criss-crossing the airspace, punctuated by sarcastic comments by the daughter Xuyen, that I realised that artistic blood flowed freely through the veins of everybody here. Of the two teachers upstairs one sang and one painted. Downstairs there was poetry and the occasional drama. As I came down the stairs the girls were trying to calm Tuyet down, holding her at the waist as if trying to keep her guts from spilling out. They might well have been able to hold her guts but nobody could ever hold back her tongue. Normally even Tuyet's brand of language had its own punctuation, but when she had a fit it knew no full stops. You had to be a resident of Saigon Tailor to really know what it was like. Even the kerbside cigarette vendor or those across the street selling Russian electrical goods were no match for Tuyet. I came down the stairs straight into the middle of her sentence, 'making a mess and not tidying up after yourself finishing with the iron and not unplugging it is just like going to the toilet and not flushing, like shitting and not shovelling it away leaving this old woman to clean up after you, you little young sluts so that you can sit and chat amongst yourselves don't say that you've come here to learn not one of you can manage to sew a straight line your buttons are uneven like the dirt tracks of your paddy fields your button-holes are as coarse and hairy as your cunts don't bother calling yourself students I'll send you all packing this is a place for serious learning we are all educated and cultured here this is not a bloody brothel this is not a market that you can come and go as you bloody please in this day and age nobody cares about anybody if I don't look after you who would...'

I stood there, immersed in her sentence, not wanting to leave. I felt happy because compared to her my lot was quite lucky. My waistline was still sixty-two and a half and I spoke a kind of gentle Vietnamese punctuated with well-defined pauses. The package in my hand, the pair of shorts cut quickly and uncreatively by Quyet, was a very minor tragedy. If Lan helped me to sew them together the situation could still be salvaged as her stitches were beautiful, smooth and straight. Right then Lan stepped in, followed by Teacher Tuc. She ran, half-skipping, up the stairs. Tuc stayed downstairs. His fat gut and Tuyet's large girth were just about evenly matched. He said to Tuyet: 'Calm down – people must be laughing.' But Tuyet continued her terrifying unending lines of poetry, changing the topic slightly to make a footnote, 'so you think you are gifted and you can do anything you like I'll tell you what I pay you good money to teach not to take them to cafés this is not a brothel this is not a market...'. Lan came down the stairs wearing her favourite pink and white outfit. High heels, red lips and cascading hair. She took the stairs one by one. Each step revealed a portion of her thighs which then disappeared at the completion of the step. Revealing and concealing, in this mesmerising fashion she climbed down the stairs and came face to face with Tuyet. 'Mum, if you don't stop I am going to throw myself in front of the train.' Tuyet wanted to but she was unable to stop. Once started, her language did not know how to generate its own full stops. Lan went out to the street, bent down and got through under the lowered boom gate. When we heard the screeching sound of the train braking and rushed outside, it was too late. She had been cut into three sections, her lovely mesmerising thighs pointed to our tailor shop and her hair cascading towards the flower shop on the other side of the railway lines. Her clothes were all bloodstained dark red. You had to look closely to tell what had been pink and what had been white. She must have been lying there looking up at the spot where a bunch of traffic lights was hanging from electrical wires. She must have been lying there counting silently, 'One, two, three, I bet Tuyet is going to stop. One, two, three, I bet somebody will run out and pick me up and whisk me off the track.' The poor girl had been in Hanoi for only three months, not long enough to know that here nobody cared. Even if I was there, on the spot, I would have just stood and watched. This time the train didn't avoid her. It was the Reunification Express, running non-stop all the way to Saigon. Little Lan had not paid her course fee so she mortgaged her body in Hanoi, but her soul could now catch a free ride directly to Saigon. There she could use her real name. There her father would have next to no chance of finding her. Somebody once said that whereas Saigon girls were modern and showy Hanoi's were aristocratic and classical. There was nothing aristocratic or classical about Lan so that's probably why she had to go. Her tendency to show off her body too willingly was not really appreciated in our Hanoi.

The dressmaking shop closed for a day for Lan's funeral. She wasn't a registered resident but Tuyet adopted her to enable her to be buried at the Van Dien Cemetery. She bought incense and flowers and placed them at the spot. Each time a train passed, the incense and flowers would be squashed, and she would bring fresh ones, a dozen or so times each day. Each time – a dozen or so times a day – she would slap herself across the mouth, vowing to temper her poisonous tongue with her heart of gold. The girls would line up inside the shop to watch Tuyet flagellating herself – they had never seen anything quite like it. I saw Lan having to interrupt her trip to the South dozens of times a day to return here to witness Tuyet's repentance. Teacher Tuc said that he had taken Lan to have a look at the College of Fine Arts where there was a course in fashion design. After that they went to a café to discuss the possibilities of Lan working as a model for the drawing class until she made up her mind what to do. He did not burn incense at the railway lines. Instead he laid himself down next to Quyet on the table and cried, 'Why did you do it Lan, why did you have to be so stubborn and proud?' I did not have any pride left after unsuccessfully dropping so many hints of marriage to Dung, so I felt quite overwhelmed by Lan's sense of pride. Now and again I felt goose pimples rise just thinking that she might come back, not to witness Tuyet's self-flagellation, but to ask me, 'What does *design* mean, my friend?'

The day after the funeral I took the material to the shop and began to sew the pair of shorts. There were nine machines downstairs but only one worked properly without breaking the cotton thread. Normally whoever got there first would claim that machine and never let go of it. But that day it was empty downstairs. I threaded the cotton through the needle and dropped the guiding slot down to claim the machine, and went upstairs. The girls were crowding around Tuc, all asking him to cut a pink jacket. One for each of them. I thought they had all gone mad. Jackets and then miniskirts. My poor body would have to stand twenty times as a model for twenty jackets and twenty miniskirts. Twenty times I was to be a pink piece of chalk with a white rubber band around me. And then they would all change their names, throwing away their harsh sounding names in the same way they had thrown their needles on the floor for Tuyet's grandson to pick up and put in his mouth. I told myself to stay calm, not to panic and not to go to the College of Fine Arts with them.

Instead I went downstairs. I sewed the shorts together, cut the cotton threads, ironed the sewn shorts, unplugged the iron, sewed the elastic band on and then wrapped the shorts in a copy of *Ha Noi Moi* newspaper, the one that carried the news of Lan's death. I would give the package to Dung later and tell him to open it after he got home. I knew that they were a terrible pair of shorts, as terrible as this railway intersection.

The day after, when I came to the shop, the girls were all busy getting in and out of their pink and white outfits. Tuyet, her daughter and daughters in-law and the four teachers and the cook stood there helpless, stunned and speechless, watching the twenty opium intoxicated butterflies flapping their fannies. The intoxication even infected several passers-by in the street, causing them to stagger. When I completed the duty of standing as a model for twenty pairs of pink and white outfits Tuyet called me, gave me a package wrapped in newspaper and said, 'A man gave this to you.' Inside Dung had left a message, 'Thank you but there's no need.' The night before we had kissed and again our lips glued together and our tongues tasted sweet but I didn't disentangle my lips to mention marriage. I knew that was the last kiss.

I plan to ask Tuyet for a part refund. I'll say that I've been sent away unexpectedly. A special assignment to Saigon. But she is throwing another fit and her sentences cannot be interrupted. Prostrating herself in front of the twenty girls, each and every one of them in a pink and white outfit, beating her head on the ground, Tuyet pleads in a loud voice, 'Oh my dear Lan, my dear Chut or whatever your name was, please rest in peace and don't come back and haunt me like this, please please all you girls don't you play games like this please please.'

I go out into the street, on a special assignment to Saigon. In the near future perhaps I'll take an Executive Secretary course.

Translated into English by Ton-That Quynh-Du

Hoa Pham

The Daughters of Au Co

Hanoi

Before hopping on her moped, she pulls on her long gloves and plain shirt to cover her arms from the sunlight. A hat goes on her head, and a little kitten facemask shields her nose and mouth. Then sunglasses to ensure she does not get wrinkles at the corners of her eyes.

She has class today, on American literature. The story she understands the most is 'The Story of an Hour' by Kate Chopin. The heroine imagines her life without her husband, unfolding into days of freedom. Then when he appears alive her heart stops with gladness.

She would like a husband one day, once she finishes college. A rich husband to support her so she can have children and do the housework just like she does the housework for her father.

She gets to school and the class rumbles into the classroom. Chairs are knocked asunder as the students crowd behind their wooden desks.

The professor stands there, bent over and wrinkled, writing something on the board.

Mistranslation. The ending of 'The Story of an Hour' is wrong. The heroine died of a heart attack and they say she died of joy. But it is ironic, a fact the original translation missed. She felt chained by her marriage to her husband.

She reads the board again, trying to understand.

San Francisco

She folds down her eyelid and places transparent tape artfully over the folded skin. Now she has an epicanthic fold, and looks more European. She dabs her fingertips in vaseline and smoothes the gel on her eyelashes. They glitter in the light when she blinks.

Smoothing back her hair she critically inspects the blonde streaks that are growing amber day by day. She wishes she was a natural blonde, then she wouldn't have so many problems dyeing her hair. She ignores the clenching of her stomach, complaining because she has not eaten. The tight t-shirt she wears forms her breasts like round perfect apples. She does not dare wear a tank top, she's aware that you can see her ribs and this is not attractive.

Sydney

I cannot stand Hanoi women who cross their legs when riding their mopeds. It bores me. In Little Saigon in Cabramatta the young gaggles of Vietnamese girls giggle with their pierced ears and cool streaked hair. They call the ones in tight jeans and white ugg boots 'fresh off the boat'. They are cooler, uber cool, too cool to go to Asian nights or associate with other Vietnamese that are FOB. I'm of the generation before, generation 1.5, caught in the middle. When being Vietnamese was not cool, and *pho* was not available everywhere. Chinese girls told me that I wouldn't get anywhere because I was Vietnamese. Now it is my Vietnamese ethnicity that I draw on, that gets the most attention.

Melbourne

She lives in a big house in the suburbs. Every day she walks to the shopping centre to buy fruit and sometimes vegetables. It's the only place that seems like home, the grocery section with the fruit and vegetables on display and people jostling back and forth. Otherwise the concrete pavements are empty, the green kerbside lifeless. She spends the day time alone when her husband is at work. The neighbours do not understand her English and only the cat seems to talk to her, meow, meow, meow.

She tries not to regret leaving Saigon for this suburban emptiness. She misses the market stalls, the buzz of mopeds, the friendliness of neighbours and passers by. She tries to retain her sense of wonder at the excess space, for a study, a kitchen, a dining room and a lounge room, when she had been used to sleeping on the floor of a multipurpose room used for eating, sleeping and watching TV with her sister.

She tries to think of her husband's good intentions and tries not to hate him for bringing her here.

San Francisco

She is a banana girl, white on the inside yellow on the outside. She clatters downstairs in her high heels, ready to go out now.

Her mother is standing in the kitchen cooking up one of her godawful Chinese medicine messes.

Why doesn't her mother take better care of her appearance? She looks like a steamed dumpling in her cooking shirt, wrinkled and white.

Her mother looks at her pretty daughter with pride. She has worked long hours at the factory to ensure her daughter can go to college and afford salubrious things like the jewellery she wears around her neck and her rings on her slender fingers. Her mother only wishes that she would come home with a suitable Vietnamese–American boy to give her grandchildren.

Hanoi

She goes to an international literature conference courtesy of her father. There is a handful of foreigners there, mostly older men and women. Professors dominate the sessions, talking in a long-winded way, posturing for the audience. A young student comes up to her and asks her if she speaks English. Haltingly she says yes. But her English is very bad compared to the Canadian's and she has trouble with her accent.

The conference is translated into English through headphones.

One conference speaker, a lively older woman, accuses modern Vietnamese literature of being too black and white, too derivative of oral Vietnamese literature, where good and evil are clearly delineated.

She does not understand quite what the speaker means.

Then she meets a woman author who writes domestic dramas. Her work is criticised for being only concerned about women's lives, about love affairs, abortions and sexuality.

She thinks about Kate Chopin and Americans. Are they, too, only concerned about domestic dramas?

Sydney

There is a Vietnamese–Australian circle of artists who all know each other and go to each other's gigs. They are the ones who I feel the most comfortable with – outsiders to both cultures who can talk to me about their heartfelt concerns. I am *Viet Kieu* and when I'm with the first generation or when I'm back in Vietnam I feel the pressure to conform – to accept unwritten codes of behaviour, to accept what is unsaid. As an artist I can say what can't be said, my next installation work will be on silence, to talk about what is silent in women's lives.

Hanoi

She takes her new Canadian friend for coffee down by West Lake where the lovers hang out in Hanoi. She tells her of her dream to go overseas but her English is too bad. She needs an IELTS score of 6.5 and it's very hard. Her Canadian friend is very confident even though she speaks no Vietnamese. The foreigners have a charmed life in Vietnam – except for the pricing. They are charged triple once the staff realise that the Canadian is paying.

Her father who is a professor earns 3 million *dong* a month. He has to do lots of tutoring on the side to keep his family in style.

The Canadian asks her whether there is a lot of censorship in Vietnam.

'No,' she says. 'That is in the past.'

Melbourne

She did not tell her sister that she was leaving for good when she left Vietnam. She told her by letter that she was staying in Melbourne, that she had fallen in love.

She knows that her in-laws think she only married for permanent residency. Better that than to suffer in a refugee camp or a detention centre. She does volunteer work for the local Vietnamese Community Association, knowing that they are conspiring for democracy in Vietnam. Someone has to campaign for freedom while they produce movies like *Indochine* which is just communist propaganda.

She hates the communists for taking her father away and breaking his spirit in the re education camps. He was too intelligent and too vocal.

There is freedom in Australia and they fly the Southern flag yellow with red stripes on festival days in the streets. The local Vietnamese who are politically active write long tracts that are published in Australia and America – anywhere but in Vietnam.

But the Australians? No one seems to care.

San Francisco

They eat *pho* in Orange County in Little Saigon. Up on the screen *Paris by Night* videos blare for the oldies. *Pho* is cheap and good and her friends giggle and laugh about the latest exploits at college. She fiddles with her earrings after eating. Her stomach complains bitterly and she goes to the restroom while the others are busy.

When she reaches the toilet she throws up.

Feeling much lighter she rinses her mouth out with water. Her ex-boyfriend isn't talked about anymore which she was dreading. She's looking for someone new but she'd rather in her secret self be alone. No one really wants to be with her or to know her properly.

No one really knows her at all.

Hanoi

At home the maid serves dinner, rice and bony chicken with fish sauce salad. She eats daintily, tonight her class mates are going out to karaoke for the last time before exams. Impatiently she waits for her father to come home. The bribes his students give him will go towards her education and entertainment. Even with her connections she still has to give a gift to her teachers to ensure that she will pass.

Sydney

It's time for Viet Community Radio – *Viet Girls Down Under.* The others have gone to Canberra to demonstrate on the anniversary of the fall of Saigon. They thought it was just an excuse to go clubbing with the Vietnamese Social Club but quickly find out that it is much more than that. On the program they play parts of *Symphony 75* by a Vietnamese expatriate which contains motifs of traditional Vietnamese folk songs.

San Francisco

The next morning her mother is beaming. She has risen early in the day after the night shift to make her breakfast.

'What's the occasion mom?' she asks.

'I've saved up enough for us both to go to Vietnam,' her mother smiles as she serves her some rice porridge.

'To Vietnam?!' She tries to hide her horror. She doesn't want to go back to a third world country. The guilt of the *Viet Kieu* escaping to a better life weighs on her. She feels the urge to throw up and chokes on it.

'We'd have to avoid our relatives though, unless you can contribute some money,' her mother continues hopefully. 'They will expect gifts from us.'

Family obligation pulls on her like an undertow. She will have to go. She will forego her allowance. There is no way out of it.

Melbourne

She visits Maribyrnong Detention Centre. A Vietnamese grandmother is there, about to be deported. She had covered up for her grandson who deals in heroin, and now the government, having had her spend time in jail, wants to deport her back to Vietnam.

Whenever she visits the detention centre she feels angry. Angry at the security measures, the plastic wristband snapped around her wrist, being told not to take any possessions into the visiting area, how the detainees are strip searched in the stress room before seeing visitors and afterwards.

Ba is resigned to her fate. It is her sacrifice for her children, to go back to a country that she has not seen for forty years. Ba will never again see the grandson she has protected.

Irrationally she too wishes she was going back. But only by choice. She clings to her Australian citizenship as a defence against bad luck.

On the way home on the tram she wonders at her freedom, being able to ride on a tram.

Hanoi

At karaoke a desperate boy in an ill-fitting shirt and slacks makes calf's eyes at her. She turns away and sings loudly to her girlfriends knowing that he is socially inept and his parents are from the country. They only tolerate him because he speaks English better than the rest of them.

'Music makes the bourgeois rebel,' she swoons like Madonna in the bright stage lights. Her friends cheer and for a moment she goes with the flow, transported, and doesn't care about what anyone else thinks.

Sydney

Identity. Hybridity. Who are you? I am Vietnamese–Aus-tray-lian. We mince our words and dance around cross-cultural concepts mining our mixed feelings for art. Cabramatta is our spawning ground.

One of my friends goes back to Vietnam on an artist's residency. She is followed by the secret police. There are four rules of writing in Vietnam she was told, by an author who had to wait six years to be published after the censors had finished with his book. Don't write against the government. Not too much sex or violence. And don't discriminate against the ethnic minorities.

Melbourne

She pens a desperate article to the local paper protesting at the treatment of refugees – knowing it won't be published. There is no censorship in Australia except market-driven desire – but this too is a form of gagging.

When she finishes she puts down her pen and stares out at her empty grassy suburban backyard. This is paradise. She bursts into tears.

Saigon

Ho Chi Minh City is a blast of hot air in the face. Full-on neon signs, mopeds, fashions and KFC. She quickly revises her ignorance, they see no paddy fields until they go for a trip out of Saigon. Her cousins flash with bright tinted fingernails take her on wild trips on the back of their mopeds. She envies them and their confidence until she realises they share a room with their brothers and sisters and parents and have no privacy to their thoughts at all. Beggars see her on the street holding out their hands and she shrinks away from them guilty of wealth. This could be her, she thinks, begging on the sidewalk, slaving away to tourists' demands, flashing by on a moped. The possibilities are endless.

Hanoi

When she gets home her father is marking papers.

'This is rubbish!' he mutters under his breath. Her father was educated in the States. He wants his students to stop copying him, but no one would dare desecrate the words of the teacher.

She goes upstairs, up the narrow staircase to their shared sleeping room.

Downstairs her father is playing an opera, of *Lac Long Quan* the dragon king and *Au Co* the mountain fairy. From the one hundred eggs they laid come fifty sons and fifty daughters. At the time of greatest need they will reunite and rejoin the Vietnamese people.

The time of greatest need has passed, she thinks.

Even if they could come, nobody believes in dragons and fairies anymore.

Le Minh Khue

The Concrete Village

The telegram from her brother had read: 'Grandma ruined. Rotten. Back soon.' Na had seen the clerk at the post office scratching her head, puzzled. But she was Roi's sister and understood his language immediately: 'Grandma sick. Dead. Come home.' Terror had stabbed her heart.

Now she is on a train, on her way home.

She is twenty-one years old and her face is as beautiful as the moon and her hair is as smooth as silk and she is tall and slim and has a twenty-four inch waist and knows if she hadn't been lamed from a fever she'd caught at birth, her mother would have made her into some kind of provincial beauty contestant. Instead, she became a teacher, and since graduating has worked in a primary school in the highlands. She considers it a soothing and suitable profession for girl like herself.

Her name, *Na*, Custard Apple, was given to her by her grandma. Grandma had been evacuated from the city during the war, to what became Na's native province. She had married Na's grandpa, a village teacher, and had remained there ever since, performing her father's traditional work, preparing medicinal herbs for the women in her neighborhood. Grandma drank tea perfumed with jasmine, enjoyed sugarcane steamed with pomelo blossoms in winter, and dressed herself in cotton and raw silk. 'An early eighteenth century antique,' Na's younger brother would call her. His name is *Roi*, Rose Apple, but at some point he decided to change it to *Thanh Hung*, meaning Green Bear. He is nineteen now and burns through three packs of cigarettes a day and when he sings karaoke, he always keeps a girl to caress and fondle at his side. He's content, he tells Na, to live day by day, 'running on idle' he calls it, letting the antiques compete with each other in preaching to him, their words 'dirt in his ears'. It pains Na to watch her brother behave like a caricature, to see him run through his life without direction, his desires coaxed only by the riot of advertisements he sees in the streets. But what can she do?

There had been, until now, five people in her family: her parents, her grandma, her brother and herself. And another under their roof who might be counted as the sixth. But Na refuses to think of Thang as Roi's sibling. He's an orphan, a distant relative of her mother's, who had taken him in after he'd lost his parents. He grew up with Na, went to school, and ever since, until he went into the army, had worked for her family like a house slave. He did everything. He was utterly different from the rest of her family. Especially Roi.

On the day she had packed her bags to leave for the teacher training college in the highlands, it had been Thang who had gone with her to the railway station. She had stood next to him in the twilight, waiting for the evening train, feeling low, conscious of her deformed foot. Thang, as always, had been comforting. Roi, on the other hand, never called her by her name, only Full-Stop-and-Comma, meaning one leg straight and the other bent. She could see it angered Thang when Roi called her that, and grandma's face would tighten whenever she heard Roi's callous laughter at Na's misfortune. Grandma and Thang. They had been her true family. What would she have now?

The train pulls into the station. She sees her father waiting, framed by her window, all dressed up in a red tie and an embroidered shirt – a black armband is the only sign on his body that someone has died. Under him is a gleaming new motorbike. Na stares at the black armband, and it hits her again that grandma has really died. She sobs as she disembarks and goes to him.

'Where is she, dad?'

'We buried her yesterday. Why did it take you so long to get here?'

'As soon as I got Roi's telegram I came straight home.'

'That damn Roi!' her father shakes his head. 'He only brings us misery. I told him to notify you immediately. He probably stopped by some bar and forgot all about it – he's hopeless.'

Na stares at her father and swallows hard. That such a task was entrusted to Roi!

She sits silently behind him on the motorbike. Eucalyptus borders the road leading to the village, and a canal runs parallel to the rows of trees. The village is the same, yet different. Two new karaoke bars stand behind some heaps of straw strewn with buffalo dung. Teenagers in jeans, their hands and feet cracked and calloused, lean against each other in front of the bars. They ogle Na and yell something filthy at her. For some reason, she remembers a phrase from *The Odyssey:* 'words on wings'. Disgusting, sticky wings. As her father drives through the village, she sees straw is still spread everywhere, drying. In spite of motorbikes, in spite of karaoke music, in spite of the stink of gasoline fumes that seeps into each kitchen.

The house where she'd grown up is near the main road, an area where the streets are all paved. There is the usual cluster of shops and restaurants, the headquarters of the People's Committee, but she's heard that several massage parlors have opened here also now, catering to men from the village and township. The houses of the people who live in this area seem to be competing with each other to imitate building styles currently fashionable in the city. Her eyes are confused by the jumble of square and pyramid roofs growing helter skelter, painted as gaudily as a circus act. Her parents' house itself has been renovated into a square cement cake, topped with a pointed squiggle of a tower, like a minaret. Her father and mother had expanded it right over the garden where Grandma used to grow vegetables to sell in the market. Looking at it hurts Na's eyes. Inside, everything is cluttered and jammed together, evoking in her the same feeling of chaos she'd had looking at the village center. She remembers that when her father and mother had modernised the place, they had moved Grandma's bed back by the wall on the west side, and Grandma had moaned to Na: 'Everywhere I look is cement. When I lie on the bed, my back aches like I've been beaten.' When she'd said that, Na's mother had given her a dirty look. 'You're only saying that to cause trouble,' she'd said. 'You want to be like a crab, stuck crawling in the same mud for its whole life.'

Now that Grandma is gone, Na thinks, the house will probably be even more chaotic.

Thang is waiting for her at the gate. When he takes her hands, she feels the grease on his and understands that, as always, her parents have assigned everything that needs to be done to Thang. He stands silently now, his face strained with grief. Next to him, Roi flashes his teeth at her and winks, as if to say see how I'm pretending to behave properly. She feels even more pity for her grandmother. But at least her mother hasn't dressed herself in her usual fancy, sweeping skirt; she wears a pair of black trousers and a white mourning blouse. Sobbing, she pulls Na to her, then wipes her nose on her sleeve. Her mother's nose, Na sees, is dry. So are her eyes. She smiles slightly at Na. Father's pretense at sorrow, mother's air of liberation from a burden, Roi's take-it-easy mood suddenly make her feel shaky, as if the earth has moved out from under her and she's trying to walk on waves. Only the sight of Thang steadies her. When Grandma was alive, she never had this feeling of being out of balance. Thang moves closer, as if he sees her distress and wants to help her. He's only a distant relative of her mother's, doesn't have a single drop of her paternal grandma's blood in him, but in this room only his eyes that are reddened from crying.

He and Na light incense sticks on grandma's altar. Looking at her photograph, both of them have the same thought. This family is broken.

Na goes into the kitchen. Roi follows her, asking if she had brought him any blackball from the highlands.

Meaning opium. 'Of course not,' she says. Her brother, she knows, will mock her empty hands, her lack of ambition. 'You fool,' he'll say, 'where you sit is where you'll rot.'

He says it now. Then whispers furtively, 'Listen, when you go back, I'll give you enough money to buy a kilo. I know a place where I can move it – we'll split the profit.'

Thang has come in, and he squats in silence now, working on a broken kerosene heater. Roi grabs a piece of rolled pâté and a handful of sticky rice from the tray being prepared for Grandma's altar, tilts his head backwards and tosses them both into his maw. He chews and swallows like a snake devouring a rat, then stands in front of the tray as if at attention and snaps his hand to his forehead in a military salute. Na silently replaces what he's taken with new pâté and sticky rice, so the offerings will be pure and untouched when they go on the altar.

'Why did you send me the telegram so late?' she reproaches him.

'You should be grateful to me. Why come back early, when all you're going to do is wear mourning clothes and roll around the cemetery all day? No fun in that.'

Exasperated, she says: 'Roi, what are you going to become if you continue to live this way?'

He grins at her. Their father, he tells her, has been getting rich with his land deals, and going out to visit his 'noodles', his girlfriends, nearly every night; their mother has taken to filling up her closet with clothes she scavenged from everywhere. 'Go up and see, you don't believe me. When you open that closet, it smells like shit. She has to wear a different skirt every evening, and don't think she isn't stepping out too, just like the old man. Now that grandma's gone, she'll be free to spread herself around, much as she wants.'

'But how do you live?' she insists.

'Me, I take whatever I want from them and they don't dare say a thing. They did and they know I'd put a word in the ear of the right people, blast apart this house like with dynamite and be long gone for Hong Kong. Not like Miss Full-Stop-and-Comma, who's so dumb and so full of all that morality bullshit passed down from Grandma, she'd never grab a boat ride out. Don't you worry about this Thanh Hung – I'll always have an exit.'

'That's enough,' Na felt sick. 'Please don't say another word.'

'Look, you want my advice – if I were you I wouldn't waste myself by holding out. You're a cripple, but your waist is small and your breasts are big – you still have value. Go to the provincial capital and let someone 'pop' you for half-an-ounce of gold. Use it as capital, and keep moving on...'

Suddenly he is flying through the air, through the door, his head hitting the concrete steps in the yard. Like a kung fu movie, Na thinks. Feeling detached, as if she truly was watching a film, she sees Thang pick up the half-repaired kerosene heater and hurl it onto Roi's back.

Her mother screams as if the house is on fire. 'We're already in mourning for an old person; what are you trying to do – put us in mourning for a young one as well? You ingrate, Thang – do you see what you've done?'

Father rolls up his sleeves and grabs a cleaver. The guests there for the third day of the funeral hold him back. The scene is as raucous as a fire in a market. Thang stands in front of the door and says calmly: 'I'll tell you, Uncle and Aunt, I don't care if I go to jail – I still want to break his jaw. He's a devil, not a human being.'

Na doesn't go to Roi, but stands between Thang and her furious parents, protecting him with her frail body. She thinks of herself that way, frail, and suddenly she sees herself as a flowering mustard green in her grandma's garden. Roi has staggered to his feet, his face gaudy with blood. The sight of it freezes the air in the room like cement. He wipes his skin with his sleeve, at once looking faded and weakened. Na thinks: So devils bleed.

Roi limps back in, sticks his finger into Thang's face. 'If you're wise, you'll disappear. I'm not a soldier like you, but I have my own teeth to bite you with – I'll come at you from behind one day, so don't wait for me to show up in your face, get it? Get lost, you old woman – I'm tired of hearing your stupid opera songs. I'm not dead yet; I still have to live out this stupid life. Get me some cloth for this blood, someone!'

Oh Grandma, Na thinks. You've only been dead for three days. When you were alive, father had to come home on time in the evening and mother had to say 'please have your dinner now,' to you, even if afterwards she did give you a dirty look. You didn't care – as long as she was polite.

And when Roi sold his motorbike to get money for the karaoke bars, he had to do it behind your back, and at home, in front of you, he kept his mouth shut since he knew that his language was no longer the language that human beings spoke to each other. And when the garden had been cemented over and you had no more vegetables to water, you worked so meticulously on your herbal medicines, and once when you were drying some herbs, Roi put a piece of dried cow dung in the middle of the tray. And you just looked at him calmly and said: 'This one is sick, but his illness is difficult to cure, so let life cure it for him.' And when Thang enlisted in the army, you said, 'Joining up is good, grandson. Trouble is everywhere, but in the military, people still know how to be afraid. When one knows how to fear, things are still in order.' And it was because of your advice, grandma, that I overcame my doubts about going to the highlands and becoming a teacher. 'People will tell you that place gathers dust,' you'd said, 'but that job will suit you.'

Grandma, you stayed in one place all your life, but you knew everything. In the end, you hardly spoken to my parents, Father with his land development schemes with state land and dressing himself up like a big grasshopper, and mother with her own under-the-table business, and tawdry second-hand clothes, and blue eye shadow, and gambling. You would only shake your head and cluck your tongue. Oh, Grandma. Life drifted by your white hair like a filthy ghost. It thrived in spite of your goodness and you were alone in it except for Thang and me.

Now Thang gathers the few clothes he'd left in the house. Roi goes and lies down. Mother sits on an armchair, stretching out her legs. 'All my life, I've been a horse and a donkey, carrying all of them on my back,' she sighs. 'And as soon as one grows feathers and wings, then he betrays me immediately. I'll tell you, if my Roi dies, I'll destroy everything and flee!'

'Enough, Mum,' Na says. 'He's all right now.'

'Daughter, you may be lame, but your head is hard as ironwood. I've told you over and over to quit that lousy job and come take care of my shop. But you don't care a bit. You're infected by the morality of all those old generation crabs that crawl around in the mud – all you want to do is sneak back into those mountains and jungles and get bitten by mosquitoes. I'll tell you – don't crawl back and expect me to care for you when you get sick. You're a donkey that loves to strap on its own heavy load.'

Thang slings his knapsack over his shoulder and walks out to the small yard. He turns back to look at the cement box of a house. Father's fury has passed. Both he and Na's mother turn away, as if there never had been a Thang, at once nephew and servant, working for them for years like a beast of burden, and now leaving without a word of farewell from anyone.

'I think you were right,' Na says. 'That kick you gave Roi was too generous – much less than he deserved.'

'What else could I do?'

Oh, Grandma. Both Na and Thang let out a sigh and look around. On the right side of the village, now being paved over, the remnants of a sandy hillock rise from the middle of the rice fields. For many years, a grove of kapok trees had grown here, and it was rumored to be haunted by ghosts, so that for a long time the land gangsters hadn't dared touch it. A small, moss-covered shrine to the man who had planted the kapok trees had stood in the middle of the grove; it was always covered with flowers and incense sticks left as offerings. In the season when the kapok blooms, the whole hillock would turn red as if the green rice paddy had caught fire down its middle. It was so beautiful that Na would have to tighten her heart to repress her sobs. She was a small girl then and Grandma would hold her hand as they walked along the field of mustard greens, laced with brightly colored flowers, Grandma's hair a white cloud floating through reds and yellows. At the shrine, Grandma would light incense sticks while Na wandered about picking up the kapok flowers that carpeted the ground. Around them, birds would fly up from their nests.

Until recently that hillock had remained an intact mystery in the middle of a world of noisy trucks transporting lime and sand back and forth, transforming the village into a heap of concrete. Then last year, the sandy rise and its grove of kapok trees came under attack. First, branches were cut for firewood. Then people began tearing up the soil to look for treasure – a story had gone around that during the resistance against the French, people had buried their gold and jewelry there. No one knew from where the rumor came, but it seemed to drive many villagers mad with greed. It was said that a whole family had died because of their suspicions about each other's discovery of treasure. One member of the family – Cuong – had poured gasoline over the others and burnt them alive, then disappeared. According to Roi, he snuck out of the country by boat, heading for Hong Kong, but on the way, death found him, and his corpse was thrown into the sea. At least that was the story that had reached the village.

Oh, Grandma. Na and Thang remain standing, looking over at what had been the kapok grove. Finally, Thang says: 'Last month some foreigners came and staked out that whole area, including the grove. Now it's gone.'

'Why do they keep tearing up the land like that?'

Thang shrugged 'I heard they're going to build a motorbike factory there. So there will be plenty of motorbikes for people to ride. Grandma felt terribly sorry for that grove.

She told me she might leave this earth with the kapoks. And she did just that.'

It is a half hour before the evening train arrives. They are at the railroad station now. For the first time Na senses that Thang is nervous. Keeping his knapsack on his back, he paces to and fro while Na sits on a cement bench near the tracks. She wants to cry. Her lame foot hurts and she misses her grandma and she'll be far away from Thang – how will she manage in this world?

'How is the area where you work?' Thang asks.

'It no longer seems tranquil,' she blurted. 'The gold miners have started pouring in. I can't keep the children calmed down so they can study. But I won't come back here to take care of mother's shop.'

'No, don't do that. Keep on teaching. Then I'll see what I can do.'

'What can you do, Thang? You're a soldier; you're about to be sent to an island.'

'I'll be away for two years. But I'll write, and when I take my annual leave, I'll visit you. Only I won't return to this family anymore. Grandma is gone.'

'I feel like life is the same as in wartime,' Na says. 'I'm frightened all the time – the same fear that I have when I think of Roi.'

'No, don't be afraid,' Thang says. As if to say that with him in the world, she has nothing to fear. Na shakes hands with him when the train arrives. A little dazed from grief, but feeling a tiny spark of hope.

The next day, as she packs to return to her school, she finds a crumpled paper inside her handbag, scrawled with some hasty lines, a date. A note from Thang.

Roi snatches it up, reads it. 'Careful – he's your long-range gun cousin, sis. If you have kids, they may be full-stops-and-commas, just like you. Hey, maybe our old man and old lady are distant relatives too — maybe that's why they gave birth to a cripple, right?'

Na looks into her brother's shameless face. There are so many like him now, she thinks. People who are no longer human. But what are they then? It wasn't fair to call them animals. Animals didn't now how to be cruel.

'Take care, my brother,' she says. 'You still have a long life in front of you.'

'Hey, my sister, what do I care about my little piece of life? Old Grandma is dead, and there's no one who feels pity for me anymore. The only feelings the old man and old lady have are for money.'

'At least you still have me,' Na whispers, her eyes brimming with tears. All Roi has, she knows, is his own self-pity.

She lights incense sticks and bows down to say goodbye to her grandma's spirit. She leaves. The grove of kapok trees and its hill have been devastated and levelled and are about to be covered with concrete. Soon lines of motorbikes will pour out, spewing their chaotic noises. Will Grandma be at peace in the other world?

Translated by Phan Thanh Hao and Wayne Karlin

Steve Kelen

Hanoi Girls

Hanoi most sensible of cities –
at night the traffic finally does stop
and a great hush of sleeping
descends: a curtain drawn
down by good spirits
and ghosts about to start work.
Not a sound for kilometres
except a cough deep in a house
a lonely bicycle bell, a word called
out from a dream, a stray bird drunk.
It's dark on the pavement
but the sky glows with smog.
Quiet all night until a rooster crows
sunrise somewhere in the rice fields
behind the rebuilt suburbs
north of the river.
The people who sleep
in the street hammocks are first up
and busy. Everyone's going to work
in an office, school, a sweatshop
or a street stall, hot days get louder
with all the talking it's as if everyone's shouting.
Slow rivers of traffic meander.
Suddenly the girls are there, dozens
then hundreds riding motor scooters

braking gently at the traffic light in Ly Thai To Street
now the traffic flows like ripples on a quiet lake.
Cyclo drivers and labourers
might stop for a moment, consider
the day's hot slog is almost worth it,
to see their city's young women growing beautiful
and rich. They remember to be kind to strangers
who try to compare their less cultivated worlds.
What greater joy could there be than to see
Hanoi girls ride motor scooters,
pillion sisters sitting side saddle.
When the traffic slows they gossip
like tigresses with girls on the other scooters.
Silks and nylon made sure the war
was won by the miniskirt allied with knee-high
leather boots or diaphanous sandals.
Hanoi girls out-glamour the Italians
they fit imitation Gucci so much better
and bring a sense of reticence to leather.
Their mobile phones ring urgently –
lightning strikes Hanoi's holy mountain
friendly rain clouds gather.
Dial an ancestor – mothers and grandmothers
were the bravest women warriors
Vietnam had seen for centuries.
They fought the invaders and lost husbands,
brothers and sons, sisters and daughters.
Everyone lost somebody
when the heartless and stupid ruled America
sent over soldiers and bombers.
The war ended, and lots of granddaughters,
lots of grandsons came into the world.
Over time the hard times got better
there was food for almost everyone.

The population skyrocketed, as they say, and
Hanoi's granddaughters grew up and dressed to kill.
Commuting on their scooters they chatter: are love poems
more romantic more sincere than a gift of flowers,
or just cheaper? There's the wicked past of a Government
Minister who used to be a Saigon pop singer –
too wicked to mention. French football stars
are heading to Vietnam to help improve the local game
ha ha it won't work – the boom in Hanoi's real estate
goes through the roof, So-and-so is starting up
a new business, the new style of Hué cooking
is not so new, those horoscopes in *Sport and Culture*
magazine are so vague to be nearly always right
and the interview with David Beckham
is almost the same as last month's.
To ensure good daughters have everything their mothers
and fathers missed, the sacrifices made are tougher
than to much loved ancestors –
money to buy a good scooter comes harder
than fake banknotes burnt at an altar.
Hanoi girls pull up at the traffic light
knee-high boots and sheer sandals
rest on the road, mobile phones ring in
a business deal, an old apartment to renovate,
lunch at West Lake. As grandma said,
'when no bombs fall on the polity
it's fine to indulge frivolity.'
Hanoi girls are serious, study and work
their way to the top if that's where life leads.

Nguyen Thi Thu Hue

Believe Me

'Don't go, darling. Believe me! Please forgive me! I love you so much,' Hoai cried. Her beautiful face was soaked with tears.

'Forget it; I'm out of here. Good-bye! Don't waste your time coming after me,' Thang said. He was a well-dressed, bookish young man whose face at the moment was flushed with rage. He snatched his bag off the table and strode to the door.

'Please listen to me. I have never in my life asked anyone for forgiveness, but now I'm begging you. You have to believe me!' She grabbed his right arm.

He cast off her hand violently and continued towards the gate. Outside, a brand new blue motorbike, a Model 82-89, was parked, waiting for him. He mounted it and roared away.

★   ★   ★

Hoai leaned her forehead against the windowpane and continued to weep. She stood for a long time, miserable, her heart breaking inside her chest. She didn't hear her classmates come back into the dorm.

'Hey everyone, come here, look at this – it's our own 'PM Thatcher' standing here and crying her eyes out,' shouted Loudmouth Phuong, pointing at Hoai. 'What a bolt from the blue! A storm must be brewing,' she teased. Everyone laughed.

They rushed into the room, piling their books onto their bunk beds, then gathering around Hoai, hugging her. She tightened her lips and pushed them away, fell on her bed and wept. Her friends left the room quietly, realising now that the situation was serious. Only Thanh lingered behind, changing her clothes. She sang to herself in a low voice:

> Darling, you still live in Hanoi
> Amid the fragrance of the ylang-ylang blossoms
> And the sweet scent of the milk flowers
> That waft here to me and tell me you are still mine…

'Shut up!' Hoai shouted. 'Go away and leave me some peace.'

'Where should I go? I just bought some vegetables and the bathroom's crowded, and I may as well just stay here and cook some dinner for my greedy boyfriend. Whenever he gets hungry, he gets angry at me,' Thanh said.

'He's rich – why do you have to cook for him? Why doesn't he take you out?' Hoai said. She had stopped crying.

'He's stingy and eating out costs a lot of money. Besides he doesn't make that much money.'

'Then why do you cling to him?'

'Well, he's not that tight with me. He shares whatever he earns. Maybe he's a little rude, but at least he's honest. He only eats with me, and he only sleeps with me and never even thinks about other women. What else can I expect to find here? We're fifth year students and we're going to graduate soon; our glory days are over. Now's the time to grab some young Hanoian and marry him, so we can stay here for good.' Thanh was getting emotional. 'Now tell me why you're crying? I don't remember you crying this much even when you heard about your mother's illness back in the country.'

'Thang broke up with me.'

'Really? But he loves you so much.' Thanh's surprise was genuine.

'It's my fault, Thanh, all my fault. What can I do now?' Hoai started to cry again.

'Beg him for forgiveness. He'd be an ideal husband! If you married him after graduation, you'd be all set to live in Hanoi for the rest of your life, not in that provincial, impoverished little village you came from. His father would find a good position for you for sure. It's a golden opportunity, Hoai, make sure you don't miss it – you'd be the luckiest girl in our class. I have no idea what's in store for me – maybe my boyfriend will only enjoy me until graduation, and then take a French leave. God knows!'

'No, everything's over for me.'

'Our fate is so cruel! Why were we born and raised in the country? Who will look twice at us here? And it will be even worse if we go back home. Where will we find a university graduate to marry? And those ignorant country bumpkins at home – which of them has the guts to ask for the hand of refined young ladies like us? We wouldn't fit in either world. All the time, we dream about wonderful love affairs, like yours, and yet...'

'Hello girls! What are you talking about?' Dam wheeled his Chinese bicycle into the hallway. There was a bunch of juicy mulberries in the bike basket.

'Boring stuff, Greedy Dam.' Thanh kissed his cheek. Hoai turned away, her shoulders trembling with tension.

A sneezing fit overcame her. She heard Dam talking to Thanh: 'I'm really hungry. Got anything for me to eat? Look, tonight we'll go see that new American flick, *The Corpse in the Mountains*. We saw half of it already, remember – over milkshakes at the coffee house.'

'Dinner's ready. You're going to have a fantastic meal tonight.'

Dam told her what he had earned that day. Thanh told him about her classes. Neither paid attention to Hoai. In the middle of this female dormitory, they were behaving like a married couple. They kept nothing from her, even the most sensitive issues.

Hoai stood up and left.

A wind was blowing violently through the campus. The last rays of the sun had vanished somewhere in the twilight sky. Students were busy with their routines. Some were taking pails out to fetch water from the pump; others were bringing back meals from the kitchen. From the first floor of the dormitory she could hear a catchy tune sung by a carefree girl.

Hoai's eyes brimmed with tears.

* * *

'Who can beat our champion, Hoai! I'll be the judge – whoever wins gets a pack of 555s, and the loser treats us for sugarcane juice. As for me, I'll egg on the competitors and buy the cigarettes.'

'That's not enough!' chimed another. 'Don't be so cunning. Let's just see who the winner is: Hoai the Beautiful or Toan the Short.'

'How can you compare shrimpy Toan to me? You'd better just give up now, Toan. I'm going to beat everyone. I just made a whole bunch of money,' Hoai said proudly.

'I've never been defeated by anyone – let alone some pretty girl,' Toan said defiantly.

Five water pipes were brought out and filled with tobacco. The two contestants were off. They smoked and smoked and, as usual, Hoai won.

'Well done, bravo…Hoai!' everyone shouted.

'OK, then, I'll treat you to all the beer you can drink and all the dog-meat you can eat. To the restaurant!' cried the judge.

That was the carefree life Hoai had been leading for two years. After her first term at the university, she began to act like the Vinh City girl – born and bred – that she was. Competitive. Thriving. An intelligent but lazy student with round eyes, a charming smile and a pretty face. Liked more by young men than her female classmates.

At one point, she had become notorious when she behaved atrociously after she'd received a 'two-mark' on a Russian test. In fact, she utterly hated Russian, while she loved English very much, and could sing some tunes in English beautifully. She had been called to the Dean's office to discuss her problems.

'It's true, I drink rice wine and smoke tobacco,' she said. 'But I haven't caused anyone any problems. And I haven't done anything wrong.'

When she got back to her room, she began to scream at her friends. 'Who snitched on me to the Dean? Even if I want to make out with some guy in this room, that's my business. If I steal any of your stuff, or seduce your sweethearts, then report me – otherwise keep out of my life!' she shouted. Then she left and stayed out all night.

By her second year, everyone knew about her. She drank brandy, smoked tobacco and danced all night with her favourite boys.

One day, she led a strange young man into the dormitory. Hoai's roommates were surprised at his innocent air. He had manners. He was well dressed, elegant, soft-spoken. And he was very considerate to Hoai.

'This is Thang,' Hoai introduced him. 'He's a radio engineer, working for a research firm.' She had met him through her older sister, when he had been in Vinh on a short business trip.

The new Hoai amazed everyone. No longer was she 'Hoai the Brazen.' She had overnight become a well-educated young lady from a refined family.

The two fell in love.

★ ★ ★

Love was a magic wand. Hoai had been transformed in every way. In the past, her parents would send her a few words of advice and some money they saved from their hard labour in the country, whenever they heard about their daughter's carousing. She would grab the money, discard the note. Now everything was different. Since Tet she'd sent them scores of letters, saved up most of the money they had sent. She was like a crab shedding its former shell. Her friends and teachers were happy to see the change, and loved seeing the blissful couple together. That afternoon, their love affair had reached its one-year anniversary.

Now everything had come apart so quickly. She didn't understand any of it.

★ ★ ★

The previous evening, Thang had told her: 'Tomorrow is Mum's birthday. It'll be a good chance to introduce you to my family and friends. Then next week, you're going to have several days off to prepare your long essay, so we can go to your hometown and I can ask your parents for permission to marry you. We can have the wedding party at the end of the second semester, just before you leave university. That will give all our friends and your teachers a chance to attend the ceremony, and we can leave a fine impression on everyone when we go.'

Nestled in Thang's arms, Hoai was beside herself with joy. She had never dreamt a day would come when she would wear a bridal dress, cradle a big, beautiful bouquet of white flowers in her arms, ascend into a festooned wedding car to the strains of Mendelssohn's *March*, and then live happily ever after in Hanoi. She would be the luckiest of all her classmates.

The next evening, she arrived at Thang's house carrying a huge, decorated cake for his mother's birthday. Every member of Thang's clan gazed at her tenderly. Champagne was poured and toasts made and Hoai felt she was entering a dream, filled with the scents of perfume and of the foreign cigarettes she had given up. She laughed, spoke naturally, and soon began to smoke as well. For the first time in Thang's presence, she drank, one glass after another. What was the point of concealing her true self when she would soon be his wife? As she became drunker, she started to dance the lambada and disco with other young men, under the dim, coloured light.

'Why not a waltz or tango?' Thang asked her, his voice strange.

'Those are for beginners. I like exciting rhythms.'

'I've never seen you dance like that before. At your friends' birthdays, you would only eat and drink and stand around.'

'Times have changed – I'm about to become your wife. I can't hide things anymore.'

Thang tightened his lips.

Another waltz came to its end. Next was a disco. Hoai stepped out onto the floor, feeling a bit dizzy. She felt as if she were being lifted off the ground, as her feet glided over the floor. Her body convulsed with the beat. She tossed her hair and flapped her arms to the quick, sharp beat. Looking at her, amazed, Thang thought: why she looks like one of those whores who make their livings at sleazy bars.

'Let's have a lambada,' he suggested.

Under the dim veil of smoke, under the coloured lights, in that air thick with perfume and smoke, Hoai swung her body so gracefully that every eye in the room was fixed on her.

'My God, what have you brought home?' Thang's mother asked. She went upstairs without saying another word.

Thang told everyone to leave. He turned off the hi-fi. Everyone stopped dancing and silently filed out. Only Hoai was still on the floor, still swinging her body. Madly swinging.

'Excuse me!' Thang said icily. 'Allow me to take you home.'

Suddenly she understood what had happened.

★ ★ ★

On the way home, she told him everything about her past life. She had thought that since they were to be married, she should hide nothing. She had changed for the better, and that should be what mattered. But Thang was bitter. 'I thought you were someone else. I want to marry a decent girl, not a whore. You were very clever; you took me in.' He took a deep breath. 'There will be nothing more between us. Don't bother me again.'

★ ★ ★

'Come on, get up, Hoai. Join us for dinner,' Thanh urged. Her boyfriend was sitting behind her.

Once Hoai had asked: 'Why do you always call him 'greedy' if you love him so much?' And Thanh answered: 'Because I do love him. And I have nothing to lose as long as he gives me money. All I have to do is prepare delicious meals and satisfy his carnal desires. I only fall in love with well-off men.'

'Why?'

'With such men, we have nothing to worry about. They can afford everything. Girls like us can't just go back to our villages with just a tertiary degree, but here in Hanoi there are swarms of postgraduates. Our motto is: 'once we've arrived, we're here forever'. And besides guys like Dam, who would ever even look at us country girls?'

Now Hoai said: 'I've lost my appetite.'

'Forget about him! Well…anyhow, we still have a long way to go. I'll find you another guy like mine, from the same town. Okay? It's our destiny! What else can we do? Forget all your fairy tales. Get real. You were in love with him for over a year. That'll do. Poor country girls! Come to the movies with us and forget about him.'

Hoai's eyes brimmed with tears.

She lamented her life. 'Mum and Dad, why couldn't you be here with me, so I could be less lonely? What's the use of all my studying now? My future is nothing but emptiness.'

A sad tune drifted up from the first floor.

I still have you, my solitary almond tree
Growing on an isolated street corner
Under a lonely winter moon that year

Hoai rushed out of her room. She went down the street, to her favourite hangout. The bartender recognised her right away, even though she'd been gone for a year.

Translated by Tran Ngoc and Wayne Karlin

N. B. Najima

At the Mermaid Stairwell

The three boys are inseparable. When I ride up they are standing at the gate, their heads wrapped in black and white scarves. Two are smoking. The smoke twists up straight and stands beside them like porcelain shadows. There is no wind. I walk straight at them – exaggeratedly so, each coming heel placed in a line with each leaving set of toes. They don't speak but the short one, the sweet-eyed one, smiles slightly as they lead me to the house where their father, the ambassador, reclines on a lemon yellow hassock.

The moment I enter he stands and cries, 'You look delightful!' kisses my cheeks and motions gracefully to the parlour. We sit in one motion, at right angles, the ambassador on the lemon hassock and me on a chair. He is a distinguished man. Slight, greying and a bit stooped. Shortsighted.

The maid brings us glasses of mint sherbet; I taste mine with my lips and set it down. The table between us is draped with an embroidered silk runner. It has squares of blue and yellow and orange and green and I worry about staining it but no one reacts. The ceilings are high, lost. The walls lean away and lean back again through mirrors shaped like daggers and surrounded by tiny red embroidered arabesques.

The boys never pass over the threshold. I see them through the open doorway out back, crossing the courtyard between the kitchen and the braziers, their black and white scarves hanging down their backs like misplaced tails, their heels striking the flagstones at all angles. I never hear them speaking, only laughing. They must think together without speech.

They reach in through the doorway to hand platters to the maids, who then kneel at our table to serve us. No one moves to draw back the silk runner. I eat cautiously with a white napkin spread over my lap. The ambassador picks dreamily, directly off the platters, his eyes lost in the lost corners of the ceiling, telling me all about his wife. She isn't here. She's back in that country of his that does not exist.

When I was younger, men would talk about the wives they hoped to have or have not. Or they talked of their own mothers or their aspirations. That was polite foreplay then; opening shutters between intelligent people.

Later they spoke of ex-wives – theirs or their friends'. They talked of love and marriage and children and their syllables had hard edges that cut around the silverware and the sweating water glasses. There was so little whimsy; so much hurt couched inside of gruff orders.

Now, these men (like the distinguished, affable ambassador) talk about their wives in the present tense, but often removed. They play Brahms or Coltrane as background music and they don't fuss to apologise or explain. They just state the obvious and portage any judgements cluttering the path of their very linear brains.

'She is there but not here. She is a mother. A tired mother. You are here and I feel fresh. I also feel like olives. Don't you? Let me call for some.'

He claps his hands and the maid runs off to the kitchen where I imagine, but do not see, the three boys smoking into life three slender parallel beasts and telling stories with their thick black eyebrows.

The little sweet-eyed one is a full head shorter than the rest. Once he asked me for the time and when I told it to him he forgot to walk away.

The ambassador sucks on two olives, his eyes closed and his cheeks trembling. Here is a man who knows the value of pleasure. He puts an olive in my mouth and I eat it slowly so that he can pleasure from my pleasure; the pleasure he wants to think he has given me.

'Warda,' he calls me, which means rose. 'You're as beautiful,' he says, 'as the desert in springtime.'

I have never seen the desert but I know that it is dry. 'How can such a dry thing be beautiful?' I ask him.

He laughs. I don't, because I don't understand. It might have been the language – his English is poor, so we use French; my French is not rich but it's enough – but tomorrow I'll understand and still not laugh because it isn't funny. Buffoonery is embarrassing. Wit, now is entirely another matter; something to aspire to.

The ambassador is finished eating and he starts to smoke a tall water pipe with cappuccino-flavoured tobacco. The scent makes me dizzy. He strokes my hair and I remove his gold ring. It is heavy. 'Sapphire,' he tells me, 'from Burma. The embargo keeps the prices down.'

I set it on the checked silk runner next to my sherbet, which has melted, and slip his hand into my dress. He sighs deeply, from his core, long and aching. He sighs so long it takes several minutes for the sigh to reach his nose, vibrate his nostrils and stir his thick white moustache.

He will love me forever, he swears it. Anything I need, anything at all.

Now I *do* laugh, because irony has some wit after all. I need so much! From him, from me, from life. Where do I begin? But I will remember his oath, however insincere, and bank on it for later.

The maid brings our dessert: fresh mango and pineapple in crystal bowls with cream and black, sweet cardamom coffee in demitasse.

'Wouldn't you like a sapphire?' he asks me. 'A heavy, brilliant one like I have on my ring?' He promises me: 'One ruby the colour of a ripe pomegranate seed, one the colour of the flecks of red in a peacock's tail, and one the exact blush of your blood.' He cuts the soft skin between my little and ring fingers with a paring knife and sucks it, hard, his cheeks flattening against his teeth and his eyes closed with that same expression of deep, abandoned pleasure.

It stings and I pull away, gently.

Later I climb down from the lost high corners of the ceiling to fetch some water from the kitchen. It's dark and quiet and I am on my way home. The sweet-eyed boy is still in the courtyard, warming his hands over the brazier's dying coals. This is the first time I have ever seen him alone. He pretends not to have noticed me.

I drink two full glasses of ice water, one after the other, standing at the water bottle with my hand on the spigot. It freezes me through to my arteries. I rinse the glass, put it back in the cupboard and turn to find him standing there with nothing in his hands and nowhere to put his honey eyes.

'I'm on my way home,' I tell him finally.

He says 'I'll drive you' and I'm not sure where to go with that so I agree.

His motorbike is a dark green Piaggio with leather seats. Expensive. He takes off his black and white scarf to strap the helmet on and I glimpse his head. It's bald, absolutely, like a sand-coloured egg. This is unexpected.

I grip the seat so I don't have to put my arms around him but I can't avoid our thighs. They fit together neatly on the soft black leather and underneath the plastic mushroom helmet I am blushing.

He drives fast and in the air – our air, his air, the Piaggio's air; the air of movement and freshness that wasn't there before – the smoke is horizontal and the streets are absolutely pure in solitude and silence.

He shouts a question but I can't hear it so I move closer and tell him, in his ear, my address. He smells of myrrh. We zoom across a roundabout that's empty and dazzling with ropes of white lights the size of acorns. Across the lawn from the Ho Chi Minh Mausoleum he stops. The lights are out here; the guards have gone to bed and the flag is put away. The monument looks like a massive dry rock. Only the flame-like torch of the war memorial still glows down the street, backlighting the flowering trees and keeping us in relief.

The grass was cut today; I smell its fragrance, strong and biting like the soul of water. I slide off and look at him curiously. He steps off too and looks back at me. Pointedly. We both look at the tomb and I wonder out loud, 'Shall we go on then? Or I can walk from here…?'

He is stroking the Piaggio. 'What do you do with the ambassador?' he asks.

'Talk politics, poetry. Sometimes gossip.'

'Like a friend?'

'Like mentor and student.'

'He is as a father to me.'

'He is a good man.'

'Yes.'

'Where is your own father?'

'Away. Do you know my name?'

I shake my head.

'It is Aziz. It means 'dear.' My grandfather gave me this name to be a spell; to endear me to anyone I meet. Including my parents, who had greeted my birth like a funeral.' He squeezes the Piaggio's handlebar and unbuckles his helmet. 'My mother and my twin died when I was born. Have you ever killed someone?'

I smile. 'Not on purpose.'

'Intent and action, you mean?' He speaks quickly. 'I don't believe in that. It's too easy. People believe themselves to be the opposite of how they act.'

I grunt.

'Do you really understand who you are? Does your idea of yourself match with the way you behave?'

Is he digging for information about the ambassador? About our evenings of mint sherbet and dark corners? How awkward. I squat to touch the new grass. I squeeze it with both hands. 'I do my best, like anyone.'

'When you sit alone with the ambassador, who does the talking?'

'He does.'

'You like to listen?'

'Always.'

'Why?'

I laugh. 'What do I learn from speaking aloud things I already know? It's a waste. I'm selfish in that way. No one's perfect.'

'I'd heard that about you; that you listen.'

I look up at him. He looks different from this angle; different as a tall man. 'Is there something you want to say?'

'Yes. And, no.'

There is a long silence. I feel chilled; I hug my knees for warmth and dream about burrowing into the soil, dream that it is warmer down there, warm and close, dream that the worms twine about me like pulsing bracelets and the grass grows from ruby and sapphire roots. So heavy, never to be blown away. Maybe Uncle Ho counts the rubies and sapphires at night, after the lights go out and the standards are rolled up; maybe he has a whole stockpile of plans for his triumphant comeback. I have no doubt that men like him will live again. The rest of us, we have a hope, if we can stop ourselves from frittering it.

'It's cold,' I say finally.

'Are you afraid of water?' Aziz asks hurriedly, as if an idea has just come to him and he's afraid it might go again.

'Only cold water.'

He starts the motorbike and holds out his hand. I climb back on without touching him. We drive up past the presidential palace and the big pagoda, cut through a park, bounce down a narrow alley and rev up a hill to the southern shore of West Lake. It's colder and colder; I grip the seat more tightly and fight the urge to throw my arms around his warm, narrow waist.

He stops at a mermaid stairwell. It is wide, baroque, crumbled and slimy. It runs straight into the water. A row of listless boats are tied in a row along its flanks. Aziz springs lightly into one, unties it and poles it to the edge of the stairs. He holds out his hand and looks up. The black and white scarf, wrapped once more around his head, is gleaming, reflecting the points of light in his eyes. I detour around his hand and board, sitting in the stern. We move out onto the lake. He poles, and then rows, the muscles in his naked forearms bulging. I watch his back and his tail. They part the mist gently.

The shore reeks of dead fish and refuse but once we move past all that it's cleaner, though the air's still so difficult to breathe; too wet; too metallic and heavy, like the ambassador's garish gold ring that I left on the checked silk beside my melted sherbet. His ill-begotten sapphire; didn't he think about labour rights for mine workers? Typical.

Aziz lays a sheet of metal on the bottom of the boat and lights a fire with candle wax and sugar cane stalks. I wonder if he is planning to kill me, and if death will be wet and cold or if it will just taste like worms. I have never minded worms. They have no eyes, no ears, no tongues; they are life whittled down to its essentials.

'You're not afraid?' he asks me.

'No. Why haven't you got any hair?'

'It never grew in. My twin brother pulled it out when I passed him in the womb. He couldn't get to air in time. They pulled his body out to try and save my mother. He was already dead and they found my hair clenched in his fists. My mother died but my aunts remembered the hair. They made it into a myth and then it became truth and none ever grew again on my head. I was a curiosity in school, so I never wanted to go.'

'That must have been difficult.'

'Only at first. My father let me stay at home and take a tutor instead. The tutor taught Abdel as well as me – you know him, the taller one, the ambassador's son. We learned together and became like brothers. When their family left for Paris Abdel became sick without me. My aunts said he was trying to take the place of my dead twin and they quarrelled over it – was it bad luck or good luck? But the ambassador convinced my father to let me go and join them and I did and Abdel was cured and I have travelled with the family ever since.'

'You never went home?'

'Where is home? Home is family, no? Now my family is here.'

The fire burns without smoke. Instead of smoke it gives off sparks and those sparks spiral straight up and make an endless, streaming golden wraith that blocks his face but lights up his eyes. The whole little boat, this funny canoe, is warmed by the fire. I never want to move back into the cold.

He says, 'Just before coming here, in Albania, my brother caught a snake that was crawling in our garden. He pressed its head down with a stick, trapping it there, and called out to me to help him. We watched it thrashing and didn't know what to do: kill it or let it go.'

'Why did he trap it then?' I interrupted. 'Why not just let it be in the first place?'

'Exactly.'

We are quiet, watching the fire.

'You go often to see the ambassador, don't you?'

'I'm not sure what often means.' I don't want to be defensive with him; I don't want to explain myself. I want to watch the fire. I look to see how far away the shore is but cannot find it. The light from the fire isolates us, makes the night around us darker, binds us to each other and we both to this circling dinghy. We are the only drop of light in the world. 'What did you do then, with the snake?' I ask.

'We spoke to it. Calmly, slowly. With feeling. And we let up on the stick incrementally, so that the snake barely noticed. We hypnotised it. By the time it was free we had befriended it and it didn't want to hurt us anymore.'

'Nor did you want to kill it.'

'Exactly.'

'Have you trapped another snake now?'

He smiles, a flash of white in his dark face. 'Do you think a snake is lucky or unlucky?' he asks.

'I don't know.' I swallow. 'Look, the ambassador is my friend. I know that's unlikely, but I think friendship is found in unlikely places.'

'I would have said it grows in unlikely places.'

I dip my fingers into the water, absently, forgetting how dirty it is. The cold is extreme but I leave my fingers where they are, leave them until the cold burns them like fire.

'We kept the snake for a long time,' he says. 'It spied for us – on girls we liked, on our tutor, on boys in the neighbourhood. We were always foreigners so we needed to keep our guard up. It brought us messages and stung anyone who crossed us. I used to sleep with it coiled around my arm.'

'What happened to it?'

'It passed on, of course. Mortal things pass from one shape to another.'

'You mean they die.'

'No. They move.'

'Move where?'

'When you pass through a moment,' he explains slowly, 'it changes you. Sometimes it is so obvious, it is visible – like a shadow, for example, which can leave you and be replaced by someone else's. Other times not visible, just inside, like the change in the snake when we hypnotised it. Dying is the same. For mortal creatures. We change outside and inside, more or less, depending on the creature, on their strength and merit and passion and energy – well, those are all the same maybe. Creatures who are the weakest, they don't even change when they die. You won't know that they are dead unless you see their marker.'

'Their marker?'

'Yes. But markers are personal – that is to say, not personal to who they are marking but personal to who is seeing them. I know what points out death to me. I don't know what shows it to you. Not everyone sees them but I believe that you do; I see it in your eyes, in your mixed-up shadow; I saw it when you came tonight. I wanted right away to talk to you about it but where to start?'

'What marks death for you?'

'Bats,' he says without hesitation. 'Bats eat death. They come to feed on dying souls. When I see them flying around something, or someone, I know.'

'Do you see bats around me?'

'Of course not.'

'What did the snake become, then?'

'Different things. But it still spies for us and sleeps with me, whispering its secrets in my ear. In our father's house it stays near the ceiling. The ceilings are so high, didn't you see? So high that they become lost, they never end; their corners are an illusion. Light and shadow. The snake climbed down before you did and it told me about you, about why you visit the ambassador.'

'Dear God,' I whisper, pulling my hand back from the water. I can't feel my fingers anymore. 'Whatever you understand…it isn't what you think.' I won't look through the sparks – those strange, upright, smokeless sparks – to him and his feverish eyes. Why am I here? 'It feels like we are the only drop of light in the world,' I murmur without thinking.

He puts another stack of cane on the fire.

Why have I said that? My mind is unbending like a fan; strange pictures are coming out of my mouth. 'Aziz,' I say, 'did the charm of your name work as your grandfather hoped?'

He stands – so smoothly that the boat stays as it is, as flat as earth – cranes his head back and embraces the column of sparks; they separate and pass around him like a lambent, golden fog. 'It didn't work with my father. It only works with things that have changed. Like the snake. Like you.'

'But I haven't changed!'

'What happened to your shadow then?'

'There's nothing wrong with my shadow. Why doesn't smoke touch you?'

He laughs and sits again. 'Because I don't let it. Smoke is a changer; I want to stay like this a while longer.'

'What else is a…changer'?'

'Mirrors. Mountain passes. Some dreams. Some sex.'

'Experiences?'

'Of course. But those are more predictable and parts don't get lost in the exchange.'

'What about your twin?'

His bright, sweet eyes become sad. The corners turn down like raindrops. 'That's what I wanted to speak to you about,' he says. 'I can't find him. Will you help me?'

My answer is never in doubt. He has hypnotised me, just like the living-dead snake. He will lift the stick gently, gradually, and by the time I am free he will possess me. His dark face below the white turban, the ebony night and the sparks he swirls with his lazy fingertips have paralysed me. Where among the living does one go to seek the dead?

I agree.

He nods, satisfied, and picks up the oars. We return to the mermaid staircase and he helps me up it, one warm hand gripping my elbow. We ride to my place and I hold on to the back of his jacket to steady myself. The only light on the road is our headlamp. We shine it aloft and burrow into the night behind it, like moles. I want, desperately, the morning. And the street market. And noise.

I climb off at my gate and say good night. He touches two fingers to his lips and promises, 'Call you soon.'

I undo the padlock by feel. My housemates are in bed and the dregs in their wine glasses have dried. I have no idea of the time. I imagine that out there on the water we were like two astronauts, beyond light, beyond seconds, the night expanding and contracting like a room that let us in and pushed us out without ever making us leave the room where we started; the room where a party was happening and people were drinking and flirting while we were ensconced in a window seat enjoying a tête-à-tête about football and the price of airfare; we never moved from there, we were always there, spinning out the reel of a conversation so old it spins on its own like a player piano; we left a quarter there and spent the rest on the fringes of reason.

That must be what happened. Because the dead remain dead, every fire has smoke, there are no mermaids in West Lake and what's more, baldness is becoming, these days, quite the fashion.

Adam Aitken

The War Never Ends

A woman sheltering under a rattan mat
in a storm of Hueys
by the banks of the Mekong,
her last recollection of home.

Your story won't translate
if no-one can read the cards
or can recall
the exact sound of a five hundred pounder
hitting a storehouse of rice.

Who here would want to?
Books like those
now bestsellers in the States,
but here

Temple bells and roosters
will always wake you
from your dream,
sounding just when the poem
needs them.

Cut! the bells say, Silence!
in that jump-cut montage
of heroes fighting for the village

threatened now
by an influx of Gangsta Rap
and foreigners who fall in love
with the way you tease them
about their size, their impatience,
their fake ragged clothes,

the way they say they care for you
and you can't resist.
How about that happy ending
he enquired about at the front desk?
Is it still available?
I want to help, they say
and don't come back.

Phan Huyen Thu

Doll Funeral

I became insane when I blurted out to my friends my preference for waking up during a thunderstorm. A thunderstorm. Waking up alone. Clearly I was insane.

I sang out loud the lines of poet Hoang Hung in a hip-hop rhythm the beats originating from a secretary's typewriter. Suddenly shuddering because of a raindrop suddenly shuddering because of a raindrop suddenly shuddering because… everyone stood up abruptly. The transition meeting ended on the eighth suddenly shuddering I did not intend to sing any more maybe I could shudder about something else.

In a Western backpackers' café, I was the only homegrown backpacker. What was usable there was not coffee was not cold cuts was not anything that could be sold. I was addicted to the alien casual egalitarianism belonging to those who could not be without a backpack.

His kind brown eyes were mocking that which was not kind. Me. The sort of backpacks which appear to be imported yet are sewn domestically one hundred percent, here and there where the threads have come loose were jumbles of blue and red threads intended to conceal yet revealing.

His kind brown eyes, all the brownness and kindness belonged to the eyes. He smoked he talked he looked around, I so craved a kiss I became jittery. I released a sigh onto the slippery table, and entered a vague exotic storyline imagined to be echoing from his table.

I often shuddered because of a raindrop and only because of a raindrop. He came out of me with all the personal skill of someone appearing to a strange woman. I blurted out the most tactful greeting on this earth because dear god there was not a raindrop to be had.

I recited a song by Trinh Cong Son dicated in the To Huu manner: leaving you that day my soul was in stitches my grief like a pack of worms...I stitched myself with leftover threads from past loves, a nest-building endeavor to hide the sad worm.

He had kind brown eyes, all the brownness and gentleness belonged to the eyes. I admired myself for not shuddering during an entire day of rain a week of rain a season of rain. But then again my corny folk operatic root shuddering Mr. Trinh Cong Son had declared to the world before I was made that even rocks and pebbles need each other.

You already knew that I lied to myself, ignored your sly games with women. You already knew that I was the most ignorant girl because I was the most infatuated and most desperate for a kiss. Besides I was also exceptional in my hysterical craving to be able to cook, wash and sew for an organisation of no more than three. I longed to be fruitful to be a mother to be able to raise children. You already knew I was fearful of the sounds of typewriters fearful of transition meetings fearful of compliments about my beauty sensitivity intelligence or any other kinds of compliments. You knew my fears even more clearly than what others already knew the fact that I liked you tender and brown. All the tender brownness belonged to the eyes. More than a thousand times two three or four times I had been painfully deceived happily deceived assiduously deceived. Jail me along with the jinglings of keys nail clippers ear wax removers dinosaurs shimmering bikinis inside a brown purse so tender you called longing and love. I had next to me an entire brown universe.

Finally you did come with all that I craved. The first time after so much yearning you did not brown me in the tender or kind manner belonging to your always brown eyes.

A blissful ignorant excursion. I cried and believed I had conquered all that was brown. All the material pain of the beginning was only an experiment to discover a way to track you down and to stash you away.

The doll funeral of the nighttime FM broadcast had poured into me a painful awareness of my endless virginity. Even in death I will not forget the clever union to the point of cadishness between you and Tchaikovsky. Outside the wind and the dry leaves were entangled on the sidewalks, naked I clung tightly to the sheet and you still brown still blue still pink still white still drilling into me a possessive force of a brown suffering an early death.

I became addicted to backpacks from that day, addicted to alien casualness from that day. You were still tenderly brown. All the brownness and tenderness belonged to the eyes, coming out of me with all the personal skill already mentioned you could not give me the manikin I was craving.

I have not forgotten that it was the only morning when I woke up with you during a thunderstorm. The bedsheet was smeared with extremely delicate brown stains. All the tender brownness belonged...

I no longer sing lines of poetry or recite in poetry lyrics from songs nor do I confuse the various shades and densities of brown.

I became insane when I blurted out to my friends my preference for waking up during a thunderstorm. A thunderstorm. Waking up alone. Clearly I was insane.

Translated by Linh Dinh

Isabelle Thuy Pelaud

Eurasian

I was born in a place
Where I was not supposed to be born
Native, girl, other
My ancestor, I was taught,
Was Vercingetorix
A man
With red hair
And a red moustache
Brandishing a sword in his left hand

I was Alone
Without a land
A people
Whose gaze
Defined my
Existence

I now think of my Mother,
And me
Standing back to back
You look toward Vietnam
Your family, your home
A time when you were free
From husband and child,

This leaf
Floating down a river
Without strings
Anchor
Intensely quiet
Walking forward
And away
Trusting no one
But the Dead

And yet
We are tied to each other
Like two branches
Of a tree
With the will to sacrifice all
For the other

You do not think I see you
But I do
You too stand alone
You have been away
For too long
Having had no choice
But to take refuge among the enemy
Mimicking
The woman child
Of his fantasy
Your family looks at you
Sideways

Our silence is our gift
This imperfect tool
Of survival

But with his words
On the tips of my fingers
I aim to clear your shadow.

About the Authors

ADAM AITKEN

Adam Aitken spent his early childhood in London, Thailand and Malaysia, before settling in Sydney. As well as numerous articles on poetry, works of creative non-fiction, a PhD thesis and academic articles on Asian–Australian literature, he is the author of four full-length collections of poetry. He recently spent a year in Cambodia working on *Eighth Habitation* (Giramondo). He taught English in Indonesia and lectures in Writing and Communications at the University of Technology, Sydney.

BAO NINH

Bao Ninh was born in Hanoi in 1952. During the Vietnam War he served with the Glorious 27th Youth Brigade. Of the five hundred who went to war with the brigade in 1969, he is one of ten who survived. A huge bestseller in Vietnam, *The Sorrow of War* won The Independent Foreign Fiction Prize for 1994. It is Bao Ninh's first novel.

PAM BROWN

The Australian poet, Pam Brown, has published fourteen books of poetry and prose, and from 1997 to 2002 was the poetry editor for *Overland* magazine. In 2004 she became Associate Editor of *Jacket* magazine.

CATHERINE COLE

Catherine Cole is Professor of Creative Writing at RMIT University in Melbourne. She has published three novels, (*Dry Dock*, *Skin Deep* and *The Grave at Thu Le*), two non-fiction books, *Private Dicks and Feisty Chicks: An Interrogation of Crime Fiction* and *The Poet Who Forgot*. She is co-editor with McNeil and Karaminas of *Fashion in Fiction: Text and Clothing in Literature, Film and Television* (Berg UK and USA, May 2009). She has also has published poetry, short stories, essays and reviews. She has been a Writing and Research Fellow at the University of East Anglia, UK, a resident of the Keesing Studio, Cité International des Arts in Paris, and an Asialink writer-in-residence in Hanoi, Vietnam.

CHI VU

Chi Vu was born in Vietnam and came to Australia in 1979. Her stories have been published widely in *Meanjin*, *The Age*, *Refo* and in anthologies, most recently the *PEN Anthology of Australian Literature*. She has been a writer, artist, performer, lecturer and writer-in-residence. In 2000 on an Asialink writer's residency in Vietnam she wrote 'Vietnam: A psychic guide'.

JANE GIBIAN

Jane Gibian is a Sydney poet whose most recent collection is *Ardent* (Giramondo, 2007). In 2002 she was an Asialink Literature Resident in Hanoi, Vietnam. Her previous publications include *The Body's Navigation* (Five Islands Press, 1998) and a chapbook of haiku, *long shadows* (Vagabond Press, 2005). She works as a librarian and ESL teacher, and studies Vietnamese.

CHRISTOPHER KREMMER

Christopher Kremmer's books on modern Asia include *Bamboo Palace, The Carpet Wars* and *Inhaling the Mahatma*. He is currently a research scholar with the University of Western Sydney's Writing & Society Research Group. The story in this collection appeared in a different form in *Travel & Leisure* magazine.

ANDREW LAM

Andrew Lam was born in Vietnam and went to the US in 1975 when he was 11 years old, has a Master in Fine Arts from San Francisco State University in creative writing, and a BA Degree in Biochemistry from

UC Berkeley. He is a syndicated writer and an editor with the Pacific News Service, a short story writer and a commentator on National Public Radio's 'All Things Considered'. He co-founded New America Media, an association of over 2000 ethnic media in America. His essays have appeared in dozens of newspapers across the country, including the *New York Times*, *The Los Angeles Times*, the *San Francisco Chronicle*, *The Baltimore Sun*, *The Atlanta Journal* and the *Chicago Tribune*. He has also written essays for magazines like *Mother Jones*, *The Nation*, *San Francisco Focus*, *Proult Journal*, *In Context*, *Utne Magazine*, *California Magazine* and many others.

Lam's awards include the Society of Professional Journalist Outstanding Young Journalist Award (1993) and Best Commentator in 2004, The Media Alliance Meritorious awards (1994), The World Affairs Council's Excellence in International Journalism Award (1992), the Rockefeller Fellowship in UCLA (1992), and the Asian American Journalist Association National Award (1993; 1995). He was honoured and profiled on KQED television in May 1996 during Asian American Heritage Month. He won twice the Literary Death Match West Coast competition in 2008.

VINCENT LAM

Dr Vincent Lam was born in London, Ontario. He lives in Toronto with his wife and son, where he is an emergency physician. *Bloodletting & Miraculous Cures* won the prestigious Giller Prize and was a number one bestseller in Canada.

LAM THI MY DA

Lam Thi My Da was born in Le Thuy District, Quang Binh Province, in the central part of Vietnam. She graduated from the Writer's College in Vietnam in 1983, and received a Certificate for Advanced Studies in Literature at Moscow's Gorky University in 1988. She has worked as a reporter and a literary editor, and serves as an executive board member of the Vietnamese Writers' Association and Chairperson of the Thua Thien Hue Writers' Association. She has published five collections of poems in Vietnam: *Trai tim sinh no* (*The Fertile Heart*, 1974), *Bai tho khong nam thang* (*Poem without Date*, 1983), *Hai tuoi em day tay* (*Gathering My Years*, 1990), *Me va con* (*Mother and Child*, 1994) and *De tang mot giac mo* (*Dedicated to a Dream*, 1998). She has won several major prizes for poetry, including two awards from the Vietnamese Writers' Association and, for her 1998 book, highest honours from the National United Board of Vietnamese Literature and the Arts.

N. B. NAJIMA

N. B. Najima is a writer, journalist and development worker based in Hanoi, Vietnam. She has lived in Asia for six years and works as a speechwriter for the United Nations.

HOA PHAM

Hoa Pham is the author of four books, *Vixen*, *Quicksilver*, *No One Like Me* and *49 Ghosts*. She is also the founding editor of *Peril* – an on line Asian–Australian arts and culture magazine, <www.peril.com.au>. She has also written three plays, and numerous short stories that have appeared in *HEAT*, *Griffith Review* and others. Her work can be viewed at <www.hoapham.net>.

HO ANH THAI

Ho Anh Thai is presently the elected President of the Hanoi Writers' Association and member of the Central Committee of Vietnam Writers' Association. He is a writer best known for the novels *Behind the Red Mist* (Curbstone Press, 1998), *The Women on the Island* (University of Washington Press, 2001) and *L'île aux femmes* (Editions de L'aube); and his short story collections *Aventures en Inde* (Kailash Editions), *Fragment of a Man* and *The Goat Meat Special* – he has published about thirty novels and story collections. His books have been translated into ten languages. Ho Anh Thai has won several awards of the Vietnam Writers' Association and prestigious newspapers in Vietnam.

STEVE KELEN

Steve Kelen is a Canberra-based poet. He was Asialink fellow in Vietnam in 1998 where his chapbook, *Dragon Rising*, was published by The Gioi in Hanoi. Kelen's most recent books are *Goddess of Mercy* (Brandl & Schlesinger, 2002) and *Earthly Delights* (Pandanus, 2006).

LE MINH KHUE

Le Minh Khue was born in 1949 in Thanh Hoa. She joined the Youth Volunteers Brigade at the age of sixteen and spent much of her youth on the Ho Chi Minh Trail, later serving as a war correspondent for Tien Phong (Vanguard) newspaper and Giai Phong (Liberation) Radio. She's an editor at the Vietnam Writers' Association Publishing House. A short story writer and novelist, her works include *The Stars, The Earth, The River; Summer's Peak; The Distant Stars; A Small Tragedy; An Evening away from the City.*

NAM LE

Nam Le was born in Vietnam and raised in Australia. He has received the Dylan Thomas Prize; the (US) National Book Foundation's '5 under 35' Award; the Pushcart Prize, the Michener-Copernicus Society of America Award; and fellowships from the Iowa Writers' Workshop, the Fine Arts Work Center in Provincetown, Phillips Exeter Academy, and the University of East Anglia. His fiction has appeared in *Zoetrope: All-Story, A Public Space, Conjunctions, One Story,* NPR's *Selected Shorts, Prospect Magazine,* and the *Best American Nonrequired Reading, Best New American Voices, Best Australian Stories,* and Pushcart Prize anthologies. He is the fiction editor of the *Harvard Review.*

NGUYEN THE HOANG LINH

Nguyen The Hoang Linh was born in 1982 in Hanoi. He's regarded as a literary phenomenon when hundreds of his poems posted in the websites from 2003. His first novel, The tale of a Genius, won the annual award of Hanoi Writers' Association in 2005. He has two published collection of poems: *The Simple Reason* and *Every Nation is a Country of the World.*

NGUYEN THI THU HUE

Nguyen Thi Thu Hue was born in 1966 in Hanoi. Her father, a journalist from Ben Tre province, repatriated to the North after the Geneva Agreement had been signed in 1954. Her mother is a well-known writer, Nguyen Thi Ngoc Tu. Also a scriptwriter, Nguyen Thi Thu Hue is the director of the VTC9 (Let's Viet) television channel and is the Vice-President of the Hanoi Writers' Association. Her published works include *After Going to the Paradise, The Witch, The Waiting Sand, Let us Forget it etc.*

NGUYEN NGOC THUAN

Nguyen Ngoc Thuan was born in 1972 in Binh Thuan province. He graduated from Ho Chi Minh College of Fine Arts and works as an artist for *Tuoi Tre* (Youth) newspaper in Ho Chi Minh City. He won best novel prize in the Contest of Book for the Youth in 2000 with

Opened the Window When Shutting Your Eyes. Later, he won first prizes in the Book Contests of two prestigious publishing houses with *A Story of Dreams* and *The Angels are Herded in the High Hill.*

ISABELLE THUY PELAUD
Isabelle Thuy Pelaud is Associate Professor in Asian American Studies at San Francisco State University and co-director of the Diasporic Vietnamese Artists Network (DVAN). Her essays, short stories and poetry have been published in *Making More Waves, Tilting the Continent, Vietnam Dialogue Inside/Out* and *Forbidden Grounds.* Her academic work can be found in *Mixed Race Literature, The New Face of Asian Pacific America, Amerasia Journal* and *Michigan Quarterly Review.* Her book manuscript *History, Identity and Survival: Reading Vietnamese American Literature* is currently under review by Temple University Press.

PHAM DUY KHIEM
Pham Duy Khiem was born in Hanoi and educated in Paris. He served in the French Army, 1939–1940, and was Ambassador to France during the 1950s. His collection, *Légendes des terres sereines* was first published in Hanoi in 1942, and in an enlarged form in Paris in 1951 (republished in 1989).

PHAM THI HOAI
Pham Thi Hoai, one of contemporary Vietnam's most influential writers, was born in Hai Duong province. Her first novel, *Thien Su (The Crystal Messenger)*, first published in Hanoi in 1988, has since been translated into ten languages and was awarded the Frankfurt LiBeraturpreis in 1993. Pham Thi Hoai has also written two other novels and three collections of short stories, and has translated works by Kafka, Brecht and Durrenmatt into Vietnamese.

PHAN HUYEN THU
Phan Huyen Thu was born in 1972 in Hanoi, where she still lives. A journalist by trade, she has published poems and short stories in many journals in Vietnam, France and the United States. She was awarded First Prize in poetry by the prestigious Hue journal, *Perfume River,* in 1997.

VIET LÊ
Viet Lê is an artist, creative writer and curator. His work has been featured in *Fuse, Amerasia Journal, Art in Asia, corpus, Asia Pacific American*

Journal, nhà magazine, Blue Arc Anthology of California Poets, West Coast Line, CONSEQUENCE Journal, Love, West Hollywood anthology and *Asia Art Archive* among others. Lê's artwork has been exhibited in Korea, Vietnam, Canada, the United States and Italy. Lê has received fellowships from the Civitella Ranieri Foundation, Fulbright-Hays, Fine Arts Work Center, Center for Khmer Studies and PEN Center USA. Lê curated *Charlie Don't Surf!* (Centre A, Vancouver, BC) and *transPOP: Korea Việt Nam Remix* (Seoul, Sài Gòn, Irvine, San Francisco). He has co-edited special issues of *BOL Journal* (*Việt Nam and Us*, 2008) and *Reflections: A Journal of Writing, Service Learning, and Community Literacy* (2008). Lê received his MFA from the University of California, Irvine, where he has also taught the Studio Art and Visual Culture courses. He is currently a doctoral candidate at the University of Southern California. <vietle.net>

VO CHUONG DAI

Vo Chuong Dai is a poet, cultural critic and freelance editor based in the United States. She is interested in memory, storytelling, movement and motion, and diasporic dislocations. She has a PhD in Comparative Literature from the University of California, San Diego. Her research interests focus on twentieth-century Vietnamese national and diasporic literature and films.

The Translators

Harry Aveling
Kevin Bowen
Ho Anh Thai
Wayne Karlin
Linh Dinh
Ngo Vinh Hai
Phan Thanh Hao
Ton-That Quynh-Du
Tran Ngoc

Permissions and Acknowledgements

Extract from Nguyen Trong Tao's *Memory of Black Eyes*, The Gioi Publishers, Hanoi, 2009.

Bao Ninh's *The Sorrow of War* (extract) was first published in English in 1994. This extract is from Phan Thanh Hao's translation, Penguin, USA, 1996.

Nam Le's 'Love and Honour and Pity and Pride and Compassion and Sacrifice' was first published in *The Boat*, Penguin Australia, June, 2008. It is reproduced with permission by Penguin Group (Australia).

Lam Thi My Da's 'A Sky in Bomb Crater' is from *The Vietnam Literature Review*, Number 1, 1999, and was translated by Ngo Vinh Hai and Kevin Bowen.

Chi Vu's 'Vietnam: A psychic guide' was first published in *Meanjin: Fine Writing and Provocative Ideas*, Volume 60, Number 1, 2001.

'Hue' first appeared in the *Song Huong* magazine of the Hue Arts and Literature Association, 1997.

'The War Never Ends' was posted on *X connect*, a magazine of literature of the Pennsylvania University.

Ho Anh Thai's 'Installation' was first published in *Heritage*, the in-flight magazine of Vietnam Airlines, in 2008.

Steve Kelen's 'The No-Food Restaurant', 'Red Dzao Village', 'At the Ho Chi Minh Mausoleum' and 'Hanoi Girls' are from *Dragon Rising: Poems* which was published by The Gioi Publishers, Hanoi, 1998.

Le Minh Khue's 'The Professor of Philosophy' was first published in the *Vietnam News* in 2002, then in *Love After War: Contemporary Fiction from Vietnam*, edited by Wayne Karlin and Ho Anh Thai, Curbstone Press, 2003. 'The Concrete Village', was first published in *Vietnam News*, 2004.

Pham Thi Hoai's stories 'Sunday Menu', 'Vision Impaired' and 'Saigon Tailor' were translated by Ton-That Quynh-Du and were published in *Sunday Menu: Selected Short Stories of Pham Thi Hoai*, Pandanus Books, ANU, 2005, <http://rspas.anu.edu.au>.

Nguyen Ngoc Thuan's 'Her Schedule on Saturday' was first published in *Heritage Magazine*, Number 46, June and July 2008.

'Long Live Peace' by Catherine Cole is an extract from *The Grave at Thu Le*, Picador, Sydney, 2006.

Pham Duy Khiem's 'Tu Uyên or The Portrait of a *Tiên*', was translated from the French by Harry Aveling in *Legends from Serene Lands, Classical Vietnamese Stories*, Prestige Publishing, 2008.

Viet Lê's 'Haunting' was first published in *Crab Orchard Review*, 'Color Wheel' Issue, Volume 14, Number 2, Summer/Fall 2009. Carbondale: University of Illinois, 2009. 'Hot Dogs for Dinner' and 'Strawberries for Sale' are previously unpublished.

Andrew Lam's 'The Palmist' was published in *Manoa Journal*, Volume 16, Number 2, 2004, pp. 163–7. 'Saigon in our Prayers' is a new, unpublished work.

Jane Gibian's 'Carp', 'planted' and 'Footpath (Hanoi)' are reprinted from *Ardent* Giramondo, 2007. 'Vietnam Haiku' and 'Further Haiku' are from *long shadows*, Vagabond Press, 2005.

Vincent Lam's 'A Long Migration' is from *Bloodletting & Miraculous Cures* published by the Fourth Estate/HarperCollins UK and Australia, 2008.

Pam Brown's 'The Hanoi Cycle' was first published in *This World. This Place*, University of Queensland Press, 1994.

'The Watchman' by Nguyen Ngoc Thuan appeared in *Vietnam News*, Hanoi, 25 February 2007.

Adam Aitken's 'Beyond Khe Sanh' and 'The War Never Ends' are new, unpublished works.

Vo Chuong Dai's 'The Remains of the Dead' and 'After the War' are original unpublished works.

Nguyen The Hoang Linh's 'Gun and Flower', 'Save and Delete' and 'About Vietnam' were first published in *Chuyen cua thien tai* (A Genius's Story), by Hoi Nha Van Publishing House, Hanoi, 2005.

Christopher Kremmer's 'The City of Darkness and Light' is an original unpublished work.

Hoa Pham's 'The Daughters of Au Co' is reprinted with permission from *Inner Nebulae, HEAT 16*, new series, Giramondo, 2008.

'Believe Me' by Nguyen Thi Thu Hue is previously unpublished in English.

'At the Mermaid Stairwell' is a new work by N. B. Najima.

'Eurasian' by Isabelle Thuy Pelaud is a new, unpublished work.